I0760777

The SCENT *of* HEAT

E. P. SERY

TESTIMONIALS

"*The Scent of Heat* transports you to 1950's Israel, and into the heart of a tangled love affair. Thrilling, passionate, and shocking. This bold debut novel will keep you guessing and leave you wanting more." –**Jessica Therrien**, best-selling author of *Oppression (Children of the Gods)*

"A tightly crafted story of forbidden love and broken promises. The culture and customs of Israel and Israelis are carefully woven in to provide a delightful and complete background to Ariella's life. Very gripping conclusion that keeps the reader engaged to the very end!" - **Dr. Sally Pollack**, Professor and Emmy recipient

"I loved everything about this sensual, exotic story. I felt a special kinship with the main character, Ariella, who discovers the painful truth about the people she loves most and must search for the strength to stand on her own.

I was rooting for her dream to come true, all throughout *The Scent of Heat*. This coming of age love story is a must read!" – **Holly Kammier**, author of best-selling *Kingston Court* and *Choosing Hope*

"You can't help but fall for Ariella Paz when grief and a covert romance stand between her and her dream. She stares down misfortune that threatens her future and her inner strength moves her forward. I loved E. P. Sery's crafty debut novel, *The Scent of Heat*. It engaged me fully and left me yearning for a sequel." – **R. D. Kardon**, author of *Flygirl*

FROM THE TINY ACORN
GROWS THE MIGHTY OAK

Publishers' Note

Although the author is using her own family as a point of departure, this is a work of fiction. Names, characters, places, events, and incidents either are the product of the author's imagination or are used fictitiously, and any resemblance to actual persons, living or dead, is entirely coincidental.

The Scent of Heat
First Edition

Cover design by Mae I Design
www.reginawamba.com

Book formatted by Christa Yelich-Koth
www.christayelichkoth.com

ISBN: 978-1-947392-20-5

www.epseryauthor.com

DEDICATION

To all the breast cancer survivors and the ones still fighting.
We've come a long way since 1957.

And to the memory of **Ron Tsafrir Sery, z"l**

Chapter One

AUTUMN made its way southeast from Europe, and the light winds floated over the calm Mediterranean Sea toward the Israeli shores. The sun spread its last rays across the white-washed four-story buildings of Tel Aviv, as its round golden body glided into the cool blue waters.

Nineteen-year-old Ariella Paz made her way home from the army base after a nine-hour day in the office. It was a cool Sunday evening in November 1957, a regular work day. She walked erect and proud; she was serving the final months of her mandatory military service, just like any other Israeli who was enlisted at eighteen. Boys served for three years; girls for two.

It was after five, and the streetlights came on. Ariella looked up at the low buildings with their small apartment balconies. Most of the blankets and rugs that hung over the railings for airing during the day were now pulled back in for the night. But some people hadn't taken down their laundry yet; shirts and underwear, hooked to thin laundry lines strung across the verandas, were still flying in the breeze like decorations. She smiled and tucked a stray hair behind her ear.

Ariella had decided not to take the bus home today but to enjoy the crisp, refreshing air. Goosebumps formed under her khaki long-sleeved army uniform, so she stopped by a building entrance and pulled her olive-green sweater over her head. She used the shelter to light a cigarette and inhaled deeply. She smoothed the A-line khaki skirt that came down almost to her knees, ironed with two pleats in the front. Her khaki shirt was well starched and tucked in under her sweater. That morning she'd brushed her long, brown, sleek hair before she rolled it up in a French twist, banana-style, exposing her tanned neck, as per army regulations. Now her military beret sat on the left side of her head like a little capsized boat. She continued walking.

Ariella was getting hungry; the smell of falafel balls being fried by a street vendor and the fragrant fresh pita they were going to nestle in made her salivate. She couldn't wait to get home to her own mother's delicious cooking.

Stepping into the apartment where she lived with her parents and siblings, Ariella's large brown eyes widened as she took in the scene in the living room: her *Ima*, mother in

Hebrew, a seamstress, was twirling around in a brown summer dress with little pink flowers; her *Abba*, father, wore a navy jacket that was too long for him, and her sister Yael hugged a new doll.

"*Shalom*, what's going on?" Hello. She smiled at the funny sight.

"We got another 'Parcel from America'!" eleven-year-old Yael called out cheerfully. "And I got a new doll!"

"Aren't you a bit old for dolls?" Ariella gazed fondly at her little sister while removing her military cap. "What did Eitan and I get?" she asked, pulling off the army sweater and placing it on a chair.

Ariella looked at the crumpled brown wrapping paper and rope resting on the floor. A white dress shirt lay neatly folded on the coffee table, most likely for her twenty-three-year-old brother Eitan. Where would he wear it? To a wedding, a funeral? Next to it lay a pink sweater.

"Is this for me?" Ariella asked. Nobody answered. Her parents were already in the bedroom she shared with her little sister. She could hear them laughing and fighting over the tall, narrow mirror that stood on three legs between the girls' beds.

Ariella and Eitan lived at home with their parents, like most young Israelis did in 1957, until they either got married or moved to another city. The newly-established country was poor, made up primarily of Jewish immigrants from the tortured European continent and hostile Muslim countries that had ejected them. It was the "promised land," but there weren't enough dwellings. There wasn't enough money to go around either. Many families with one or two children shared apartments, usually *one* bedroom per family. All the families shared the kitchen and one bathroom.

Ariella's family was fortunate; they had a two-bedroom apartment all to themselves. The bigger bedroom was given to the two girls, Ariella and her little sister Yael, and Eitan had the smaller one to himself. Every night Abba and Ima converted the living room sofa into a bed for themselves. They paid rent to Uncle Gabriel, Abba's older brother, who owned several apartments. He also owned the bakery where Abba worked. Being wealthy was rare; Uncle Gabriel was the exception.

Ariella tried the pink sweater on top of her long-sleeved army shirt. It fit somewhat tightly, pulling over her arms and chest. She wondered if it could be worn without a starched shirt underneath, just button it up. She noticed a small stain on the sleeve, by the cuff, and made a face. She examined it. Most probably coffee. Darn, why couldn't it be a new sweater? Always hand-me-downs. She folded the cuff back to hide the stain. It looked better.

The truth was, she felt a mixture of anticipation and humiliation when those "Parcels from America" arrived; feeling poor and in need, although she never said a word about it; she didn't want to sound ungrateful. Ariella knew Abba would write his cousin in California to thank her for the gifts, but secondhand clothing wasn't Ariella's idea of luxury, even from America. She loved beautiful clothes even if she couldn't afford them. Everything new she wore was made by her mother's own hands.

Ariella envisioned Los Angeles full of rich people, the land of the movie stars she so admired. The twenty Israeli *lira* she earned in the army each month was just enough for cigarettes, a weekly *The World of Cinema* magazine, and her beloved movies. Babysitting money bought a quarter kilo of pistachio nuts to eat while reading the magazine on Friday afternoons after work. Those were her current precious luxuries.

"How do you like your sweater, Ariella?" Ima came back to the living room, wearing an old housedress. She must've changed in the girls' bedroom, where she shared their closet. Abba's clothes were stored in Eitan's room, in a shared armoire.

"It's lovely. Please thank Cousin Sonia for me," Ariella said, not wanting to upset Ima. She didn't show her the stain; she knew that being poor wasn't what Ima had expected after living in Israel for twenty-four years, but what could she do?

"How is your dress?"

"Too big," Ima replied, the sides of her mouth drooping with sadness. "I've lost some weight lately, not sure why. But you know me, I can alter it. Did you see Yael's doll? Cute, isn't it? And Eitan's shirt? Very decent. But Abba is too short for his jacket. He wants to give it to my brother."

"Well, that's a good idea." Uncle Rafael was tall and handsome, and the jacket would serve him well in his current job at the bank. She adored Uncle Rafael.

Ariella smiled, and headed to her bedroom to change her

clothes, but turned back to Ima and added, "I'm going out to the movies with Rachel." Rachel was Ariella's best friend.

"Again? What are you going to see?" Ima asked, a hint of jealousy in her voice.

"It's an American movie with subtitles, called *Daddy Long Legs*, with Fred Astaire and Leslie Caron. It's a romantic—"

"*Beseder, beseder.*" All right, all right. Ima said, sounding suddenly impatient. "You can go, but first come help me make dinner. Eitan should be back from university soon, and Abba is hungry."

* * *

The pink sweater looked just right with her striped gray-and-pink, three-quarters pants that Ima had made last year on her eighteenth birthday. She wore her flat black shoes, which she got from her parents for her nineteenth birthday two months ago, and held a small, black clutch bag in her hand, a gift from Uncle Rafael and his wife Dalia. She combed her hair to its full length, letting it fall over her shoulders; her scalp hurt from the bobby pins.

People at the bus stop turned to look at her, and two soldiers in uniform stopped talking as she boarded the bus. Ariella smiled and sat down just behind the driver. She was used to people staring at her; repeatedly telling her that she was beautiful. Young men would turn around to look at her when she walked down the street, and young teenagers whistled often when she passed by.

When she arrived at the Mugrabi movie theater on the corner of Allenby and Ben-Yehuda Streets, Ariella spotted Rachel buying tickets. Sweet Rachel. She had short red hair and fair skin, just like Eitan and Yael. Funny, she could pass for their sister more than Ariella could. Rachel, a new immigrant, came to Israel from Poland only three years ago, at the same time Ariella and her family returned from their two-year adventure in Argentina.

"*Shalom*, you got here before me!" Ariella smiled.

"Well, my parents weren't home when I got back from base, so instead of a sit-down dinner, I grabbed the schnitzel my mother left for me and wolfed it down, cold. But don't you ever tell her!" Rachel and Ariella shared a laugh.

Two hours later, Ariella and Rachel walked down the wide stairs of the majestic Mugrabi movie house. The theater, with its long, vertical Art Deco windows, rested on the pointy corner on Allenby, between Pinsker Street and its famous Café Noga, and Ben-Yehuda Street. Directly across stood a large clock on a streetlight, a favorite rendezvous for teenagers.

Ariella had felt hot in the theater, although its roof opened during intermission to allow fresh air in and the cigarette smoke out. But she loved the movie; it had fueled the fire that had been burning within her for a long time. Invigorated, she couldn't contain her daring idea any longer. She needed a cigarette to calm herself and offered one to Rachel, who declined this time.

"Listen, Rachel, I have to tell you something." She struck

a match and inhaled deeply as she lit her cigarette. "But you must keep it a secret."

"Oh, I *love* secrets!" Rachel exclaimed, her face lighting up. "Do you want to sit somewhere and talk?"

"Oh no, thanks, let's walk," Ariella tapped the edge of her cigarette, nervous energy coursing through her veins. She needed to move, the excitement welling up inside her. She was about to say something she'd never said out loud, or even written in her diary. Ever.

"I want to go to America." She exhaled.

"Everybody wants to go to America. What's the big secret?"

"No, I *really* want to go. And stay. I want to *live* in America."

"Live there?" Rachel's warm breath billowed in the cool night air. "But you're in the army...we still have six more months to serve."

"I know, silly, I'm not going now, although I wish I were." Ariella sighed. "Once I'm discharged, I'll need to work and save," she said. "What I really want is to go to university in America. Study there, live there. This is my *biggest* dream. Did you see what fun it was for the girl in the movie?"

"Yeah, it really looked like fun, but she was lonely, too. Won't you be lonely? You don't really know anybody there." Rachel frowned. "And besides, what do you want to study that you can't study here in Israel?"

"As a matter of fact, I do know somebody there. Cousin Sonia, a distant relative, lives in Los Angeles. She visited last year during Hanukkah, remember? And she invited me to come. I won't be lonely. Maybe I'll study to become a nurse, or a social worker, or something. But *imagine*, living in Los Angeles! Hollywood! I miss the wide streets of Buenos Aires, the large department stores, the beautiful buildings. I know they have them in America too!"

"*Oy*, Ariella. It sounds so glamorous, but I don't know. I'll miss you. And your parents? Do they know? Won't you miss *them*?" Rachel sounded worried.

It was past eleven o'clock at night, as they were headed north from the movie theater on Ben-Yehuda Street. There weren't too many people out, but they felt safe. They could roam the streets of Tel Aviv until the wee hours of the morning with no worries. Ariella didn't feel that safe in Buenos Aires just a few years ago and wondered what it was like in Los Angeles.

"No, I didn't tell my parents, not yet, and yes, of course I will miss them, but I want to be independent. I want to find a good job first, save, and go when I have money for a ticket and some savings. That's my plan," Ariella said decisively, feeling more confident by the minute. She wished she could go right then.

"My parents and I feel lucky that we could come and live in Israel, and you want *to leave*?" Rachel shook her head.

Ariella didn't reply, not wanting to sound like a snob, but hating the idea of living in a one-room apartment once she found the 'right man' and got married. There were no prospects of ever getting wealthy, and it was important to her.

Memories of the large, comfortable house they had rented in Rosario, Argentina after she finished her studies in Buenos Aires flooded her.

Ariella let her imagination run wild as they walked toward home. In America she'd be independent and might even learn to drive. She'd be speaking English. Imagine that! What if she bumped into a movie star in in the streets of Los Angeles? She might even cut her hair, like Aunt Pearl, her mother's youngest sister, or like Ava Gardner in *The Barefoot Contessa.*

She would make it happen. Living again in the big world she had tasted. Out there. Tired of being poor and accepting handouts. She wanted to go to a university in America, earn a degree, and send gifts to her relatives in Israel. *She* wanted to be the giver.

It was almost midnight when Ariella entered the apartment on tiptoe, careful not to wake her parents, who were sleeping in the living room. She sat down at the kitchen table to write the letter to Cousin Sonia she'd already composed in her mind, thanking her for the sweater and asking for help and advice, as she was the only one Ariella knew in America. Her only way out.

Ariella gave Rachel's address for a reply. She disclosed it was too early to discuss her plans with her parents. Rachel was right; she still had to complete her military service. She also needed money.

Chapter Two

ON a Friday afternoon in December, Ariella sat in the living room reading her magazine and eating pistachios. Eitan didn't want any, although she had offered. He was reading a geography book as though it were a novel, and Yael was reading a book from school, all snuggled in Ima's favorite soft armchair.

Ariella put her magazine down as her thoughts drifted back to five years ago, 1952. The new State of Israel was only four years old and the economy had plummeted. People could hardly afford bare necessities. Going out for coffee when you were unemployed was impossible. Her father sold only bread and rolls, and the occasional cookies, as a baked-goods vendor. His brother Gabriel needed to fire two of his bakers.

Times were so tough Abba got food stamps for her then six-year-old sister Yael, so she could get powdered milk and powdered eggs. They had to mix the powdered eggs with water to make scrambled eggs. "It's disgusting," Yael would complain after spitting it out.

"I've had it," she remembered Abba announcing one day. He and Ima started arguing late into the nights, which was a new thing. Sometimes they called Eitan to join them. But not Ariella, and of course, never little Yael.

"I'm tired of struggling for almost twenty years, Ariella." At long last Abba confided in her. "I want a better life for my children. I want to go to America, or at least, Canada," Abba said about two months after she turned fourteen. "But we need to go to Europe first, for visas. It's not so easy to get in."

Ariella had felt as if the ground had dropped from beneath her.

Looking up now as the aroma of heated chicken soup penetrated her consciousness, Ariella noticed she was alone in the room. She heard Eitan and Yael in the kitchen chatting with Abba and Ima. How could she have slipped so deep into thought and missed her parents return? She got up and joined them all in the kitchen.

* * *

That night, when Ariella climbed into bed with a book, she read the same half page three times. A sense of adventure engulfed her. When she was certain that Yael had fallen asleep, Ariella quietly unveiled an old shoe box, hidden under all the old blankets and feather pillows, from the closet. She opened the box and removed an old, torn sweater, and there it was. Right at the bottom. Her old journal. She wanted to read her entries from five years ago, when she was fourteen and they had left Israel, thinking they were going to America, "or at least, Canada," as Abba had said.

21 December 1952
Dear Diary,

I'm desperate. I'm telling. I'm telling my 8th grade teacher Morah Dvorah today. I must go to school now. Bye.

I told her. I had to. I told her my parents said we're leaving Israel for America, but I'm not allowed to tell anybody.

I said it's top secret. I know I can trust her. She gave me a hug and said, "Ariella Paz, you'll be fine. We'll miss you, but you'll be fine, I know that." I froze and tried hard not to cry.

23 December 1952
Dear Diary,

Eitan is eighteen. He is taller than Abba, who looks up at him admiringly. Like he is a prince or something. The heir. I'm sure Abba wants to protect him and keep him close, but isn't it the law to go to the military at eighteen? What if they catch my brother leaving? What will they do to him? I'm so scared. I'm shivering.

24 December 1952
Dear Diary,

I heard that there is a change coming in "financial policy" in Israel, whatever that means. I hear it all the time.

My father tells me that the price of food, furniture, clothes, everything, is going up by sixty percent. It will cause massive unemployment, and we better leave. It sounds serious, but I don't really understand it all. How come my friend Liora's father knew to buy things before the increase? Because he works for the government?

1 or 2 January 1953
Dear Diary,

I don't even know what date it is. All I'm told is that we're sailing to France. I think we dock in Marseille. But I'm not feeling well. I'm sleepy and nauseated. I keep waking up and falling asleep. My eyes are burning, and I can't hold the pen. Bye.

5 January 1953

Dear Diary,

We're on land again, Marseilles, France, to be exact, and now we must take the train to Munich in Germany to see my father's cousin and get our visas to America or Canada; we'll see. My head is aching, and I still feel sick.
I felt sick on the train, too. All I remember is muttering "the trunk, the trunk, don't forget the trunk" again and again.

We arrived this evening in Munich by train! I can't believe I was on a train in Germany!!!!! I felt a chill. People around us on the train were speaking German. The sound of the language gave me the shivers. I was expecting to hear "*Raus*! Get out!" every time we stopped at a station, just what the Jews heard when the Nazis wanted them out of the trains when they'd arrived in Auschwitz and other concentration camps. My stomach was in a knot all the time. I wanted to block my ears.
I wonder, how can my father's family live in Germany? Aren't they afraid?

Ariella placed her diary on her chest and closed her eyes. Yes, she wanted badly to go to America. But not via Germany this time. Maybe London, England. She'd love to see London.

Chapter Three

IT was a dark night with no stars in the sky when Ariella smelled the cigarette smoke before she could see his silhouette. Abba stepped into the girls' bedroom and whispered, "We need to see you in the kitchen, now." He turned around and left.

Yael was asleep already, but Ariella sat reading in bed with a little lamp on. She stared at his back for a moment before setting down her book. She got up quietly, put on her old quilted red dressing gown, and followed Abba into the kitchen.

Ima and Eitan were already sitting at the table. Ariella looked from one to the other, trying to read their poker faces. "I don't know how to tell you this," Ima said in a quivering voice before Ariella had time to assess the situation. "But I'm sick." Ima took a deep breath. "I've known about it for a while but thought nothing of it. I thought it would go away; so, I tried to ignore it. I didn't think it was serious until...until I went to the doctor."

"What's wrong?" Ariella looked from her mother to her father, feeling her pulse throb in her neck.

Neither of them answered her question. Instead Abba walked behind Ima, put both hands over her shoulders, and squeezed gently. He moved his hands closer together and massaged Ima's neck. Soft sighs escaped her lips; her eyes closed, and she stopped sniffling.

Eitan stared at his own hands placed before him on the table, fingers linked together, his knuckles white.

"What is going on?" Ariella asked again, the heat rising to her throat, her mouth dry.

"Ima has a lump in her breast," Abba disclosed. "She used the blue light lamp, and we thought it would go away, dissolve the cyst, but it didn't." He sighed deeply, as if he'd been holding his breath the whole time. "Eventually I persuaded her to see the doctor. He said she'd need a biopsy." Abba swallowed hard; he wasn't a talker, and Ariella was used to it, but now she needed more.

"What's a biopsy?" She was afraid to hear the reply.

"All we want you both to know is that Ima is going to the hospital for tests tomorrow. We need to decide what to tell Yael," Abba said, looking from Ariella to Eitan, and back. He looked pale. He seemed lost.

Poor Yulinka, thought Ariella, using her parents' nickname for her little sister, forgetting her own fear for a moment and thinking of how an eleven-year-old would feel.

"I'll talk to her," Eitan volunteered. "Don't worry, I'll try to make it not a big deal." Abba patted him on the back and kissed the top of his head. He helped Ima get up from her seat, and they both shuffled into the living room to make their bed.

Ariella and Eitan stayed seated in the kitchen for a few minutes, not speaking a word. When her brother got up and trudged off to his room, Ariella barely made her way back to bed, her head hung low, fear invading every cell in her body.

What's a biopsy?

* * *

The following morning Ariella did her best to feel optimistic. She told herself everything looked worse at night.

She removed her military cap as she entered her office at the army base, and stood for a moment by the window, looking out. She took a deep breath. It was a weird January day. The air was different, and the ground felt like it was on fire, as if the tarmac would melt. The sky shone an eerie silvery blue, almost white, and a warm haze floated about.

Ariella liked the Israeli summers, but this was January, and unusual. Still, it was very welcome, as she loved the dry heat-waves, the engulfing *Hamsin*. She breathed in the dry air with its ancient desert scent. The heat felt like a warm, caressing hug.

She even tolerated the small particles of sand that stuck to the tiny hairs on her exposed neck. A shiver of pleasure ran through her body.

She heard her boss, Major Amos Yom-Tov, talking to someone in his office. She didn't want to interrupt, so she sat down at her desk and gazed at the blue-and-white Israeli flag flapping in the hot wind. She tried to focus on the flag as not to think of Ima. Her chest tightened; *oy*, Ima, what will the tests show? Is a biopsy a test?

Yom-Tov and his visitor walked out of his office into hers, Yom-Tov's arm around his handsome guest's shoulders, hugging him affectionately. Ariella jumped to her feet to greet them.

"*Boker tov*, Ariella." Good morning. The Major was first to speak, but Ariella focused on the tall stranger.

The visitor's eyes locked on to hers. With a smile and a raised eyebrow, he turned to Yom-Tov, awaiting an introduction. Just then the phone rang. Ariella hurried to answer while the two men looked at her in anticipation. She listened and nodded to her boss, who quickly returned to his office to take the call, yelling over his shoulder, "*Shalom*, Arik, *Le'hitraot.*" See you later.

Ariella replaced the receiver gently. The visitor walked straight to her, extended his hand, and introduced himself with a wide and charming grin, tilting his head.

"*Shalom*, I'm Arik."

She smiled and said politely, "Ariella. Very pleased to meet you." She shook his hand.

Arik's palm was large, soft, and warm. She noticed deep-set, light brown eyes surrounded by thin smile lines; a tiny brown beauty spot at the edge of his right eye; well-cut, slightly graying hair above his ears; the straight nose; the chiseled jawline; the engaging smile, broad and friendly, displaying white, healthy teeth.

Ariella dropped her gaze, worried she was staring. She noticed his light khaki pants, brown and dusty shoes, his light blue, short-sleeved shirt, and, as she slowly raised her eyes again, she saw his tanned and slightly hairy arms. A faint whiff of musk-scented aftershave reached her nose. She still felt his soft palm in her hand.

"Ariella," he repeated, as if tasting her name. He smiled. "What time do you get off duty?"

Ariella gave Arik a surprised and lingering look, not sure if he was joking.

"Excuse me, why?" She frowned and tucked her chin in. This time she noticed the unbuttoned top of his shirt, which disclosed some dark hair. Still— *Hutzpah!* What audacity.

Arik smiled again, unabashed, the lines by his eyes deepened. "Can I invite you out for coffee sometime after work?"

He wasn't joking! Israelis were known for their straightforwardness, but he had some cheek; she wasn't sure she disliked it though, but still, his line sounded rehearsed. Ariella took a quick breath and said, "Maybe someday," her cheeks reddening.

When Arik left, Ariella remained standing and thinking.

He was gorgeous, like a film star, and he must have known it; but still, they'd just met, and he invited her to go out for coffee? *Shtuyot*, nonsense. He probably said it to many women.

Now she cocked her head. He must be her boss's friend, his age, too, around forty, not an army man though; he wasn't in uniform. She had no time to wonder any longer as Yom-Tov called her in for a dictation. The day had begun.

Did he have a dimple?

* * *

When Ariella entered the apartment that evening, she found Abba seated at the kitchen table smoking Dubek 10, an Israeli cigarette, and reading the paper. Yael sat next to him in a swirl of smoke, doing her homework. One could be fooled by the idyllic scenery; they looked peaceful, with Mozart's piano concerto playing on the big radio in the living room.

Ariella hated to disturb them, but she had no choice.

"*Shalom*, Abba. *Shalom*, Yael. Can I talk with you, Abba?"

Her father took his reading glasses off and looked at Ariella. She motioned to the bedroom with her head. He seemed to understand, got up, and followed her to her room.

"Where are you two going?" Yael raised her head from her homework.

"I just need to show Abba something," Ariella said quickly. "We'll be right back."

* * *

"What did the doctor say today? How bad is it?" Ariella didn't mince words once they were in her bedroom. "How long will she stay in the hospital?"

"They're not sure. They may have to operate on her soon. We'll find out the results tomorrow."

"What do you think? Will they have to cut her breast off?" Ariella couldn't help it; she remembered reading about the Black American actress Hattie McDaniel from her favorite movie, *Gone with the Wind*, who died of breast cancer. And the amazing British contralto singer Kathleen Ferrier. Those talented stars she'd read about! Those beautiful women!

"Shh...enough! Not around Yael, Ella," Abba hissed and grimaced, glancing back in the direction of the kitchen.

"But Abba—"

"Enough, I said." He raised his voice. "She's in the doctors' hands." He stormed out of the bedroom and lit another cigarette in the kitchen. She saw his hands shake as she followed. The frustration in his voice scared her.

An hour later, the three of them sat at the kitchen table, both Ariella and Yael staring at their dinner plates. Ariella could hardly swallow. Yael's eyes filled with tears that started dropping into her chicken soup. Ariella wondered if Yael had heard anything earlier and placed her hand on her sister's.

"When can we see Ima?" Ariella thought that a visit might cheer up her sister.

"Visiting hours are from two to four in the afternoon," Abba replied without looking up. "The hospital is very strict about it. You can't visit any other time; I was told today that it disrupts the work of the doctors and nurses. Will you be able to get special permission from the military to go visit?"

"I will ask," Ariella said, but she wasn't sure it would be that easy.

"Maybe you can stay two extra hours on the days that you take the two hours' break to go to the hospital," Yom-Tov said the following day. "I'll talk to First Sergeant Cohen, but you'll need to get it in writing from him to show the guard at the gate."

Ariella teared up. "Thank you," she said quietly, her eyes cast down.

The following day Abba, Ariella, and Eitan stood by Ima's hospital bed when a mousy blonde nurse stepped into the room and asked them to come and see Dr. Brill. They kissed Ima goodbye and slouched into the doctor's office.

Ariella stared at the short, chubby, bald man. He had small hands with short fingers.

"I'm sorry, Mr. Paz." Dr. Brill ignored the young people as all three of them took a seat in front of his desk. "We've been x-raying and running blood tests, and the biopsy wasn't good. Hmm. It's a malignant tumor, and it has spread. I'm afraid your wife will have to undergo surgery." He looked up and seemed to notice Eitan and Ariella now. "We need to get the whole growth out now."

Ariella instinctively crossed her arms over her chest and held an opposite shoulder in each hand, missing what the doctor said next. Then his voice reached her again "...hope she'll recover and return home to you and your children." He looked from Eitan to Ariella, before he looked back at the thick file. "We'll scheduled the surgery very soon." He stood up to shake Abba's hand goodbye, indicating the meeting was over.

Was that it? She needed to speak with Ima. She needed her to explain; why, if she had known that something was wrong, hadn't she said anything? Had she been hiding it longer than she'd led on? Was she scared to hear the truth? Ariella felt sick and wasn't sure if it was from the smell in the hospital or something she'd eaten. She thought she tasted bile.

She looked at Abba.

All he said was "Thank you, Doctor" and then walked out of the doctor's office and headed toward the hospital's exit. Ariella and Eitan followed him quietly. At the hospital's main doors, Abba turned to them as if to say something, making eye contact with each of them, but then looked at the ground, seeming to regret it. He remained silent.

Ariella and Eitan looked at each other, not sure what to do next. She noticed her father's color. He was unusually red, as if angry, as if wanting to say something but thinking it was better not to. Once again, she felt her stomach heave.

Abba started moving again, picking up speed on his way to his van, as if he couldn't get away fast enough.

"Wait!" Ariella called out from behind him. "Can we go

somewhere and talk, Abba?" Her head felt hot and cold at the same time, but her hands were frozen.

Abba stopped, looked back at her and Eitan, then continued walking.

"Eitan..." she tried.

Her brother increased his pace and made his way next to Abba's side.

Ariella managed to whisper to no one in particular, "I have to go back to base." Neither Abba nor Eitan seemed willing to talk. She turned around and walked away to the bus stop.

What about Yael? Should she talk with Yael? What did Abba tell her? Ariella thought as she stood in the full bus with her feet far apart, rocking from side to side, holding on for dear life, feeling nauseated. The ride back to the military base seemed endless.

Does Ima know? Who had told her? The doctor? How? When? Was she by herself? Was Abba with her when she was told? Maybe she doesn't even know yet?

Ariella needed to talk to somebody...Rachel! She needed to speak with Rachel.

The pain in her heart made it want to explode. She tried to focus on Abba. Don't think of Ima, not Ima, she commanded her brain.

Abba left home every morning before dawn to stand in front of the hot oven at his brother's bakery. Then he delivered baked goods to the coffeehouses and confectionaries in his small, gray van. Now he'd have to go sit by Ima's bed after work—

The bus arrived at her stop.

Ariella walked as if in a dream to the base and rushed to her office. It was after four thirty, and Yom-Tov was already gone. There was nothing on her desk. Did he forget that she was returning? She picked up the phone and dialed Rachel's office. She was glad to have her so close by.

"First Sergeant Cohen's office, *shalom*."

"Rachel, it's...me..." Ariella started crying as soon as she heard her friend's voice.

"Ella? Are you back? I'm on my way."

"My mother has cancer. *CANCER*!" Ariella yelled hysterically the minute Rachel walked into her office, as if she'd bottled it all up in the past hour and had to release the venom.

"What am I going to do if Ima died?" she asked Rachel. Who would put a cold hand on her feverish forehead when she'd get sick? Would she never feel Ima's soft hands again? Would Ima not be by her side when she gets married one day? Will Ima never come and visit her in America?

Ariella collapsed into the chair by her desk, beating its top with the sides of her fists, making the heavy, black phone jump.

"Why?" She whimpered like a wounded animal, hitting her thighs.

"Ariella..." Rachel sounded helpless. She knelt by her friend and tried to hug her waist. Placing her head on Ariella's thighs made Ariella stop beating them. She held Rachel's head and let the tears fall onto her best friend's hair. Rachel cried, too.

"Cancer...cancer...cancer..." Ariella whispered. She knew that the word wasn't usually uttered out loud. People said, "that thing, you know..." or "that awful illness," but *cancer*? They didn't say *cancer.*

"I'm so worried, Rachel."

"I know, me too..."

"I still don't know what a biopsy is, but Ima has cancer." Suddenly she felt lighter, as if saying again and again the word nobody wanted to say lifted some weight off. Her head pounded. "Will my mother die?" she asked Rachel, as if *she* had the answer. "Do you think they will be able to save her? How can I live without Ima?"

Rachel held both of Ariella's hands in hers and pulled her up to standing, but Ariella pulled away in anger.

"She knew, and Abba did too...I'm sure of it," Ariella started pacing her small office. "They kept it a secret for a long time, but why? They were afraid to find out the truth! Did they want to protect us? And Yael, what about Yael? Who will raise my little sister? She's not even twelve years old, and if Ima dies...? I can't raise her... she needs Ima! I need Ima!" She tasted bile again and swallowed hard.

Ariella thought about how Ima shopped and cooked for them all, sewed the girls' clothes and did everybody's laundry. How she waited for them with a hot meal when they returned home from school or work, how she took them to the doctor and nursed them when they were sick. What will Abba do? And Eitan?

"We all need Ima," Ariella whispered, her spirit broken.

Rachel reached to hug her friend, but Ariella plopped on her chair again, refusing to be consoled.

"I know," Rachel said, "it's too damn hard. I'm here, Ariella. Always remember this: I'll always be by your side. I may not be able to help your mother, but I'm here for you and for Eitan, and for Yael. Let's be strong, let's be hopeful, maybe she'll be all right."

Ariella was in a haze when she took the bus home. She couldn't speak to her father nor her brother about Ima, but at least she had Rachel. Good, sweet Rachel.

Chapter Four

ON Sunday Ariella was back on the army base, relieved to be working, trying to keep her thoughts away from Ima's upcoming surgery.

After work, as dark, swollen clouds gathered and threatened to pour heavy rain on her head, Ariella rushed to the falafel stand to wait for Rachel. She took her place in line behind two customers under the canopy, where she was going to order her *hahtzi-mahnah*, half-portion falafel in pita. As Ariella needed a distraction, Rachel had suggested they go to see Hitchcock's movie *To Catch a Thief* with Cary Grant and Grace Kelly. It had just come out with Hebrew subtitles and in color, too! Abba and Yael were home with Ima, and she told them that she'd be late.

"Yes, what will it be, *buba*?"

Ariella smiled awkwardly. It made her uneasy when strangers, especially men she didn't know, used terms of endearment like "doll" when they spoke to her.

"*Hahtzi-mahnah* with a little salad and a drop of *T'hina*," Ariella said. The vendor smiled at her warmly. She knew he meant no harm, but still, he sized her up.

"Why do you look so serious, *motek*?" Sweetie. The vendor asked as he was filling her pita.

Someone pushed her from behind and she shot around to see who it was.

"Stop it, donkey," she heard the boy who pushed her yell to the boy behind him. "Why are you pushing me?" He turned back to face her. "*Sliha*," he mumbled. Sorry.

Ariella eyed the group of high school boys who stood behind her, about four or five of them, all bunched up together. Israeli style, she thought, never standing in line behind each other. The lack of order upset her. One of the boys, probably the one who had pushed his friend into her, smiled and winked at her.

Ariella narrowed her eyes at him in response; she was impatient to leave. "What's with you, kids?" she asked, though she couldn't be more than two or three years older than they were.

The teenager at the end of the line wolf-whistled, and Ariella hurried to pay, wanting to get away.

"Stop bothering this lady-soldier!" the vendor yelled at the teenagers as he handed her the half-pita wrapped in a napkin with one hand, taking her money with the other. "Don't you have any respect for a uniform? Soon enough you'll be wearing one and protecting this country! God help me if you guys have to protect me!" He winked at Ariella, half smiling. She quickly turned to walk away when she bumped into a man.

"*Sliha*," Sorry, Ariella mumbled, her eyes cast down.

"Ariella...?" she heard the man say.

Ariella looked up into smiling brown eyes. She almost dropped her dinner.

"Oh, Arik," she said, surprised. Yes, Yom-Tov's handsome friend. She remembered.

"Uh-ah! Look, her father just arrived! Beware, *kids*, he'll beat you up!" one of the teenagers called out, laughing.

Arik walked up to them. "What kind of behavior is that?" he said in an authoritative tone. Then he turned to Ariella and said, "Are you in a hurry? Can you wait five minutes for me while I get my falafel?"

"I'm waiting for a friend," she said reluctantly, looking at her watch. Noticing the boys were listening intently, she added, "*beseder*," all right, and walked away to wait for him.

Ariella's tummy rumbled with hunger, so she stood on the sidewalk eating her falafel and scanning the people on the street. Where was Rachel? A middle-aged woman approached with two heavy shopping bags, an old man with a small dog and holding an umbrella walked by. Not too much traffic passed on the small street, but she could see King George Street and the bus stop in the corner. About ten people stood there in a group.

No line, of course. She stared at the gray buildings, all three or four stories high, as if the ground in Tel Aviv couldn't handle taller ones. Was the city built on beach sand?

By the time Arik walked toward her, holding his falafel in one hand and his briefcase in the other, she had finished eating. He smiled and said, "Thanks for waiting, Ariella. Those boys can be really rude, so I gave them a little lecture back there."

"Oh, forget it," she waved her hand as if it were nothing. Goodness, he was so good-looking and well-mannered. She felt a bit uncomfortable suddenly, her hands sweaty. Where was Rachel? She had an urge to run away and didn't know why.

"Although, I can't blame them too much," Arik continued. "It's hard to see a beautiful woman and not express one's appreciation. I guess men always look at you this way." He seemed to have muttered the last sentence to himself.

Which way? And did he just call her a beautiful *woman*? Ariella didn't know how to reply and kept quiet, feeling more uneasy as they walked side by side toward a nearby bench.

"Should we sit down?" he suggested.

Ariella sat at the edge of the bench, watching out for Rachel.

"So how is Yom-Tov treating you?" Arik asked. "He's an old friend of mine, so you can tell me the truth." He smiled and tilted his head, squinting a bit as he faced the sun setting behind her. She liked the way he wiped his mouth after each bite, and that he finished chewing before he spoke.

"He is a good man, you know, and a wonderful boss," Ariella replied politely.

"And what are your plans for after the service?"

Three soldiers stood by smoking and talking, one openly staring at Ariella. She blushed and averted her eyes from his. To Arik she said, "I'm going to find a job, save my money, and go to America." Ariella realized what she'd just said. Even her parents and brother didn't know of her plans. But he didn't know her family, so whom could he tell?

"America?! Have you ever been overseas?" Arik seemed genuinely interested.

The bus arrived at the corner stop, and Ariella observed people pushing each other to get on. The smoking soldiers threw their cigarette stubs onto the sidewalk and hurried to board the bus. The sidewalk by the bus stop looked like a giant ashtray to her, but she turned to answer Arik's question.

"Actually, yes. When I was fourteen, we went to Argentina for two years. We were supposed to go to America but landed in *South* America." She smiled. "Not the same thing. On our way back, we stopped in Italy. I really liked that country; I'd like to visit there again someday." She looked longingly into the distance, remembering Giovanni, the Italian sailor.

"I go to Europe often on business. Maybe when you're done with your service, I'll be needing an assistant, and you can join me." Arik smiled mischievously.

Did he just offer her a job? Like Arik's first offer to have coffee together, Ariella wasn't sure if he was joking. He was straightforward, but he had that charming smile that threw her.

"Here you are!" Rachel said. "What are you doing on the

bench? I was looking for you at the falafel stand!" Rachel got hold of Ariella's wrist and pulled her up.

Arik stood. "*Shalom*, Ariella. It was nice seeing you again. Maybe we'll have that coffee one day, or I'll see you in the office." He lifted his hand to wave and walked in the opposite direction.

"*Shalom*!" Ariella waved with her free hand, the other still held by Rachel.

"Coffee? Office?" Rachel asked as they were walking. She turned back to look at Arik as he walked away, and remarked, "He's good-looking, almost as handsome as Cary Grant. Who is he? Where do you know him from?" The girls walked in sync, their arms entwined.

"He's Yom-Tov's friend. I bumped into him at the falafel stand. Hey, why were you so late? Cohen kept you locked in? Isn't it against regulations?" It started drizzling, and they had no umbrellas, so they huddled closer as if that way they could walk between the drops.

"Regulations, shmegulations, I had some work I needed to finish, sorry. But forget it...let's first buy tickets, and then I need to eat something."

The sky opened over their heads and they started running.

Chapter Five

THE following evening, the night before Ima's surgery, Uncle Rafael's wife Dalia came to visit.

Ariella was home alone; her father had gone to visit his younger sister, Leah, and had taken Yael with him. He needed some moral support, Ariella understood, and his sister knew how to comfort him. She was waiting for Eitan to get back from university.

"I wish your Aunt Pearl were here, don't you?" Dalia was referring to Ima and Uncle Rafael's sister. "We need your mother's little sister to be with us now. I doubt that life in South Africa is good for her. Rafael is a bit worried. We haven't seen her in how long now, two years? And he doesn't have a good feeling about her life in Johannesburg. Leaving Israel for South Africa...it's a different world out there!"

"Yes," Ariella said. "Ima would be so happy to have her sister here, and we'd like that, too. We love Aunt Pearl and I was so sad when she left after her wedding two years ago."

"We all were. I'm not sure how happy she is; money isn't everything." A look of doubt spread across Dalia's face.

"Why do you say that?"

They sat at the kitchen table snacking on Aunt Dalia's homemade butter cookies.

"Never mind," Dalia said as she smiled warmly and waved her hand. "You remind me of your aunt; you two look so much alike."

"We haven't heard from her in a while," Ariella said thoughtfully.

"Well, enough of that. Your mother's surgery is tomorrow, and let's hope it will be a good day. I must go now, sweetie. We can't sit here all day eating my cookies, right?" She stood up. "I need to go and put the girls to bed. Will you be okay? Eitan is coming home soon, right?" A look of concern appeared on Dalia's face. Ariella nodded.

Aunt Dalia left, and Ariella sat drinking coffee with a lot of milk, just like Ima used to make for her when she was little. She decided to have a second dessert, so she sliced the chocolate *babka* Abba had brought fresh from the bakery. Thoughts of the surgery came flooding in again, and a huge lump clogged her throat. The cake remained on the plate. "*Oy*, Ima, Ima," she mumbled. You're all alone in the hospital. Are you scared?

By the time Eitan walked in, he found Ariella sitting with her elbows on the table, her head resting between her hands, tears collecting below her chin and dripping onto the Formica tabletop.

* * *

The following day, the day of Ima's surgery, the clock refused to move. Ariella couldn't concentrate and had to type Yom-Tov's letters again and again. He never said a word.

By the time she arrived at the hospital after work, she found Abba and Eitan standing by Ima's bed. Ima lay fast asleep when Doctor Brill walked in.

"I'm sorry, Mr. Paz." Doctor Brill's mouth rested in a tight line. He looked at their father, as did Eitan, while Ariella stared at the doctor's moving lips, noticing his yellowing teeth. She didn't understand much of what he was explaining. He must be a smoker, she thought, distracted. Squashed between her father's and brother's shoulders, as they formed a small circle with the surgeon, she could feel their body heat. She didn't really hear the doctor's voice; her whole being rejected his words; her head was in a fog. Then suddenly it reached her.

"...the best we could do. As you can see, she is sleeping now, heavily sedated, no point in waking her. Now that most of the tumor has been removed, we're more hopeful of recovery." The doctor looked at the two youngsters as if realizing for the first time that they were also present. "We had to remove the whole right breast and lymph nodes. The growth was much larger than we'd anticipated. We'll treat it with radiation as soon as the scar heals. Come back tomorrow. Only time will tell, Mr. Paz. Let's be hopeful. I'll see you tomorrow, *shalom.*" He walked away with his gaze averted, not looking at Ariella nor at Eitan even once.

Ariella hung her head. Damn. She looked at Ima. The whole breast. Lymph nodes.

Ima slept peacefully. She couldn't have heard the doctor, right? Her face looked pale, her lips thin and bloodless and her hair a mess. Ariella couldn't believe that this beautiful human being could walk out of her life. Impossible. Women could live with one breast, right? Just like one lung or one kidney. Ima would live. She had to. They all relied on her, needed her. Ariella wouldn't accept that Ima was dying. Not *her* mother.

"Let's go, Ella." Eitan's voice penetrated her thoughts.

Ariella looked up, as if seeing him for the first time. She looked back at Ima. Her chest rose and fell in a steady rhythm. That was a good sign.

Abba walked slowly toward the hospital exit, so slowly, as if some force was pulling him back. Eitan and Ariella followed. Everybody stared at the white tiled floor.

Ariella remembered Yael was with Rachel's mother. As if reading her mind, Eitan nodded. "I'll take the bus to Rachel's and pick up Yael. You two can go home. I'll tell Yael that Ima had her surgery and everything's fine...the doctors are happy. I'll say that she'll be home soon and will recover and get better."

Ariella said nothing; she was surprised at her reserved

brother's initiative. He was usually so quiet and serious.

Ariella walked with Abba in silence to his small van, and they drove toward home. Staring blankly outside, the world looked foggy to her, a blur of whites and greys.

"Abba," Ariella began. "Can we talk about...I'm so—"

"Not now, Ariella, I can't talk right now." Abba sighed. He sounded exhausted.

* * *

The next day, when Ariella, her father, brother, and sister visited Ima, her room smelled like disinfectants, medications, alcohol; all the scents mixed together almost made her gag.

When she saw Ima in her washed-out, undignified hospital gown, sadness enveloped her. Ima, the woman who loved makeup and nail polish, the seamstress who adored beautiful clothes. The loving mother who taught her to dress nicely, and who guided her to look in magazines to try and emulate the models. Since Ariella was young, she'd watched Ima leaf through fashion magazines. Ima sewed for herself and for her daughters, lovingly laboring over a pattern, choosing the right fabric and making them try the clothes on again and again, wanting them to look perfect.

She was only forty-seven for heavens' sake, Ariella yelled in her head to the God she no longer believed in, but everybody said was there. He was a cruel and vengeful God, *if* he existed.

A week after surgery Ariella got off the bus just in time for visiting hours. She straightened her khaki skirt, and made sure her starched shirt was well tucked in. The winter sun felt hot on her skin and she felt sweat drops trickle down her back. She shivered at the thought of another visit into that sterile hospital.

The minute Ariella stepped into Ima's room, the smell of sickness and sterility hit her nostrils, nauseating her. The light grey walls, the darker gray floor tiles, and Ima's pale face surrounded by white bed linens made her want to cry.

Ima moaned. "My hand...it's so painful...look," she said and tried to lift her right arm but couldn't. "It's swollen..."

Ariella could see Ima had an infusion in her right arm. She didn't really understand what was wrong, but she could see that Ima's left hand wasn't as puffy.

"Don't move, Ima. It really looks painful. I'll call the nurse."

The nurse followed Ariella and yanked the needle out of the back of Ima's hand. Ima winced. "Sorry, Mrs. Paz, the fluid must have escaped. We'll find another vein, maybe in the other hand? Don't worry, love, I'll take care of it."

Ima tried to smile when Ariella bent down to kiss her cheek.

"Good to see you, Ariella, and thanks for calling the nurse; she never came when I rang the bell." Ima took a deep breath. "Must be busy." Ima closed her eyes.

Ariella sat down on the stiff chair and gently slid her fingers into her mother's half-closed hand. Ima squeezed her fingers and smiled a sad smile, as if apologizing. Was she scared?

Was the scar painful? Did she regret not going to the doctor sooner?

"Ima, I need to ask you something," Ariella found the courage to say.

Ima opened her eyes.

"How long have you known about the, eh, about the lump in your breast?" Ariella thought that if Ima would have gone to the doctor sooner, maybe her breast wouldn't have had to be removed.

Ima closed her eyes again.

"Ima, Ima," Ariella urged, giving her mother's fingers a gentle squeeze. "You have to tell me…I need to know." She was so scared she might also develop a lump one day and discover it too late.

Ima opened her watery green eyes and looked at Ariella, whose heart almost stopped. She had never seen her mother's eyes turn so dark, almost black. Ariella found it hard to breathe, but she couldn't stop staring.

"About a year, Ella."

Ariella had to take in a breath, but it felt as if an elephant had stepped on her chest. "A year?! Would it have made a difference if you saw the doctor sooner?"

"I don't know. I used to get cysts and they would go away. We thought it was another one of those. I hope it's not too late. Maybe the radiation will help," Ima said, sounding tired.

"Is your bandaged chest painful?" Ariella needed to know the details.

"Yes, it is. It's burning and pulling. The stitches must be

drying, and the tubes—" Ima closed her eyes again. She seemed to have fallen asleep mid-sentence.

Ariella winced. The thought of having a breast removed and donning an unsightly six-inch scar on her chest made her want to scream. But what if it could help? What if they took the cancer out and Ima would survive?

Ariella double checked to see if Ima had fallen asleep and couldn't see her cry. Ima, Ima. She gently and carefully pulled her fingers out of Ima's weak grip. What am I going to do without you? she thought. What if you're dying, Ima! You waited a year! Ariella screamed in her head as she held it in both her hands and sobbed.

Chapter Six

ARIELLA sat in her office watching the clock tick. In just over an hour she could leave for the hospital to visit her mother. So she got up to make herself a cup of Nescafé instant coffee while her boss was away in a meeting. Then the phone rang.

"Major Yom-Tov's office, *shalom,*" she said politely.

"Hello," she heard a cheerful, deep male voice which she didn't recognize. "Is this Ariella?"

"Uh...yes, sir," she said, surprised.

"Hello, is Major Yom-Tov there?"

"I'm sorry, sir, but Major Yom-Tov is out. May I help you?"

"Ariella? This is Arik. You don't need to call me sir."

She could hear him smile. "Oh, *shalom*, Arik. In the office, everyone is called sir."

"Yes, I know, but I'm not in the military. Listen, I'm in the area and have a meeting close to the base later so I thought I'd come say hello. But if he's not there, I guess I can come say hello to you."

Ariella's cheeks flushed; that was nice of him. She remembered bumping into him at the falafel stand. But why was he coming to see *her*? She worried he could hear her heart beating through the phone, so she put her left palm on the mouth piece.

"Hello, are you there?"

"Uh, yes, eh, Arik, I'm here," she said quickly as she removed her hand. "It would be very nice to say hello again." She felt so stupid; she couldn't say even one sentence without stuttering. "I'm making coffee." She finally managed to compose herself. "I'll be glad to make you a cup, too, army style."

"Oh, I haven't had one of those in a while. I'm on my way."

Ariella had to sit down and place her sweaty hands under her thighs. She was flattered that such a handsome, sophisticated man seemed to be interested in her. It was normally the younger guys, the soldiers, who paid attention to her, but Ariella wasn't excited about any of them. She wasn't interested in immature twenty-something-year-olds; she preferred older boyfriends. Yigal, an older guy she'd met on the *kibbutz*, was her last boyfriend almost two years ago. Since she enlisted, she hadn't met anybody interesting enough.

Stop it! She commanded her hands. Don't be so stupid. It

was a compliment, yes, but he was only coming in for coffee, no big deal; he couldn't really be interested in her; she was too young for him. She jumped as the phone rang again. Here, he'd changed his mind!

Ariella picked up the phone. "Major Yom-Tov's office, *shalom.*" She tried to keep calm, ready for the disappointment.

"*Shalom,* Ariella." It was Yom-Tov. "I just needed to make sure that all three letters are typed and ready to be sent."

"Yes, Major, all ready to go. And the telegrams were sent already, sir."

"Good, I have meetings all afternoon, and I won't be back in the office. I'll see you tomorrow morning. And, thank you, Ariella."

"Yes sir, you're welcome, my pleasure, sir." He was already gone. Thank goodness! She knew she was babbling, but she could hardly contain her excitement. Ariella quickly plugged the kettle in and boiled the water again, took another cup and placed a full teaspoon of instant coffee and two teaspoons of sugar in it.

She poured a few drops of water into the cup and started stirring fervently, crushing the sugar against the sides until white foam began to appear. As soon as the water came to a boil, she started pouring. At that moment Arik walked in.

She jumped. Boiling water splattered on the tray between the two cups. Luckily her hand was out of the way.

"*Shalom,* Ariella. I didn't mean to startle you." His voice had a laughing ring to it.

"Oh, *shalom.* Just in time." She handed him his cup, then

picked up hers.

"Mmm," Arik said, closing his eyes for a second. She could see he was enjoying his drink. "Thank you, you really make this coffee taste good. You know, I bring Italian coffee from Europe when I go on business, so I haven't had instant coffee for a really long time."

"Sorry," she blushed. "I have nothing better."

"I have to go to a meeting soon, and I'd love to see you again, not just bump into you at the falafel stand or have coffee in the office. But right now, I'm sure you have some work to do."

"Not too much work, I'm almost done. I'm actually on my way soon to Tel-Ha'Shomer Hospital," Ariella blurted. Why was she telling him this?

"Why? Are you sick?"

"No. My mother is in the hospital for some treatment." Ariella picked at an invisible thread on her skirt, unable to hide her sadness any longer.

"Oh, what for?" His eyes crinkled in concern.

Ariella felt touched that he cared. "She has...a bad disease."

"*Oy*. I'm so sorry to hear that."

"Yeah, I hope the treatment she's getting today will help." Ariella forced a smile.

"I hope so, too. Thank you for the coffee. May I take you out for coffee one day?"

Ariella looked at him. He was warm and charming, friendly and very good-looking. Why not? "If you know of a place that makes better coffee than mine, I'll be willing to go."

They both laughed. It felt good; she hadn't laughed in a while.

* * *

"Here Ima, put your right arm in first," Ariella said as she held Ima's soft green blouse, helping her dress for the ride home.

The door opened, and Dr. Brill stepped into Ima's room. He seemed to be short of breath.

"*Shalom*, Mrs. Paz. Is your husband here?"

"No," Ariella quickly interrupted, "we're taking a taxi home."

"Well, I need to speak with him." He looked down at the papers on the clipboard and scratched his prematurely balding head.

Ima's eyes opened wide. "Why? What is it, doctor?"

"Oh, eh…I'm glad your daughter is here to accompany you."

Ima looked at Ariella. It was obvious Dr. Brill was up to something. On a Friday afternoon, just before *Shabbat*, doctors didn't usually make rounds. What was he trying to say?

"You can go home now, Mrs. Paz, *Shabbat shalom*." And he was out the door.

Ima and Ariella both sat down on the bed. Ariella took Ima's hand in hers.

"I'm sure it's nothing, Ima. Maybe something with the account? He wouldn't let you go home if there was something wrong."

"You're right. Let's go. I'm craving some fresh air. And I can't wait to see Yulinka, Eitan, and Abba, and to sleep in my own bed."

Ariella looked at her mother. You're so brave, Ima, she thought, and I love you so much. They both got up, and Ima leaned on Ariella's arm as they walked out of the building. She'd tell Abba to call the doctor on Sunday.

"I should have brought you something new, a gift, when I came to pick you up, Ima," Ariella said as they climbed into the taxi.

"Why, Ella? We didn't know I was going home today."

"That's true." Ariella smiled. "But remember what you brought when I left the hospital when I was five?" Ariella patted Ima's hand.

Ima looked as if she was trying to remember. "Was it new shoes?"

"Yes. When I had the croup, after a few days in the hospital you asked me one day what I wanted you to bring me when I got out."

"Yes." Ima smiled. "I thought a popsicle, or a balloon would do, now I remember, but you asked for red shoes and yellow socks."

"Yes! And you brought them! No questions asked."

"I was glad to take you home, Ella. I was worried and missed you so much, I would have brought you anything, no matter the cost."

"I know." Ariella kissed Ima's check.

* * *

On Sunday Ariella came home right before Abba.

"Where were you, Daniel?" Ima asked as he walked in the door, his hands clenched at his sides. He sounded irritated. "I thought you'd be home much earlier."

She sat beside Ariella and Yael at the kitchen table, sewing the hem of a new skirt she was making for Ariella. Yael lifted her head from her homework.

"I, eh, I had to go somewhere." Abba motioned with his head toward Yael.

"Come, Yael, I want to show you something," Ariella brushed the crumbs off her sweater and stood to take her sister's hand.

"What?" Yael wouldn't budge from her seat.

"Come to our room; it's in there." She had no idea what she was going to show Yael, but knew she had to let her parents be alone. She tried to ignore the lump in her throat.

"Ooph, I'm in the middle of homework..."

Ariella swallowed hard. "Come, it will be worth your while, come already." She felt that Abba had something very important to tell Ima.

She was looking for something to distract Yael, while her own heart was beating hard. Did Abba bring bad news? She found the pink sweater she got from America and asked Yael, "Do you want to try this on?"

"Really? Ima never lets me wear pink. She says it doesn't look nice with red hair and I need to wear blues and greens to show off the color of my eyes. Sometimes I can wear brown, even though I hate brown."

"I know. That's why I think you should try it on, see for yourself. You're almost twelve. Make up your own mind." Ariella said irritably. She could hear her parents talking softly in the kitchen. She thought she heard Ima gasp. Her heart quickened.

"Ima's right. I don't look nice in pink. Here, you can have it back. It looks nicer on you." Yael tossed it on Ariella's bed and strode back to the kitchen. Ariella followed, fear constricting her chest.

Abba and Ima stood in the kitchen, hugging. Both had red eyes.

Chapter Seven

"ARIELLA, can you come to my station before you leave?" the nurse asked.

Ima was back in the hospital for more tests, more radiation, and more medication that came only by infusion. She had to stay a while; the doctors weren't sure how long.

As the nurse walked out, Ima said with a smile, "Maybe she wants to tell you how to take care of me when I go home?"

Ariella smiled back, kissed Ima goodbye, and trailed behind the mousy blond nurse to her station. She didn't want to miss the bus back to base and hoped it wouldn't take too long.

Dr. Brill stood waiting for her at the nurse's station. "Would you please follow me to my office?" It was the first time she'd noticed he was wearing glasses. Her mouth went dry as she followed him. Why the doctor and not the nurse?

"Please sit down." Dr. Brill was always serious, but this time his face looked ashen. He sat down, too, and removed his round glasses, placed them on his desk and squinted into Ariella's eyes. "The prognosis is not good. I don't know what your father has told you, but he has told me that he doesn't know how to break the news to his children. I'm so sorry. But you're a big girl, a soldier. You'd give your life for this country and for its people, right? I think you can handle the truth." He rubbed the top of his bald head and pursed his lips. "Again, I'm not sure what your father is telling you, but in my opinion, you should know that," he cleared his throat, "your mother has less than six months to live. We'll make sure she's as comfortable as possible. I'm sorry to have to tell you this." He stood up. "I thought you should know," he repeated.

This was it. The dice had fallen.

"*Regah.*" Wait a minute. Ariella felt like she was underwater and not hearing clearly. She stayed seated, not trusting her legs. "What went wrong? You've operated, cut her breast off, left her with an ugly scar—I saw it. You're giving her radiation, infusions. What are you talking about? Isn't the cancer all gone?" She gulped for oxygen.

"No, Ariella, it's not." He sat down again, wiggling his small hands. "I know how hard it is for you to accept this. Maybe that's why your father didn't tell you everything. Your mother's cancer has spread to her other lymph nodes. She has a lump in her other breast, too, which we may need to remove as well, and we're not sure where else it has metastasized. I'm sorry. I thought you should know. We're doing our best to make her comfortable." He repeated, stood back up, and looked at the floor. "There is a lot we still don't know," he admitted.

Ariella couldn't return to the office. Instead, she shuffled to the public phone outside the hospital building where she managed to make two calls: Yom-Tov to say she was taking the rest of the day off because she was sick, and taxi.

Later that day, she wouldn't remember the ride home or whom she saw when she got there, how she took her uniform off or how she climbed into her bed.

In the morning, she felt her father's hand on her forehead and heard him ask if she was sick. Ariella quickly moved her head away. She was sad and angry that the doctor, not her father, had broken the news to her. Had he told Eitan?

"I'm fine, just tired," she snapped. "I want to sleep in."

"What about the army?"

"I told Yom-Tov yesterday that I was sick. He'll understand I'm still not well."

"Oh, I thought you said you were fine." Her father frowned and left the room.

She fell asleep again.

"May I come in?" Rachel opened Ariella's bedroom door just an inch.

Ariella opened her eyes, feeling groggy. It seemed dark

outside. She must've slept the whole day.

Rachel crept in and sat on the edge of the bed. She was still in uniform.

"What's wrong? Yom-Tov told me you were sick yesterday afternoon, but you need to get a *gimmel* (a day's rest) from an army doctor, or you'll be an absentee, you know that. You have to come in tomorrow."

Ariella didn't care. What would they do to her? Imprison her?

"Do you have your period again? Didn't you have it two weeks ago, when I got mine?"

Ariella turned her face to the side, her eyes filling with tears. Everything was collapsing.

Rachel waved a blue envelope in her hand. "Do you have a secret lover?" She smiled sheepishly and put it down.

Ariella's head pounded. "What's that?" She picked up the blue aerogram Rachel placed on her blanket. "It's from our relative in America. It's, it's..." Ariella started crying openly. Her world was shattered.

She'll *never* go to America.

"What's wrong? What is it? Ella, what happened? You haven't even opened the letter yet. How do you know it's bad news?" Rachel's eyebrows knitted together in concern.

"I...I...I can't do it...I...I can't go..." Ariella's sobbing increased. "It's...it's not fair..."

"I don't know what you're talking about. You can't go where?"

Eitan walked in.

"Ariella, do you want to come with us to the movies? It might help you feel better. There's this John Wayne movie called *The High and The Mighty* we want to see." Eitan paused.

"Eitan asked me to go to the movies with him," Rachel said, blushing, and looked apologetically at Ariella.

Were they trying to distract her? Were they dating? Didn't Eitan know about Ima?!

"Go, you...you...two go...I want to stay in bed." Ariella didn't have the heart to tell her brother, so she turned her back on them and pulled the blanket over her head, the letter falling on the floor. She heard them tiptoe out of the room but couldn't care about them now.

Ima, Ima, Ima. Ariella covered her face with both hands. You're still so young. You're my mom; what am I going to do without you? I'm so confused. You're leaving me again, even if you don't want to. But this time for good. It isn't fair, damn it!

Her anger increasing, she sat up in bed, her face wet but hot with frustration. It was quiet in the house. Abba and Yael must have been out visiting his sister again. Did they go to see Ima today? Did she miss visiting hours?

Ariella shot out of bed, rubbed her swollen eyes and went to wash her face. The pain was too much; she needed a distraction. She decided to take a walk on the *Tayelet*, the boardwalk by the Mediterranean Sea.

Chapter Eight

IT was March, and spring was battling to come early when the phone rang in the office. Yom-Tov was out.

"Ariella, would you like to clear your head and walk on the beach later? Maybe talk a bit?" It was Arik. "The weather is getting warmer," he continued, trying to persuade her, but she didn't need much persuasion, and his voice sounded so soft and gentle. She was ready to get out of the office and avoid home and the hospital.

She was tired. With fate and with doctors. In desperation she tried praying, but she wasn't convinced anybody was listening. She was willing to start keeping kosher, not ride on Shabbat or go to the beach, if only her mother would survive.

But deep inside, she felt almost certain it wouldn't make a difference. Should she give up her dream to go to America if Ima lived? It would be a huge sacrifice, but yes, she would even do that; she'd stay to look after her, after all of them.

She heard Arik's voice as if it was reaching from far away. "I can pick you up outside the camp's gate at six fifteen if you'd like."

Ariella realized that Arik was being forward again, but she didn't mind; she needed someone to push her, someone straight and honest, and he was it.

"I have a yellow Chevy...you can't miss it," he added.

Ariella's head swirled; Arik was so warm and attentive. But how could she have a nice time while Ima was suffering? She liked him and felt comfortable in his company, like an old friend. He was easy to laugh with and good-natured; it felt like he could bring some light into her life. Why not?

"*Beseder,*" alright, she said, "see you after six."

* * *

At ten minutes to six Ariella readjusted her hair; she took out some bobby pins from the chignon she had formed that morning, pulled it tight, and reapplied the pins. She placed her military cap on top of her head, a bit to the left. After applying new lipstick to her full lips, she took a good look in the small mirror she kept in her purse.

"*Que Sera, Sera,*" Doris Day's new song spun in her head and her mood shifted. She would let fate take control.

Ariella realized she was smiling by the time she reached the base's gate and decided to have a good time tonight. "Put it all out of your mind for a while," she said out loud to herself. Just for one night. There was nothing she could do to save Ima.

The yellow Chevrolet sat waiting, and she slid into the passenger seat with a smile for Arik. His car was warm, and again she smelled the musky aftershave she'd noticed before. She felt a bit nervous; it was already dark outside. The light on the *Tayelet*, boardwalk, at the Tel Aviv beach would be dim. Arik reached into the back seat of his car and handed her a small box wrapped in silver paper. Ariella looked at him in surprise.

"Open it," Arik prompted, smiling as he started the car. She tore the silver paper. It was a box of chocolates. Lindt Chocolate! Ariella couldn't believe it; imported Swiss chocolates, a rarity in Israel those days.

"Thank you!" she said.

Arik laughed; he seemed delighted. His laughter sounded like the waves outside the car window licking the beach, rolling and chasing one another.

"Well, now open the box," he urged her, looking at the road while driving. "I also want a piece, if I may."

Ariella opened the box and stared at the assorted chocolates nestled in their specific indentations. There were so many choices.

"Want to taste a piece and then give me one?"

Ariella chose one and placed it in her mouth. Milk chocolate with a small hazelnut in the center. She closed her eyes for a moment. Heaven.

"Good, right?" Arik sounded pleased. "I'm ready for mine now," he said and opened his mouth, still looking ahead.

Ariella took another piece, and as she popped it quickly into his mouth, she accidentally touched his bottom lip. It was soft, and it made her shiver.

"Hmmmm, isn't it pure delight?" he asked with his mouth full.

"Yes, it's divine. Where did you get it?" She hadn't tasted anything like it for a long time; not since they traveled through Germany six years ago.

"I'm in the import-export business. I bought this one in Paris, although it's Swiss. There's nothing like Swiss chocolate. And Italian coffee, of course."

"Oh, you mean you don't like Israeli Nescafé?" It was her turn to tease him. Her mood had improved already.

"I only love it when you make it." He smiled at her.

Ariella blushed in the darkness of the car.

They arrived at Bugrashov Street, and he found parking easily. As they got out of the car, she felt the wind picking up. Concerned it might rain, Ariella quickly put on her army sweater, and Arik yanked a light jacket from the back seat. The *Tayelet* was almost deserted.

"It's not as warm as I thought it would be. The wind is back. How about walking on the *Tayelet* instead of the sand? I don't want you to catch a cold the first time I take you out."

First time?

He moved in closer and wrapped his right arm lightly around her shoulders. "Are you cold? May I hold you like this?"

Ariella felt grateful for his body heat. He held her gently but firmly, not too tight but close enough for her to feel warm and comfortable.

She smiled up at him. She was 5'3" to his...what? Almost 6'? Over?

"Being in the import-export business, does it take you to South America?" Ariella asked.

"Unfortunately, not, I only work in Europe. Do you feel like telling me about your experience in Argentina?" Arik asked as they walked.

Ariella shivered. "We left Israel in '52 and returned in '54," Ariella said as they walked slowly. "We left at the *Tsena* time, the economic austerity. We were supposed to go to America but ended up in Argentina. I went to a teachers' college and had to live apart from my family. I was very young, only fourteen. When we returned, I went to a kibbutz." She stared at the ground, trying to protect her face from the wind that blew over from the Mediterranean Sea.

"Which kibbutz?"

"Tel-Yitzhak, by Netanya. You see, in Argentina my parents left me in Buenos Aires at the teachers' college hostel and went to a small town called Basavilbaso, where my father got a job as a Yiddish teacher. They were desperate for Hebrew and Yiddish teachers in Argentina, so they trained us all, my father, my brother, and me."

As the wind blew, Arik ran his free hand through his thick

silvering hair. "So why did you return two years later?"

"My mother's parents died in Israel while we were away, and she became full of remorse. My little sister was learning about Christianity in the public school and kept crying that 'the Jews killed Jesus,' as she was taught, so my parents decided it was enough. They were Zionist in their youth in Poland and stayed Zionists in their hearts, I guess. They felt they were betraying Israel by not living here, so we returned." She took a deep breath.

"So why did you go to Tel-Yitzhak?" Arik stopped walking, took his jacket off, and placed it over her shoulders. Ariella smiled and accepted the jacket; the wind was picking up. Arik placed his arm around her shoulders again, and now she felt like she ought to warm him.

"Tel-Yitzhak was where most Argentinian youth went when they wanted to make *Aliyah*, immigrating to Israel. So, I went with some friends from the Zionist Movement. I belonged to the *Movimiento Zionista*—that's Spanish." She looked at him. "After being independent at fourteen, it was hard to go back home and live with my parents, so I joined the kibbutz until I went to the army."

"You're all teachers now?"

"No." She giggled. "My brother is studying economics at night and works as a teller in a bank during the day. My father went back to work in his brother's bakery. He's a baker." Ariella looked in the direction of the rolling sea, far into the darkness. "You should meet my father." Ariella smiled again. "He is self-educated. He's very quiet, reads a lot in four languages: Polish,

Yiddish, Spanish, and Hebrew. He *loves* books. More than people, I think. He isn't a great communicator, though." A gust of wind hit their faces, and she instinctively snugged closer to Arik. They walked in silence after that, but it didn't feel odd. The familiar scent of salt soothed her senses.

"Should we find a place to sit in the park? It may be more sheltered from this wind," Arik suggested. The Independence Park, *Gan Ha'atzma'ut*, the biggest park in Tel Aviv, was only eight years old. The trees were young and the grass untrampled.

They found a bench that wasn't occupied and sat down, thigh to thigh. Arik hugged Ariella's shoulder, pulling her closer.

"I know that the youngsters come here for necking," he said. "I personally prefer the indoors, but for now it will do, I think." He turned to look at her and took her chin in his hand. Looking straight into her eyes, he said, "I hope it's okay with you, too." He bent down and kissed her lightly on the lips.

Not sure she was ready for his advances, she smiled nervously. Arik kissed her gently again, and Ariella could smell the sweet scent of the chocolate he'd eaten in the car. Giving in to her resistance, she returned his kiss this time. He pulled her in and she melted into his chest, feeling a familiar tingling at the pit of her stomach.

"Should we get back to the car?" Arik asked, his voice hoarse.

Ariella wasn't sure if she was disappointed or relieved. She wanted more but felt scared, too. She wasn't sure what to expect. Did he want to neck in the car?

Arik got up and took her hand in his. His palm was surprisingly warm, and very soft.

Seated in the car, moonlight filtered through the windows, bathing them in a soft glow. Arik turned to look at her. "I'm not sure I'm doing the right thing, Ariella." He placed his hand gently on her cheek. "But you're so beautiful," he whispered. He cleared his throat and said louder, "I'm going to Europe tomorrow for an extended business trip. When I get back next month I'd like to see you again. Would you want to? May I call you in the office?"

"Yes," Ariella was quick to reply. She felt nervous but also completely enchanted with the kind, sophisticated man. She didn't want to wait a whole month, and she knew she'd miss him: his soft touch, his sweet smell.

Ariella gave Arik her address and directed him to her home. He parked behind a large truck on a side street.

"I think I better drop you off here. You live just around the block, right? I'm not sure how inquisitive your neighbors are...?" He looked worried and somewhat embarrassed, but still he pulled her gently into his arms; it was easy to do in the car's front bench. He hugged her warmly and whispered into her ear, "It's going to be the longest month of my life." He kissed her softly and let go.

Ariella was touched; he didn't want her neighbors to see him hug her and didn't want to embarrass her. People might gossip. She was grateful for his decency. She opened the car door and turned to look at him.

"Have a good trip," she said before shutting the car door.

He was holding the wheel in both hands, staring out the front windshield, deep in thought. He turned to smile at her, absentmindedly, as if his thoughts were elsewhere already.

Come back safely, she thought.

As she turned the corner to her street, her lips spread into a deep smile.

Chapter Nine

IMA moved in and out of the hospital. Every time, it was another treatment, another test, a relapse, and suddenly, a surge of energy. The whole process exhausted them all. They went from highs to lows, and back again.

It had only been three weeks since Ima had come home, but she was becoming weaker by the day. She lay in bed all day, never even trying to get up to sit in the living room.

Yael would return from school and snuggle with her in her bed, and Ariella often came home to find them both asleep. Abba was always reading the newspaper in the kitchen, and the smell of chicken soup mixed with cigarette smoke filled the house.

It seemed peaceful, but the day came when they realized that they couldn't take care of Ima properly any longer. She had lost her appetite and hardly ate. Occasionally, she would sip some chicken soup. But when she didn't even want that, they panicked and called the doctor.

"You have to admit her back to the hospital, Mr. Paz. She needs an infusion both for food and for the pain" was all the doctor had said to Abba.

Ariella was relieved and ashamed. She had wished somebody else would take over. She was at the end of her strength: the stress, the looking after Ima at home after work, bathing her, helping Abba dress her, seeing to Yael's needs. She was losing weight, too.

* * *

When Ariella came to visit Ima, she was determined to stay in a good mood and cheer up Ima, too, no matter what condition she was in. She stopped outside Ima's door, reapplied her lipstick, sprayed a tiny bit of perfume on her wrist to help with the hospital scent, and entered.

"*Shalom*, Ima. I have some news for you," Ariella announced.

Ima opened her eyes and waited.

"Are you ready for this?" She sat on the edge of Ima's bed and took her hand. "Yael got her period last night!"

Ima smiled faintly.

"She got a bit of a fright, you know." Ariella continued. "She came to me and showed me her panties. She didn't panic but looked very surprised and a little scared. So, of course, I explained what it was."

"*Mazal tov*. Congratulations. I hope I'll remember to say *mazal tov* when I see her. She is almost twelve, my baby, just in time," Ima managed.

"Do you remember, Ima, what you did to me when I got *my* period?"

Her mother raised her thin eyebrows in surprised. "What did I do?"

Ariella chuckled. "You said mazal tov and slapped me."

"Oh, that." Ima rested her eyes again. "That was to scare the evil eye, you know, to make sure nothing bad happened to you. My mother did it to all of us girls back in Poland. It's a tradition."

"I think this is one superstitious tradition my generation can do without."

Ima seemed to be sleeping again.

Chapter Ten

ARIELLA was walking toward her office with a large pile of files nestled in her arms when she heard Major Yom-Tov talking. She stopped in her tracks.

"…was going to leave the office in five minutes. So good to see you, you busy man! How was your trip? And what are you doing here? I thought we were going to meet at the restaurant."

She entered her office and dropped the top two files. Arik rushed to help her and took the files from her arms as Yom-Tov raised his eyebrows. She picked up the two files that had fallen, feeling dizzy as she stood up again.

"You can place them all on my desk, Ariella. I'm going out for lunch with my friend here. Arik, have you met Ariella Paz?

She just became a sergeant—you should congratulate her. I have three more months before I lose her. It's not going to be a happy day when she's dismissed."

Arik and Ariella placed the files on her desk and moved awkwardly toward each other; Ariella's heart leaping into her throat.

"Nice to meet you. I'm Arik Emmanuel," he said formally, extending his hand to shake hers as he looked at the three stripes on her shirt-sleeve. She stared at him wide-eyed and tongue tied.

"And congratulations, Sergeant Ariella." He flashed his white teeth.

She liked the game of secrecy, pretending they had never met.

"Ariella?" Yom-Tov looked at her, his eyebrows raised.

She shook her head as if waking up. "Nice to meet you. I'm Ariella. Uh, and thank you. Yes, thank you."

She scurried to her own office and pretended to be busy with some papers on her desk, her hands shaking.

"You've made an impression, Arik," she heard Yom-Tov say with a chuckle.

She waited. Arik didn't reply.

"I wondered why you came in. It wasn't so you could see my assistant, was it?" Yom-Tov laughed warmly. "Let's go; I'm starving. See you later, Ariella." And they were gone. Arik didn't even look back her way.

What'd just happened? Why didn't he look at her when he left?

A minute later Arik was back. Alone. "Come," he whispered when he grabbed her hand and pulled her gently into Yom-Tov's office. The room had no door to the corridor, only into Ariella's office.

"I missed you so much," Arik whispered, as he cupped her small face in both his hands. "Can I see you tonight?"

Ariella placed her hands on his, as if trying to imprint his palms on her face. They stared into each other's eyes. I missed you too, she thought, but out loud only said, "Yes."

"*Yofi.*" Great. Arik took his hands off. "I'll be waiting at six thirty around the corner. Come out the base's gate and turn right. I'll be waiting there. Will you come?" he said urgently.

"Yes," she managed to whisper again, almost out of breath, before he ran back out.

Ariella sat down again, the blood pumping in her ears. He was back, and he still wanted her.

* * *

"I'm driving south of Tel Aviv, a bit out of town, I hope you don't mind," Arik said as soon as Ariella closed the car door. She didn't reply. She'd gotten back from the hospital two hours ago and found it hard to concentrate on her work. Ima had seemed so frail.

On the car radio Yafa Yarkoni sang *Ha'amini, yom yavo*, Believe, a day will come. Ariella closed her eyes. When she opened them again, she noticed Arik was driving along the beach, south of the *Tayelet*, in the direction of Old Jaffa. She opened her window, let the cold air in, and closed her eyes.

"Are you tired?" Arik asked.

"No, not at all." Ariella opened her eyes and smiled. "This song always makes me sad. I love Yafa Yarkoni. I listen to her songs all the time. This one is hopeful, but 'Please don't say goodbye to me, just say, see-you' almost makes me cry."

"You're a romantic, I see. Should I turn the radio off?" He gave her a big smile.

"No, no." She raised her hand as if in defense. "Leave it on...I promise I won't cry." She wasn't thinking romantically; she was thinking of her mother.

The restaurant in Old Jaffa looked more like a small dining room in a private home, a large and very old brick house. It must have belonged to an Israeli-Arab. She'd never been to a place like it, but she knew that mostly Arabs lived in Old Jaffa.

The soft voice of Umm Kulthum, the Egyptian female singer, filled the room. She saw eight round metal tables covered with white tablecloths and four chairs around each table. The walls were painted turquoise, accented by red-and-gold fixtures in dim lighting.

Two men occupied one of the tables. They both wore long, white *Jalabiyas,* the white cotton dresses Arab men wear, and checkered *Kafias* on their heads. One had a red rope-like band around it, and the other had a black one. They were smoking *Nargilas,* hookahs, through a long mouthpiece. The smell was strong for Ariella's sensitive nostrils, but she knew she'd get used to it soon enough.

Both men nodded to Arik as they walked in. Arik nodded

back. The waiter, also with a long white *Jalabiya* and a *Kafia*, smiled broadly. Ariella had the impression he was the owner.

"*Salaam Aleikum*, my friend," he greeted Arik in Arabic, shaking his hand and tapping his shoulder with his other hand. He smiled and nodded to Ariella. She realized that Arik must frequent this place and was much liked. "A business meeting?" He winked at Arik.

"Actually, yes," Arik said seriously. "You see, she is in uniform."

"Madam-soldier." He turned to face her now. "What can I get you to drink?" It seemed he was trying to sound respectful, but she also heard a tinge of sarcasm. "Orange juice? Lemonade? Hot tea? Maybe wine?"

"Lemonade, with a little *nahna*, please." Ariella loved peppermint in her lemonade.

The table was laden with a small dish presenting cracked green olives speckled with olive oil and hot red pepper, and a large plate with thick-cream-textured hummus holding proudly in its center a well of snow-white tahini with a dash of *S 'hug*, hot sauce. Next came the pita. Oh, the large, warm golden pita straight from the Taboon sent its delicious fragrance into the air. Later they indulged in beef kebab and large French fries.

The meal tasted out of this world. Out of *her* world.

She couldn't remember eating meat like that since Argentina. As of late, her parents could only afford chicken and some fish. Beef was reserved for special occasions.

Arik asked about her childhood, if she had siblings, her parents' origins. Ariella answered politely, not wanting to talk about her parents or even think of them.

"What about you?" she asked. "What do you do exactly? Where were *you* born and raised?" She tried to divert the conversation from her parents, specifically, her mother.

He laughed. The sound of his laughter rich, like velvet; she longed to touch it.

"I was born in Poland, like your parents, but in Warsaw, a big city. My family immigrated to Israel when I was three. What town are your parents from?"

"Katarina and Sosnowiec," Ariella replied.

Ariella thought of her mother at the repeated mention of her parents.

No, I'm not going to think of you now, Ima, please let me have this time without worry.

"I've been back to Poland, you know? They still don't like Jews there," he said.

She frowned slightly, and he continued in a different direction, thankfully. "I've been to Germany, too, to England and France for my import-export company."

"What do you import?" Ariella asked.

"Many things. From horse-pulled ploughs to iceboxes."

"And what can you export from Israel?" She was surprised; Israel was such a young country.

"Mainly oranges." Arik said. Ariella listened intently, leaning toward him. "I also arrange art exhibitions in Europe for my painter friend. He's an old army buddy."

Ariella tilted her head with interest, genuinely impressed.

"I'd like you to meet him some day. He's blind."

"Wait a minute," she said, feeling confused. "He's an artist, and he is blind?"

"Yeah, long story. He was an artist before, but we both got injured in the war and, unfortunately, he lost his sight. I'll tell you the story one day." A soft smile formed around his lips, and tiny lines spread at the corners of his eyes. "I wish he could see you. I'm sure he would have wanted to paint you, your long neck and your shining brown eyes."

Ariella blushed as Arik scanned her face, a bigger smile on his. He seemed to have noticed her embarrassment and took her hand in his, as if to console her for the uneasiness. But this didn't make her feel any calmer. His soft, warm hands, both enveloping hers, made her pulse quicken. She longed to pat his cheek, touch his lips. What was happening to her? She felt almost panicked. She hadn't experienced such a strong attraction to a man in a long time.

As if noticing her growing discomfort, Arik gently let go of her hand and said, "Hey, my friend the painter has a place not far from here, a small apartment. He actually lives in Jerusalem, but this is where he keeps some beautiful paintings. Would you like to see them?"

Ariella had to think quickly. She wasn't stupid. If she went to Arik's friend's apartment with him, that would be it. She could see the eagerness in his eyes.

Yes, she'd go; she liked him a lot. Life was going by, Ima was slipping away, America was too far. In September she'd be twenty; she had nothing more to lose, only her virginity.

Ariella was ready.

Chapter Eleven

AS they exited the restaurant, Arik took her hand and said, "Let's walk. Benny's apartment is only two blocks away."

They walked in silence. The calming air from the sea felt fresh, but different. It wasn't spring yet, though hints of it were apparent, as the days grew longer. The sun had set but the sky over the sea was still lit with a hazy grey.

Although Arik's soft hand felt strong and reassuring, Ariella's mouth went dry and her temples felt hot. She felt excitement mixed with fear, which left her legs unsteady.

They walked up two flights of stairs hand in hand before Arik unlocked the door to the apartment. Interesting, she thought. His friend gave him a key to his apartment. They must look like characters in a black and white movie, entering an unknown place, secretive and mysterious, even dangerous.

First thing, she asked where the restroom was. Two of the hallway walls were lined with deep shelves filled with large, flat sheets of paper, painting-size, and some rolled up. She had to be careful not to bump into a shelf.

She cupped her hand under the faucet and took a sip of water. Peering into the small round mirror above the sink, she noticed her cheeks were flushed and her lips were red, as if she'd been biting them. Sea breeze from a small open window caressed her face and cooled her cheeks. She could do this. There was nothing to fear. She opened the bathroom door.

That's when she heard the music. Arik must have put a record on the gramophone, as the song "The Prayer," sung by The Platters, spilled into the apartment.

When she came out, Arik stood staring out the window of the studio apartment, a cigarette in one hand and a glass with Cinzano and ice cubes in the other. The moon bathed his perfect profile in a silvery light, and Ariella stood still for a moment, taking it all in.

He turned around and stared back.

Without moving his gaze from hers, he placed his glass down on the small table, and walked slowly toward her. His nose almost touched hers. Ariella gently took the cigarette out of his hand and puffed on it, maybe to calm her nerves. Arik blinked as the smoke curled up toward his eyes. He took her other hand slowly and placed a gentle kiss inside her palm. Then he looked back into her eyes, took the cigarette back, puffed once, and put it out in his glass. *Tsssss.* She heard the cigarette die.

The Platters sang "Smoke Gets in Your Eyes," and she gave him a shy smile.

Arik put his hand out, and Ariella placed her palm in his. Slowly they moved closer to one another. He placed his free hand at the small of her back, and they began dancing, swaying in each other's arms as the words of the song floated in the air around them. Listening to the lyrics, Ariella thought, are lovers always blind?

As Arik held her tight, she felt the heat rise from her chest to her face. She moved closer. Arik narrowed his eyes, and she saw the unspoken question there. She blinked. As they swayed to the music, Arik lifted her chin with his hand and kissed her parted lips softly. She clung to him as he hugged her and kissed her bottom lip, more urgently now.

Ariella couldn't breathe; she had to gasp. She thought she heard the song "The Great Pretender" as Arik whispered, "You're so beautiful," and kissed her neck. Ariella felt him move his hand down from her chin to cup her small breast. She put her arms around his neck and once again tasted his mouth. When her body clung to his, when she felt his hardness and her own throbbing, she knew he wanted her, and she wanted him. Nothing else mattered.

Arik led Ariella to the bedroom. Her starched military uniform fell on the large, square tiles as he unbuttoned her shirt and she unzipped her khaki skirt. She stood in her simple white bra and panties in front of him. A shiver ran through her body.

He unbuttoned his long-sleeved shirt and let it drop to the floor.

With one hand, Arik yanked the covers off the bed, gently guiding Ariella to the side of it. She forced herself to look at his muscular and slightly hairy chest as he pulled off his pants. Disrobed, he lay down next to her, kissing her from her lips to the nape of her neck, from her smooth shoulder to above her breast. He pulled her bra strap down and licked her shoulder, exposing one breast. She moaned when he sucked on her nipple.

Arik unhooked her bra and threw it on the floor. Ariella stopped shivering as a wave of heat engulfed her. When his hand reached below her navel, she arched toward him.

Arik dragged her panties down over her hips, caressing and kissing her with a passion that enveloped her in a yearning haze of warmth and desire. Ariella was ready for him. He pushed her legs apart with his knee and slowly pulled himself over her body, holding on to her face and kissing her.

The sharp stabbing, the pushing, the thrusting, and the little cry that escaped her lips surprised her. She used to neck with boyfriends, even in Argentina, but never went the whole way. Now she gasped, and Arik continued his thrusts. She bit her lower lip, and he moaned and kept moving up and down. Then he shivered and pulled out, wetting her stomach and thigh. Ariella felt the cold wetness between them when he lay on top of her, panting, both his arms spread to her sides. She wanted him to hug her; she needed him to comfort her.

As if reading her mind, Arik put his arms around her back

and held her close. She didn't know what to do, so she hugged him back.

"I'm sorry, *motek*, I didn't know...eh," he said. Sweetheart. "Did it hurt?"

"I'm okay now." Ariella didn't want to disappoint him and bit her lip again. It burnt between her legs, as if she had a cut. Arik slid off her, and it seemed to her that he fell asleep in a second.

She turned on her side with her back to him, and brought her knees up to her chest, feeling confused. She wasn't sure if she had lost something or gained something. But she knew she had changed. She allowed one tear to make its way onto the pillow. At least the worst was over.

She pulled the covers over her naked body and lay back, listening to Arik's light snoring. She felt sticky but couldn't see in the dark. Making her way to the bathroom, Ariella saw blood on the tissue paper. She stepped into the tiny shower and rinsed herself, the warm water soothing her body.

Back in bed, she lay on her side, leaning on her left elbow, and looking at Arik. He slept soundly on his back, his eyes closed. She searched his face. His breath smelled so sweet, she couldn't resist licking his full lips. He twitched. Eventually her pain dissipated, and she fell asleep, too, exhausted from the emotional tide.

Ariella awoke and stretched her limbs. The sheets felt different from her own, softer. The streetlights peeped through the slats of the half-closed blinds, throwing thin lines on the walls and dark furniture.

Arik lay fast asleep next to her. Her eyes adjusted to the dark, seeing the room with its high ceiling and old furniture. What was the time? She searched for a clock and discovered one on top of the armoire, but she couldn't make out the hands in the dark, so she slanted her tiny wristwatch toward the light from the window, where the moon shone. Ten minutes to twelve. Twelve? Almost midnight! She needed to get home; her father would be worried.

Arik stirred and opened his eyes. He smiled as if surprised, and turned to her, raising his torso and leaning on his right elbow. He gently kissed her lips. Like butterflies, Ariella thought and closed her eyes. And he kissed them, too. And the tip of her nose. And her ear. And the small of her neck. She moaned and wiggled, her eyes still closed.

He kissed her mouth again, not so gently this time. She placed a hand on his chest, as if to stop him. But Arik just picked up her hand and kissed the tips of her fingers. His lips were on fire. She hoped it wouldn't hurt this time. The worst was over. And as if confirming it, Arik was as gentle as she wished he would be. He softly squeezed her small breasts as if they were tender fledglings and licked her nipples which made her groan. She forgot the time, forgot her father, and let the warmth wash over her.

Chapter Twelve

ARIELLA stood in the living room, smiling at Yael. "Get dressed, Yuli, in your nicest dress."

"Why?" Yael narrowed her eyes with suspicion.

"It's your birthday, no? You're twelve today! Just go get dressed."

"My teacher brought a cake to school, and my friends had a little party for me at break," Yael told Ariella. "The rest of the family already gave me gifts."

"That was very nice of them." Ariella knew that her father had attended a conference with Yael's teachers, and they all knew the situation with Ima. No talk of a Bat-Mitzvah celebration was discussed.

"Rachel and I are taking you to the movies." Ariella felt responsible to do something special for her younger sister.

"The movies?" Yael's eyes lit up. "With Rachel?" Yael loved Rachel.

Ariella smiled. "Go already, get dressed."

Ariella watched Yael grinning with joy throughout the Swiss movie *Heidi* with Elspeth Sigmund. Afterward, Ariella and Rachel took her out for ice cream.

"This is for you, Yuli." Rachel handed Yael a little blue velvet box. "From both of us." She looked at Ariella.

Yael looked from Ariella to the box and back to Rachel.

She opened the box. "Ohhhh!" Yael let out a surprised cry. There lay a thin gold ring with a small aquamarine, her birthstone. She placed it on her finger and smiled broadly. It fit perfectly. That night, before bed, it found a special place in the jewelry box Yael had gotten from Abba and Ima.

Maybe the last gift she'd ever get from her mother.

* * *

The thought of being discharged from the army gave Ariella a bittersweet feeling. She'd been looking forward to the day since she hung a wall calendar in her office for the last one hundred days of service, and every evening before she went home, she'd cross off one date. From tomorrow, Ariella had only forty-five days of military service, and then she'd be free.

The thought of it no longer comforted her. Instead, she felt she was ticking off Ima's days, too. She shivered as she lay in bed thinking of it. Oh my God. Tomorrow I'll tear down the calendar, she thought, fear penetrating her body. She tossed and turned for hours until she finally fell asleep.

Exactly three weeks later, the doorbell rang. Ariella looked at her watch; it was seven thirty in the evening. She got up from the armchair in the living room, placed her book down on the side table, and opened the door. She gasped.

"Aunt Pearl!" she said, falling into the young woman's arms. Her twenty-eight-year-old aunt had flown in from South Africa. "You're here!" Ariella burst out crying; all the tension, the fear, and exhaustion coming to a head when her mother's youngest sister stood before her. Pearl held Ariella tight, and they both cried from desperation, fatigue, and helplessness. But also, happy to have each other.

Uncle Rafael, who brought her from the airport, stood nearby holding her suitcase. "We surprised you, right?" His eyes shone.

"Come in, come in," Ariella said, having gotten over the initial shock. "Such a wonderful surprise! Why didn't you tell us you were coming?" She hadn't seen her aunt in more than two years. "You look beautiful!"

"You can say that again," said Uncle Rafael. "She looks just like you!"

Aunt Pearl looked at her brother. "Rafael wanted to surprise you all, and I just went along. It was a last-minute decision, and now I'm here."

"Abba went with Yael to visit Aunt Leah, and Eitan will

be home soon...he's at Rachel's. I'm so glad to see you...Oh, my God, Ima is going to be ecstatic."

"How is she?" Aunt Pearl said in a low voice, as if somebody were sleeping in the room. "Rafael says that it's pretty bad. Is it? Is it really bad?" Pearl sounded pained, and Ariella couldn't dispel the grim news; her eyes welled up again.

"Yes, Aunt Pearl, I'm afraid it's very bad."

Aunt Pearl put a hand over her mouth, stifling a cry.

The three of them sat down in the small living room, on the couch which at night became Ima and Abba's bed. Now, only Abba's.

Ariella nestled into her mother's favorite armchair. "I'm sure she'll be thrilled to see you. She may even feel better just having you beside her."

"I have to go, my dear ladies," Uncle Rafael stood up. "Dalia and the girls are waiting for me. You have room for Pearl, right, Ariella?"

Ariella nodded and hugged him goodbye. She missed the times the two of them used to spend together, just having coffee when she had visited her parents from the kibbutz. Since his daughters were born in the past three years, he became busy with work and his own family, and she felt like she had lost him.

Eitan walked in then. He hung his light jacket on a hook by the door and turned to look into the living room where three pairs of eyes followed his movements.

"Eitan, my dear boy!" Aunt Pearl got up and rushed to hug him. Ariella smiled. Aunt Pearl was only four years older than Eitan and eight years older than Ariella, but she called him *boy* because he was her first and only nephew; all the others were girls.

"Aunt Pearl!" Eitan's green eyes opened in surprise. "Thank you for coming, what a wonderful surprise. Ima will be so happy to see you."

"And you, my boy?" She smiled at him lovingly.

"Me too, of course," Eitan said shyly.

"Where should I put Pearl's bag? Where will she sleep, Ariella?" Uncle Rafael asked while hugging Eitan's shoulder.

"Here, take my room." Eitan surprised them all. "I can sleep with Abba on the couch in the living room, where Ima sleeps."

Aunt Pearl looked at Ariella, who nodded.

"Let me just take out my things and make room for you," Eitan said and went to his little room.

Yael and Abba walked in as Uncle Rafael stepped out the front door to leave. The apartment suddenly came alive; its walls hadn't heard happy cries for a long time. Yael leaped for joy at the sight of her beloved young aunt, and even Abba allowed a hint of a smile on his face.

"What a pleasant surprise," he said.

Aunt Pearl's eyes lit up when she saw him, Ariella noticed.

The next day Aunt Pearl reported that, after many loud arguments, she'd gotten special permission from the hospital administration to sit by her dying sister for two hours in the morning, on top of the two regular visiting hours in the afternoon. She told them that she had come on a long trip from another continent and would raise hell at their gate every morning if they wouldn't let her in. Ariella was happy it worked out and that there would be somebody in the apartment when her father and sister returned home every day.

At first, they could all see that Ima *loved* having her sister by her side every single day. But then Ima began falling asleep almost every time the rest of the family came to visit. Sometimes the nurse came in and checked the pain drip which was attached to her hand, and Ima would wake up and look around, but she hardly spoke to anybody.

Their mother was slipping away, the morphine taking away her pain along with her mind. Ariella knew that Ima was losing her battle. It had been four months since Ariella's talk with Dr. Brill, and she found it hard to fall asleep at night, afraid that every night would be Ima's last.

Chapter Thirteen

THE alarm clock beeped in Old Jaffa, waking Ariella from a restless sleep. Six forty-five in the morning. She smelled the brewing coffee and smiled, as she could hear Arik in the kitchen making Turkish coffee in the *Finjaan,* a Middle Eastern coffee pot. Ariella's nostrils welcomed the strong aroma filling the little studio apartment.

Was it Saturday? *Shabbat*? She wondered. Oh no, it was Wednesday! She jumped out of bed and yelled to Arik on her way to the bathroom, "I have to be at base in forty-five minutes! Why did you let me sleep so late?"

It was only her second time in the apartment in Old Jaffa, and Ariella wasn't sure which bus to take or even how long it would take her to get to the base. The night before, she had put her uniform neatly on the chair in the entrance hall so as not to crease it, and now, after she washed, she quickly dressed. It didn't look as fresh as the previous day, but she had no time to scrutinize herself.

"*Boker tov, motek.*" Good morning, sweetie. Arik handed her a cup of sweet, black coffee. "Don't worry; I'll drop you close to the base's gate. Ready?"

Ariella took only two sips and grabbed her black bag. "Oh, thank you."

While Arik drove the car, she combed her hair and put it up with bobby pins before placing her cap on top.

She showed her entry pass to the *Shin-Gimmel*, the gate-guard at the base's gate, at exactly seven thirty. At ten of eight the phone rang in her office.

"*Boker tov*, Major Yom-Tov's office," Ariella said.

"Ariella, it's me, Rafi." She recognized Uncle Rafael's urgent tone. "Please get a taxi and come to the hospital right away. We need you."

What?! Taxi? Hospital? Her head pounded and her heart beat wildly. She couldn't just walk out of the base's gate; she needed a pass. This was the military. But Yom-Tov wasn't in yet. She'd have to go to Cohen's office, and who knew if he was there. She dialed his extension.

"*Boker Tov*, First Sergeant Cohen's office," Rachel said cheerfully.

"Rachel, it's Ariella. Is Cohen in? I need to go to the hospital right away. I need a pass," she panted urgently.

"Oh no, he isn't in. What's happened?"

"I'm not sure, but my uncle just called and said I need to hurry and get there. What am I going to do? What's happening to my mother?" Ariella doubled over with panic, her stomach in a knot.

"Go to the gate and tell the *Shin-Gimmel* you have to leave the base and go to the hospital. Tell him your mother is sick and...and, I'll look for Cohen or somebody..."

Ariella didn't hear the end of Rachel's sentence. She slammed down the phone, snatched her purse, and ran.

The *Shin-Gimmel* wouldn't open the gate for her; he claimed she needed permission to leave the base.

Ariella began to cry hysterically. "My mother's in the hospital and she...she may be dying." Suddenly she got angry and yelled at him, "It will be your fault if she dies and I'm not there, you...you'll have that on your conscience."

The corporal seemed bewildered. "I'll go to jail if I let you out without a pass, I...I'm only following—" At that moment the big gate opened, and a first-lieutenant drove in. Ariella darted past his car and down the street toward the bus stop.

No, no bus, it's too slow, stopping at each bus stop, she suddenly remembered. Her uncle said to take a taxi. She ran down the block and around the corner to the taxi depot. Thank goodness there was one taxi available. By the time she got in, her hair had tumbled out of her bun and she tied it back with trembling hands, desperately trying to pull herself together. I may go to jail, she thought. She didn't care.

When Ariella arrived at the hospital, she ran to Ima's room and was met by Aunt Pearl's raised eyebrows as if asking, *Where were you the whole night?* Ariella tried to ignore her. She was too distraught and guilt-ridden, and focused on Ima. Uncle Rafael came over and hugged her shoulder.

She stood at her mother's bed, surrounded by her family, and listened to Ima gasping for air. They all stood in silence. Uncle Rafael hugged Aunt Pearl's shoulder with his other arm, and she leaned her head on him and sobbed. Ariella moved away and took Eitan's hand.

She felt nothing. Empty.

Uncle Rafael seemed to be the first to recover; he stepped out of the room to call the nurse. *Yael.* How would they tell Yael? She wished her sister was there, so they could hold each other; maybe some heat from her sister's body would thaw the ice that gripped her heart.

Ima took her final breath as the family looked on, one week before her forty-eighth birthday, and ten days before Ariella would complete her military service.

Ariella couldn't believe it. Her mother was gone. No wedding day celebrations with her mother to look forward to. No mother to comfort her when she went through troubled time. Ima only lived four months past her diagnosis, not the six the doctor had promised.

Ariella felt cheated. Her mother had been taken from her before she was ready.

* * *

Ariella knew that it would shock her sister to see her, Abba, Eitan, Uncle Rafael, and Aunt Pearl all in the living room, in the middle of the day. They had all returned only an hour ago from the hospital and were discussing the funeral that was to take place in about three hours. Jewish law required burial as soon after death as possible, to give the soul, as well as the body, a resting place.

They were all gathered together when Yael came home from school.

Aunt Pearl stood up first, wiping her wet cheeks. She hugged Yael and pulled her by the hand to sit on the couch between her and Uncle Rafael. Abba and Eitan, both sitting on dining room chairs with their hands folded in their laps, stared at the floor in discomfort. Ariella closed the circle, sitting in Ima's favorite armchair, looking at her sister. She had no words of comfort to share with anybody.

As Aunt Pearl whispered in her ear, Yael nodded but didn't speak. Ariella couldn't hear what her aunt had said but watched as Yael's sweet face crumpled and tears fell down her reddened cheeks and onto Aunt Pearl's chest.

The doorbell rang, and Eitan got up to open the door.

Ariella stumbled toward her baby sister and opened her arms, ignoring her aunts and uncles who came in. As Uncle Rafael got up to greet the new guests, Ariella took his place on the couch. Yael melted into Ariella's embrace and hugged her tightly. They sat holding each other, as if their lives depended on their embrace, as if they had to draw the will to continue living without Ima from each other's energy.

"Go change your clothes, Yael," Ariella said softly to her sister, looking into her eyes. "Put on an old shirt; we're going to the cemetery and they may tear your collar," she said sadly.

Yael looked at her sister with big, surprised eyes.

Ariella didn't have time to explain the ancient Jewish custom of *Kri'ah,* the tearing of the shirt collar of mourners as an expression of grief and anger at the loss of a loved one.

"Hurry up," she snapped as she looked for an old shirt for herself as well. She felt a nervous energy building up. Going to bury Ima wasn't an option; it had to be done.

They all dispersed into several family cars and sat in a long and slow procession to the cemetery. Nobody talked. Ariella stared outside the car's window, watching people walk the sidewalks, as if nothing had happened, as if Ima hadn't died that morning. Some men removed their hats and nodded their heads. Because the car lights were on, and they were traveling at such a slow speed and so close to each other, people must have realized it was a funeral.

As they parked and walked into the funeral home, the sadness gripped Ariella's chest like a vice. A stout woman in a kerchief and heavy black shoes walked into the room with a razor blade in her hand. "These are the daughters, and the sister," a family member whispered, pointing at Ariella, Yael, and Aunt Pearl, the deceased blood relatives. The woman approached Ariella first and sliced her collar. The sound of the fabric giving in to the sharp blade sent shivers down Ariella's spine. She grasped Yael's hand in hers when the woman repeated the *Kriah* on Yael's collar. Yael went pale when the woman came with the razor blade close to her face and neck, while muttering some sort of blessing which Ariella couldn't make out, so she whispered to Yael, "Tear your collar a bit more...this is the custom," and demonstrated on her own collar. She should have explained it to her earlier, Ariella thought with regret, squeezing Yael's hand again. Aunt Pearl tore her collar, too, and then took Yael's other hand.

Abba, Eitan, and Uncle Rafael emerged from the men's section of the funeral home, Eitan and Abba fingering their torn collars as though not sure what to do with the dangling pieces.

They all walked solemnly, following the stretcher of her dead mother's shroud-wrapped body to the open grave. She was carried on the shoulders of four men: nephews, friends, and others who wanted to partake in the *mitzvah* (commandment) of taking a loved one to their final resting place. Every few steps the men paused, and four other men took over the handles of the stretcher, placing them on their shoulders, and proceeding. In this way, they all had a chance to honor the deceased.

The women followed the procession. No casket or coffin, Ariella thought sadly, not like in the movies. In the Holy Land people were buried straight in the ground. "*For you are earth and to earth you shall return,*" it is stated in the Bible.

Ariella wondered what happened to the shrouds over time. And to the body? Her thoughts tortured her as she followed her mother's body to the freshly dug grave.

Nobody spoke; only the Rabbi's voice was heard as he chanted the prayer *El Maleh Rachamim* (Merciful God). Eitan read the Aramaic mourning *Kaddish* for their dead mother in monotone, without understanding. Ariella could hear Aunt Pearl and Dalia sniffling. But she, along with Abba, Eitan, and Yael, stood there with dry eyes, in shock. Like they didn't realize it was real. In that moment it hit her—they were only four.

Then there was nobody to visit in the hospital in the afternoons, a routine all too familiar. Ariella's chest felt hollow.

Chapter Fourteen

ARIELLA was delighted that her kind and gentle Aunt Pearl came to visit and stayed with them during those difficult times, but was surprised one day during *Shiva* when Aunt Pearl suddenly asked her, "Do you have a special someone you see when you go out, Ariella? Is that where you were when... eh...last Tuesday?"

Aunt Pearl's directness shocked Ariella. Abba never asked her about where she went or with whom, and neither did Eitan. They were all so focused on Ima's illness, the funeral arrangements, and now *Shiva*, the Jewish ritual of seven days of mourning. Ariella was usually left to her own devices; she was almost twenty, for goodness' sake, in four months!

Her father looked up.

"Nobody special," Ariella told her aunt, trying to fake indifference. Knowing she sounded nervous, she got busy in the kitchen with her back to them, and nobody bothered her anymore.

Sunday, the first of June, was Ariella's last day of service. It also happened to be the first day after *Shiva* that she could return to the office. An unfortunate coincidence.

Yom-Tov was working in his office when she came in. Early riser, as usual.

"Good to see you, Ariella. Welcome back. May you never know grief." Ariella was touched by the blessing, a customary saying directed at Jews in mourning.

She loved Yom-Tov's kindness, cheerfulness, and good manners. She was going to miss him.

"So, this is your last day here." Yom-Tov continued as a cropped-haired, bleached blonde corporal walked out of his office. "This is Mira. Mira, this is our famous Ariella."

Mira extended her hand to Ariella. "Nice to meet you. I'm sorry for your loss."

Ariella's eyes welled up. "Thank you," she managed to murmur, overwhelmed; so many losses, so many changes.

"I tried to do your job as well as I could." Mira smiled shyly. "But would you leave me a phone number or something, so I can call you in case I have questions?"

Ariella looked at Yom-Tov.

"Mira replaced you this past week and will work here until she's discharged in eight months. So, if you can leave me some kind of contact number, a friend's or maybe a family member's, I'd appreciate it." It was an unusual request, Ariella knew. Once a woman was discharged, she was done. Only men were called annually to *Milu'im*, reserve army, for a month's training.

Yom-Tov continued, "Would you like to show her a few of your tricks? She isn't bad but needs some polishing." He winked at them good-naturedly, and they both smiled.

"Sure, I'll be happy to, Major. I'll write down my uncle's phone number." She quickly jotted down Uncle Rafael's information, but before the Major had a chance to leave them to their work, the phone rang. The two soldiers reached to pick up the receiver and instantly withdrew their hands. All three laughed. Ariella nodded to Mira and pointed to the phone.

Oh, what was she going to do without a telephone? How was Arik going to contact her? Not having a phone at home was really bad. She hadn't thought about it before, being so preoccupied with her family.

"Major Yom-Tov's office, *Boker tov*." Good morning.

Ariella stood by Mira, waiting in case she needed her help. But then Mira handed her the phone and said, "For you."

Ariella took the receiver from Mira's hand, frowning. "Hello," she said.

"*Motek sheli*, (my sweetie). I knew you'd be in today. I miss you so much."

Ariella almost burst out crying. She hadn't seen him since... Mira stood right beside her, staring. Ariella turned her back to her. How could she talk to Arik while being watched so closely by a stranger?

"Mira, could you please make me some coffee?" Yom-Tov called from his office. Oh, how Ariella *loved* Yom-Tov!

Mira walked away.

"Oh, Arik," Ariella whispered, cupping the mouthpiece.

"I'm so sorry, *motek*. Yom-Tov told me about your mother. I'm devastated for you. Can I see you tonight? I so want to hold you."

"Yes, yes," Ariella said urgently but quietly into the phone, eyeing Yom-Tov's door, "but I need to have dinner with my family first. My aunt is going back to South Africa tomorrow, and it's our last dinner together."

"Is nine o'clock a good time? I can wait for you around the corner on Shimon Ha'Cohen Street. I miss you so much, my sweet."

Oh, she so wanted to be in his arms. "Make it nine thirty, alright? I miss you, too." Tears rolled down her cheeks as she replaced the receiver. She wiped her face quickly.

It was almost five o'clock when Yom-Tov called Ariella into his office. "Ariella, I want to say a proper goodbye. You've been an exemplary soldier. Here is your Discharge Certificate. And, one more thing." He cleared his throat. "My friend Arik..." She felt the blood drain from her face. "He is an old and very good friend of mine, but he has a weakness for beautiful women." He got up and looked her in the eye, adding, "make wise decisions."

Ariella averted her eyes. What did he know? Was that just a friendly warning? Yom-Tov gave her the first and only hug she had ever gotten from him.

Ariella strode out the gate. The *Shin-Gimmel,* nodded. Ariella smiled at him, not knowing if he'd ever reported her leaving the base without a pass.

Never mind—she was free!

Chapter Fifteen

WHEN Ariella got home, she headed straight to the shower and peeled off her sticky military uniform. *For the last time!*

The June humidity made her feel slimy; summer had arrived, and freedom. As the water dripped down her back, the words "make wise decisions," which had been hammering in her head for the past hour, seemed to go down the drain with it.

Wrapped in a thin, overused towel, she stood in front of her armoire, scanning her civilian clothes. After twenty-four months in uniform, it felt like she could finally show her real figure to the world; her petite silhouette, delicate looks, small feet, smooth olive skin, and well-kept long shiny hair. All she needed now were some pretty clothes. She had one new dress, the olive green, purple, and lilac sleeveless dress Aunt Pearl had brought her from South Africa. Lilac piping adorned the square neck and sleeve openings. Double pleated at the waist, it opened all the way down to just above her knees, with a thin lilac belt emphasized her small waist. She slid on her dress, put her slightly damp hair in very large rollers, and glided into the kitchen to join her aunt in preparing a chopped Israeli salad: tomato, cucumber, and onion; all cut very small, dressed in olive oil and lemon juice, salt, and black pepper.

Aunt Pearl handed her a clean apron and said, "You look beautiful, Ariella. I knew it would fit you like a glove...we're the same size. It comes from Germany, by the way. They have amazing fashion there."

Ariella kissed her aunt's cheek. "Thank you."

The family gathered at the kitchen table for dinner as soon as Eitan came home.

Ariella sensed her beloved Aunt Pearl was especially sad and withdrawn.

"I have to go back to Johannesburg tomorrow, but I'm not sure I'm going to stay there much longer," Aunt Pearl announced as they were eating.

"What do you mean?" Abba asked.

Nobody had really asked her aunt about her life in South Africa; they had all been so busy with Ima. But Ariella knew better after her talk with Dalia. She placed her fork and knife down and looked at her aunt with concern.

"I don't want to live there anymore, but Irwin doesn't want to live anywhere else," Aunt Pearl said quietly, as if to her plate.

"Live where?" Yael asked.

"In South Africa, sweetie." Aunt Pearl placed her hand on Yael's. "In the beautiful house in Johannesburg, with the maids and the gardener. I live in a golden cage."

"You mean you feel locked up? But why golden?" Ariella joined in the line of questioning, feeling for her aunt; she also felt caged in sometimes.

"It's too complicated," Aunt Pearl sighed. "I'm not sure people who don't live there can understand. Apartheid is a horrible thing. Our maids can't go home to visit their families without being afraid of being stopped and asked to show their passes, arrested even, as if they are fugitives. The ones who work in the big cities leave their children with their families back in the townships, the villages. They may see them only once a year." She lifted her head and looked around the table. "The black people are second-class citizens in their own country. I'm the immigrant, but because I'm white, or *European*, as they say, I'm supposedly superior to them. This is the law. But inside me, I feel the unfairness." She inhaled deeply before she continued, her audience captivated.

"Didn't my brother and sisters die in Europe during the Holocaust because the Jews were considered second-class citizens? I can't stand the way the police and other white people treat black people there. Separate busses, separate benches, separate entrances to banks, the post office, and other places. Even to enter my own house, they have to come through the back door while white people come through the front."

"And what about Irwin? What does he think?" Eitan asked, concerned.

"Irwin was born into it. He claims it's natural to him. 'It's the law of the land,' he justifies. He says he doesn't see anything wrong in treating people according to their education. *Education*!" Her voice rose, "Of course they're uneducated. They're not allowed in universities! His grandparents emigrated from Europe after the First World War, and both his parents were born in South Africa. He studied in London. I told him that dentists can make a living anywhere in the world: London, Tel Aviv, anywhere, but he still won't budge."

"What will you do?" Ariella asked.

"I'm not sure. I gave him an ultimatum before I left. If he isn't willing to live in Israel, I may file for divorce when I return...I have to leave him. I gave him a month to think it over. Now you all know. I didn't find the right time to tell you beforehand..." Tears glistened in her eyes.

Abba fidgeted in his seat, and Eitan stared at his hands. Such candid conversations rarely took place around their table. They all ate in silence, looking down at their own plates.

It was past nine o'clock when Ariella excused herself. "I'm sorry everybody, but I've arranged to meet with a friend," her own voice sounded strange as it broke the silence. "I'll see you tomorrow, Aunt Pearl. We'll be together the whole day until we leave for the airport. I'm not working! I'm free!" She bent down and kissed her aunt's cheek.

"Your dress is beautiful," Yael stated as a matter of fact, as if she wanted to keep Ariella there a little longer.

"Thank you, sweetie," Ariella said over her shoulder, as she walked out the kitchen door, releasing the large curlers out of her hair.

Arik waited in his yellow Chevrolet around the corner. Ariella was glad he didn't park in front of her building, just in case her brother or aunt came out. She wasn't ready to introduce him to her family. Not yet; it was too soon after Ima's death and may seem inappropriate.

The hug he gave as she climbed into his car was everything she needed at that moment. Warm, supporting, loving. She felt so fortunate to have met him, especially at such a needy time. She hoped he wasn't hungry; it was past nine o'clock, and all she wanted was to be in his arms.

It was past midnight when Ariella awoke to the scent of Arik's cigarette, realizing it was time to get out of the warm, sweaty bed, and go home. Arik placed his cigarette in the ashtray by the bed and bent over to kiss her. I'm never, never, never leaving, Ariella thought. She clung to him, covered his face with small kisses while holding his face in her hands. Then she leaned on her elbows, sighed, and whispered, "I must go home, and I hate the thought..."

"Me too," he whispered in a hoarse voice. He turned on top of her and didn't let go until she peeped at her little wrist watch and saw that it was almost one in the morning. She pushed him off and jumped out of bed, calling to him, "Come

Arik, take me home, please. It's really late."

The following evening, Uncle Rafael arrived to take his sister to the airport. Ariella, Abba, and Yael were ready to go in his car with them. Uncle Rafael placed Aunt Pearl's suitcase in the trunk and opened the car front door for her. The other three got in the back.

At the airport, after check-in and before Aunt Pearl had to stand in line for passport control, she hugged her brother-in-law. Ariella had just said a teary goodbye to her aunt, as had Yael and Uncle Rafael. She stood to one side, smoking a cigarette, giving her aunt and her father some privacy.

"Have a safe trip," Ariella heard Abba say to Aunt Pearl. "You were a great help. We'll miss you." Ariella heard the tears choking his throat. Abba? Tears? She was surprised but forced herself not to look at them.

She thought she'd heard Aunt Pearl say she'd miss him more than he could imagine, or did she say she'd miss *them all* more than he could imagine? She wasn't sure; the Hebrew words were so similar. *Otcha, Otchem.* The cigarette she was holding almost burnt her fingers.

Chapter Sixteen

AFTER Aunt Pearl left, Eitan insisted Abba take his bedroom. Ariella thought it was only fair; Eitan was out most of the time. He spent his days at work, and his evenings either at school or seeing Rachel. He came home very late, or sometimes not at all. Apparently Rachel's parents didn't mind him staying in their daughter's room overnight. Mr. and Mrs. Bernstein must be very forward thinking, Ariella thought. Maybe she should tell Abba about Arik. She felt bad for lying to him, like today, when she'd told him she was going to Jerusalem to meet with an old girlfriend from the kibbutz and would return home Saturday night. She'd be sleeping at her friend's grandmother's home in Jerusalem.

Abba never questioned her, although she wasn't sure he'd believed her. She'd tell him about Arik. Soon.

* * *

Ariella and Arik sat in a small restaurant in Jerusalem. She had on a strapless wine-colored taffeta dress with a bow at the waist. Her late mother's gold watch adorned her left wrist, and a gold bangle shone on her right—her first gift from Arik—for completing her military service. She touched it nervously with her fingers. She loved that piece of jewelry with its inscription: *To my beloved AP, with all my heart, ADE.*

Arik David Emmanuel. She loved his name.

"I can't stay away from you for too long," Arik said to Ariella. "Especially now that you're done with the army, I'd like you to join me sometimes in my travels. Would you like to go to Europe?"

She couldn't believe her ears. "Go to Europe? Are you serious?" For a moment Ariella felt like she was floating on air, but reality quickly dropped her to the hard ground. Where was her life going? In what direction?

"I need to work, Arik. I'm just taking a few weeks' vacation this summer, but I've been looking for a job in the papers. I guess I'll need to take whatever comes." Her bottom lip curled down involuntarily.

She touched Ima's watch and felt overcome with emotion. The loss of her mom and the burden of responsibility weighed heavily on her soul. It was her duty to stay home and take care of her little sister and her father. Eitan had practically moved out. There was no question about postponing her plans to go to America. She couldn't go. Not right away. It would be a complete betrayal and an act of selfishness. Besides, she had Arik. Would she leave Arik, too, just after he'd invited her to join him on a trip?

"Finding a job is never easy." Arik took her hand in his, maybe sensing her sad mood. "But it's summer now, Ella. Look on the bright side. I thought we'd go for just four days, and then you can continue your job search. Start anew and refreshed. What do you think?"

He looked so handsome with his dimple and shining brown eyes. She sighed and looked back at him. Maybe just for a few days? Maybe?

She felt torn and couldn't eat; she was too anxious. What would she say to her father? And where was her passport? It had been almost five years since they returned from Argentina...was it even still valid? And she needed money, her own money; she couldn't go penniless and just rely on Arik. It was all so complicated.

"I'm sorry, Arik. I can't just get up and go to Europe with you, not now. It's not right."

"Augh, I'm so disappointed," he said and lit a cigarette.

She knew that he went away often though, and maybe she could join him another time.

"Well, if Europe is out of the question, I have another

surprise for you," Arik said.

"Yes?" Ariella leaned forward in anticipation.

"We're going now to visit my friend Benjamin Sarkowski, Benny, the blind painter. He lives here in Jerusalem with his wife and twin boys," he said, smiling.

The blind artist! At long last. The owner of that little studio apartment in Old Jaffa. Ariella could feel the heat of excitement in her cheeks. "We're going now?" She was curious to meet Benny. But suddenly she wondered, "He has two apartments? In Jaffa and in Jerusalem? He must be rich."

Arik smiled again. "Benny lives with his family in Jerusalem but uses the apartment in Old Jaffa as a storeroom for his paintings, as you've seen. It's closer to Tel Aviv, so I don't have to drive all the way to Jerusalem whenever I need to take Benny's paintings to the galleries in Europe." Arik motioned to the waiter for the check. "Tzilla, Benny's wife, and their two boys are visiting her parents in the kibbutz and will be returning tomorrow night," he said. "So the kids' room is unoccupied, and we can sleep there. I told him about you, and he can't wait to see you—uh, meet you. I need to see him before my trip to Paris; I'm taking some of his paintings to be sold in a gallery."

He was going to Paris? she thought, but said out loud, "This *is* a great surprise, meeting Benny. I never expected it."

"I just hope the two kids' beds can be pulled together, and that their bedroom is far away from the main bedroom. He's blind, but I believe his hearing is extraordinary." He laughed.

Ariella blushed.

When they arrived at Benny's, it was almost eleven o'clock, but he sat up waiting for them.

"*Shalom, achi.*" Hello, my brother. Arik hugged Benny as soon as the door to the apartment opened.

"My one and only." Benny hugged Arik back and patted his shoulder. "Come in, come in. And what is this wonderful scent you've brought with you? Ah...flowers, hmm, smells delicious."

Ariella smiled and looked from Benny to Arik, who was beaming. Benny extended his hand her way, and she took it. He placed his other hand over it, cupping her small hand in both his large ones. He wasn't a tall man, about Abba's height, shorter than Arik by half a head. He was also plump, with a soft belly and a double chin. Looks like a man who sits a lot, Ariella thought. He was balding and had oddly thin eyebrows for a man, as if they had been burned off. His half-closed eyelids kept fluttering.

They entered a large living room, like she'd never seen in Israel before; the ceiling was so high.

"What a beautiful apartment!" Ariella said as she looked around.

"Yes, thank you, please sit down. This is a very old house. It belonged to a rich Arab who sold it to a contractor before he returned to Lebanon. The contractor divided the house into two apartments, and we were lucky to be in the market when we got married. Tzilla's parents paid the down payment, and my friend here"—Benny turned his face in Arik's direction—

"helps me pay the mortgage by selling my paintings. So, what are you guys up to? How do you enjoy my beautiful Jerusalem?"

They sat and talked for a while, the guys drinking whisky and smoking cigars, while Ariella looked around at the paintings that covered the walls, the silk Persian rugs hanging in the entrance, and the bronze artillery cartridge case full of dry wheat bunches. She also saw a colorful *Nargila*, a water-tobacco pipe, in one of the corners. But what amazed her most were the tall ceilings; she couldn't get over the eleven-foot-high walls and the antique chandelier that came down just above the mahogany coffee table. He must be filthy rich, she thought.

Ariella had to get up twice to blow her nose in the bathroom; the heavy scent of the men's cigars stung her sensitive nose. This gave her another chance to look at the beautiful, large floor tiles and colorful rugs that covered the white marble floors. The guys didn't seem to notice that she'd gotten up, and she didn't want to comment on the smell. She enjoyed the beauty around her, the large windows, and the trees outside.

It was after one in the morning when Benny showed them to his sons' bedroom. "I hope you'll be comfortable." Yes! The two single beds were pushed together; Ariella was delighted and saw Arik smile, too.

By the time Ariella and Arik slipped out of the kids' bedroom in the morning, showered and dressed, Benny had cleared off the full ashtray, the two whisky glasses, the tall juice glass Ariella had used, and the cake plates.

Benny had a secretive smile on his lips, Ariella noticed, and it made her blush.

Lucky he can't see my red face, she thought, but quickly felt embarrassed. She grabbed Arik's hand and squeezed it. She hoped she hadn't been too loud the previous night. Or had it been early morning?

"*Boker tov*, sleepy heads." Good morning. Benny turned in their direction. "*Shabbat Shalom*, it's almost lunchtime. How did you both sleep?"

"*Shabbat Shalom*. Very well, thank you." Arik was quick to reply. "May we help you in the kitchen? Do you want me to make my famous Fried *Challah* French toast?" They both smiled. Arik had told Ariella that his army buddies had crowned him King of Fried *Challah*, but she had never tasted it herself.

"Sure," said Benny, "the challah is in the bread-bin. You'll find the eggs, milk, and butter in the refrigerator. Do you mind making Turkish coffee, too? I'll sit here comfortably on the couch and tell Ariella all she wants to know about me and my paintings. I'm sure she can't wait." He laughed good-naturedly, turning toward where Ariella stood. "I'm sure Arik never told you how we met, or how we got injured. I'll have to do it myself, correct?"

"Yes," Ariella said and moved toward him.

"Okay. Let's sit." Benny patted the couch where he sat. "Let the king do his stuff."

She had been in awe earlier when she observed him maneuver around the coffee table, not bumping into anything, and sitting himself comfortably on the couch.

"So, what do you want to know, *Meydele*?" He'd called her a young girl in Yiddish, and suddenly she felt the difference in years between him and her. Between Arik and her. But she quickly dismissed it.

"I want to hear everything. Where were you born? What did you do in the army? Did you fight with Arik in the Independence War ten years ago? When did you paint? When were you—"

"*Regah, regah.* Slow down. She is one fireball, Arik. How do you tame her?" Benny called out to his friend, and Ariella blushed again.

"I don't. I love her just the way she is."

"I don't blame you." Benny said, turning back to Ariella. Suddenly he became serious. "I was born in Poland. My father died when I was a baby, and my mother had a younger sister who helped raise me. For my Bar Mitzvah, my aunt bought me a box of watercolors. I went mad. I started painting like there was no tomorrow. Maybe somewhere inside me, I knew that there wouldn't be much time for me to paint." He paused, his voice hoarse.

"Excuse me for a minute...let me get us some water." Ariella got up and brought two glasses of water to the low coffee table.

"Thank you," Benny took a sip and continued. "When I was seventeen I was already an electrician, but I loved to paint. For about ten years I painted and kept all my paintings in the basement; now they're in another place in Old Jaffa." Ariella gave Arik a quick look. Didn't Benny know that Arik took me to his studio apartment in Old Jaffa? But she returned her attention to Benny, as he continued. "I met Tzilla, my wife, here in Jerusalem, and we got married in 1947. Our beautiful twin boys were born a year later, during the Independence War. We called them Doron and Shai; both names mean *gift*, as you know. I'm grateful I was able to see their faces before I was injured."

The room went quiet. Arik approached, carrying a small, round, brass tray, elaborately decorated. A *Finjaan* and three small porcelain cups were laid on the tray, waiting to be filled with the Turkish coffee. The aroma floated in the air and filled the room. Ariella sneezed, and then laughed. She excused herself to go to the bathroom, where she blew her nose again. When she returned, three plates were laid out on the coffee table, and the guys were already digging into the fried *challah.*

Ariella could hardly see the yellow and brown edges of the toast—it was covered with so much sugar and cinnamon. She took a bite from a slice on her plate. Goodness. It was delicious; warm and soft, sweet and creamy. Arik had never made breakfast for her before. Okay, my friend, I caught you, she thought fondly, you can cook for me now.

Ariella couldn't find the courage to prompt Benny to continue his story, but she wanted to find out how he had been blinded. Benny finished wolfing down the two huge challah slices Arik put on his plate. He placed his fork and knife on the empty plate, sat back, and as if reading her mind, continued where he left off.

"In 1947, I joined the *Haganah*, the Jewish Defense that fought the Arabs. That's when I met this *shmock*." He said affectionately as he pointed in Arik's direction. "We became instant friends, and since then he makes me fried challah and brings me Italian coffee, but I prefer Turkish." It was Ariella's turn to smile.

Benny grew quiet. It seemed like he didn't want to tell her more. But Ariella was curious. "So, you use your apartment in Old Jaffa just for *storage*?"

Benny got up and placed a record on the gramophone. Didn't he hear her question? He sat down again in his armchair and relaxed.

Beethoven's Ninth symphony filled the room. Ariella's question remained hanging.

They listened for a while until Arik touched her hand. He motioned in Benny's direction, and she heard him snore lightly. They both got up quietly, but apparently not quietly enough.

"Hey, where do you think you're going?" he grumbled.

"It's getting late, Benny. We need to get going. Soon Tzilla and the boys will return so you won't be alone for long."

"Well, being alone never bothered me. I just close my eyes and I'm alone." Benny said it as a joke, but Ariella felt his anguish.

They hugged him and said goodbye. Ariella thanked Benny profusely for hosting them.

Driving back to Tel-Aviv on the long and winding road

from Jerusalem, Ariella was pleased she could ask Arik about Benny. "So what happened, Arik? How was Benny blinded?"

"Well," Arik sighed, "there was an explosion, and half of our squad was wiped out. Arms and legs were flying, and we could hardly see in the heavy smoke. I got injured in the groin—you've seen the scar—but Benny lost both his eyes. It was horrific, a real tragedy. I promised myself I would help him. As soon as I got established in my import-export business, I started setting up gallery exhibitions for him in Europe. He has hundreds of watercolor paintings."

"Hundreds? Yes, I saw some rolled up in the Jaffa apartment. And you sell them for him?"

"Yes," he said, not looking at her.

She suddenly felt uncomfortable. Was she prying? Or was he lying?

Chapter Seventeen

AS the midsummer's air lay thick with humidity, city dwellers packed Tel Aviv's white beaches: Jerusalemites and other Israelis who lived inland wanted to dip in the blue Mediterranean Sea, too, and the scent of Velvet, the best tanning cream available in Israel, permeated the already heavily laden atmosphere.

"*Artik, Kartiv, Artik, Kartiv,*" yelled the bare footed ice cream vendor, waving dripping popsicles as he walked up and down the beach, weaving in between beach chairs and oiled bodies sprawled on striped towels. "*Eskimo Limon, Eskimo Limon,*" he yelled, coming very close to Ariella.

He flicked sand onto her hair as she lay on her stomach,

her bikini top unhooked. She shut her eyes tight, covered her ears with both hands until the vendor picked up his white, wooden icebox, placed the wide, red-and-white straps back on his shoulders, and strutted away.

When Ariella heard him from a distance, she opened her eyes, re-hooked her top, stood up, and shook her hair.

Now that her military service was complete, she liked to spend several hours on the beach each morning tanning, and on her way home, just before noon, she would buy both evening papers, *Ma'ariv* and *Yedi'ot Acharonot.* Every afternoon she searched the classified sections of each paper while Yael rested. Her little sister had developed intense headaches since Aunt Pearl left the country, and Ariella never knew how Yael would feel when she returned home from summer camp each day.

Ariella felt desperate for a job. She was a quick typist; she'd learned to type in the army, in Hebrew, of course, from right to left, and Yom-Tov always praised her for her speed and precision.

Yet she had found nothing in six weeks.

Then one day on her way home from the beach, she purchased her newspapers as usual, and saw the following ad:

> A TYPIST IS NEEDED FOR A LAWYER'S OFFICE. FLUENT HEBREW AND ENGLISH TYPING ESSENTIAL. SALARY WILL BE DISCUSSED AT INTERVIEW.

She rushed home to shower and change and took the bus to Uncle Rafael's home to use the phone. Dalia, her short black hair neatly combed, opened the door. Her brown eyes opened in surprise and a wide smile spread on her face when she saw Ariella.

Excitedly, Ariella waved the paper in her hand and opened it to the classified page.

"Shalom," she said after a woman answered the phone, "I'm calling about your ad for a typist."

"How good is your English?" The woman sounded irritated, as if she'd asked that question many times before.

"Eh, well, I can type well. I was a typist for two years in the army and—"

"Yes, I understand, but did you type in English?" The woman seemed to be trying her best to remain patient.

"No, but I can learn—" Ariella suddenly felt so little.

"I'm sorry. We need an experienced typist in both languages: Hebrew *and* English." She put the receiver down.

Ariella decided she had to rent an English typewriter with her first paycheck and practice that at home. No matter which job she got.

The next day Ariella saw another ad:

> A FILING CLERK IS REQUIRED FOR THE CUSTOMS OFFICE IN THE SOUTH OF TEL AVIV-JAFFA, NEAR THE PORT.

Ariella wasn't thrilled about taking a job as a filing clerk. She used her neighbor Rita's phone this time and got called in for an interview. The man who interviewed her offered her a meager salary, the office was small and dark, and the area was so secluded that Ariella thought she'd be scared to walk there alone in the daytime, never mind at night after work.

Another week passed, and still nothing advertised was suitable. Ariella combed the papers' classified sections and found nothing.

Until finally, on the last Friday of July, she saw an ad that read:

> REQUIRED:
> A HARDWORKING FEMALE FOR AN ACCOUNTANT'S OFFICE. TYPING AND SHORTHAND ESSENTIAL. NO OTHER EXPERIENCE NECESSARY. MUST HAVE COMPLETED MILITARY SERVICE. RECOMMENDATIONS NEEDED. SPLIT WORKING HOURS. SALARY TO BE DISCUSSED AT INTERVIEW.

Ariella felt hopeful, although she wasn't crazy about a split working day; she'd much rather work straight through, from eight to four. But she couldn't be too choosy; she needed a job. She had to wait for *Shabbat* to be over.

On Sunday morning she marched into the small grocery store to ask if she could use their telephone. The owner was busy with a customer, so Ariella pointed to the phone on the counter, making eye contact with him. He shook his head. Ariella was surprised. Whom did he think she was going to call, her cousin in America?

Ariella crossed the road to the pharmacy. The owners, two old spinsters, greeted Ariella warmly, and one of them led her to the back office where the phone was. Ariella informed her it was a local call, and she was applying for a job. She called and spoke to a Mr. Goldberg, who asked her to come for an interview as soon as she could. She blushed with excitement and told the pharmacists that it was good news; she was going for a job interview that minute. They smiled and wished her good luck.

Ariella hurried home and put on the yellow sundress Arik had brought her from Europe, the one that emphasized her tan. She pinned her hair up in a bun, buckled on her last year's flat white sandals, and grabbed a small, white clutch bag that used to be Ima's. She knew that she looked like a fresh daisy. On the bus, even women turned to look at her, which made her feel confident.

* * *

"Abba, I got a job today."

Her father lifted his head from the paper. "That's very good," he said, and went back to reading. He didn't seem happy.

"What's wrong?" Ariella couldn't believe his reaction.

"It's Yuli. She's sleeping. Again." Abba motioned his head toward the girls' bedroom. "She came home early from summer camp with a splitting headache. I gave her Palgin and she fell asleep immediately." He sighed, unhappy he had to give his child a painkiller.

"What do you think it can be?" Ariella forgot about her job and excitement. She worried Yael's illness was serious and had no idea how to deal with it.

"I'm not sure. We may have to take her to the doctor again; she may need some tests. I can do it in the late afternoons, but I'll need you to help in case the appointment is in the morning."

"Sure." Ariella was quick to respond. But then she remembered. "Abba, I just got a job. I've been looking for six weeks, and now I found a job and committed to it. I'm starting next week on Friday, first of August." She almost cried; her frustration and excitement all mingled. "I'll be Mr. Goldberg's secretary. He's an accountant, and he seems like a very nice man. I'm so lucky, Abba...I don't want to lose it." She knew she should have felt like the luckiest girl alive, but her sister worried her. "Maybe it's just the summer heat, Abba. Some kids get sunstroke at camp." She hated losing her enthusiasm. "After Yom-Tov, I thought I'd never find another kind boss, but Goldberg seems so nice. The office is on Ben-Yehuda Street. I can walk there or take the bus."

Abba shook his head.

Ariella tried again. "I'll take Yael to the doctor, Abba. I'll make a plan, I promise. I still have a whole week. But I need this job, I really do." She was almost begging.

"I don't know, Ariella. I'm not sure you should take this job. Any job." He looked at her. "Maybe you should stay home and take care of Yael."

Ariella was shocked. She couldn't simply replace her mother. She had to work; she had to earn money and become independent.

"You're not serious, Abba."

"Yes, I am. I think somebody should stay home and take care of her, and I have to work."

"Abba! I must work, too. She'll be going to school soon. You don't expect me to sit at home and wait for her, do you?"

"But what if she can't go to school?"

Her breathing became shallow; she could barely talk. "Do you think it's that serious? Oh my God!"

"I don't really know."

"Okay, I'll take her to the doctor and we'll see. All right?"

Abba nodded.

That night Ariella didn't go out but sat in Ima's favorite armchair in the living room and tried to read her movie magazine but couldn't concentrate. She missed Arik, who was away on a business trip, and she missed Ima. Turning around to smell the upholstered back of the seat—hoping to catch the scent of her mother—was a new habit. Again, she smelled nothing but dust.

She got up, brought her diary, and nestled back in Ima's soft armchair.

11 April 1953
Dear Diary,

I'm back in Buenos Aires, and so is Eitan, for *Pesach*, Passover.

Ima made our favorite Pesach dishes; a large *Matzebrai* for all of us and a *Buba'le* just for my sister and me. She is so miserable here; no wonder, it's a small village and she loves big cities, but she tries very hard to conceal how lonely she is. She sews for herself and for Yael and does alterations for some women. At least she keeps herself busy.

Ariella knew she needed to keep busy, too. To try and avoid worrying constantly about Yael, she decided to take English classes at night. Learning English was important. It would be her sweet little secret. Arik was away so often, she had to fill her evenings, and this was a good cause. She'd enroll in Berlitz Language School for two nights a week.

She had so many plans. Yael couldn't be seriously ill. Could she?

Chapter Eighteen

IT was Wednesday afternoon when Ariella and Yael sat at the pediatrician's waiting room. Yael was pale and sat with her eyes closed.

Ariella had registered for night classes to perfect her English; they began in three weeks. She needed to figure out Yael's mysterious headaches soon—for Yael's sake and for her own.

The nurse showed them into the doctor's office. "You haven't had a cold lately, have you?" the middle-aged doctor asked. He wore a white coat and had several pens in his breast pocket. His blue eyes smiled at Yael as he checked her.

Yael shook her head.

"I really can't find anything wrong with your sinuses, Yael, or anything else," he said after he checked her thoroughly. He turned to face Ariella. "I would like Yael to see a neurologist for her headaches, Ariella. But I want your father to take her. Not that you're not a wonderful sister, I've known you both for years, but a parent has to be involved here."

Yael's freckled face crumbled with fear. "What's a neurologist? What will he do to me?"

"Don't worry, Yael. A neurologist is a specialist. Pain, like headaches, is the agitation of nerves. To find out the cause of your headaches, he'll run some tests on you. One such test is called an EEG, where they'll put some gel on your scalp and attach wires. Those are connected to a machine which draws lines on paper while it's moving." The doctor patted Yael's knee. "It's not painful and actually fun to watch. I'm not really worried. But I want to make sure we take good care of you, sweetie." The pediatrician got up and handed Ariella a piece of paper with the name and phone number of the neurology department in the medical building. "I'll call and make sure he sees you very soon."

What could these headaches indicate? Ariella wondered. Could she trust the doctor? Oh my God, what if the doctors couldn't find anything wrong, but it was truly bad?

With an appointment set for the following week, Ariella told Abba that she'd like to at least start the job but would quit if necessary.

"I don't think it's a good idea, Ella," Abba said again.

"What kind of person starts a job and quits a week later? You need to wait."

"I can't, Abba. This is a great opportunity. Let me start, please," she begged. "If I don't begin now, Goldberg will take somebody else. A position like this doesn't open every day. I can't wait, Abba. Let me start, please. I'll come with you to the neurologist."

On Friday Ariella started her new job. She felt excited. Her boss gave her the smaller office of the two rooms, one leading into the other, very similar to her office in the army. She felt fortunate; Goldberg was a kind boss and a patient man who clearly explained what was expected of her, and Ariella felt comfortable.

Most importantly, there was a telephone. Ariella had found it hard not to have a phone at home to keep in touch with Arik, or anybody else for that matter. The highly desired instrument that so many Israelis had been waiting for *years* to get was a rare commodity in many homes. Here, she would have one each work day.

She also decided to try and see how a split working day would work. Working from eight till one, and again from four to seven, would give her three hours to have lunch, rest, and maybe run errands. She would see.

Her first day at work was short; the office closed at one o'clock on Fridays.

On Ariella's break the following Tuesday, she joined Yael

and Abba at the neurologist, as promised.

The neurologist, a slim and tall young man, sent Ariella with Yael to the lab for an EEG and asked Abba to stay and give him Yael's medical background.

An hour later, the girls returned to the doctor's office with a tall and dark-haired nurse who carried the pile of computer paper which contained the EEG graphs.

Abba was sitting in the waiting room, reading the paper.

"It was so weird, Abba," Yael said, trying to smooth down her red curls, which were separated for the clips to be glued temporarily on her scalp. "They stuck hooks on my head and attached colored wires to it. I must have looked like someone from another planet."

"She was so brave and—" Ariella began, but the nurse called them in.

"Mr. Paz, can you come in with Yael, please?"

Ariella remained seated.

Fifteen minutes passed, and Ariella worried that she wouldn't be back in the office by four o'clock. At that moment Abba and Yael came out. Abba looked relieved; Yael looked tired.

"Would you please come in by yourself?" the tall nurse asked Ariella.

Ariella looked at Abba questioningly, and he nodded.

She walked in. The doctor smiled at her and asked her to sit down. He had warm brown eyes that put her at ease.

"This is a delicate situation. I understand that you're the older sister and have taken on the role of a mother," he said kindly. "Your father is very proud of you. Ariella, yes?" She nodded. He cleared his throat. "He told me about your mother's passing, and I'm truly sorry for your great loss. You seem to be coping well, although I don't really know how you feel, but from the outside you seem to have balance. Apparently, your little sister is struggling. There is nothing wrong with her physically. I gave her a thorough examination and spoke with her pediatrician." He was very serious now. "Your father is somewhat taciturn. Doesn't talk much, does he?" The doctor smiled again. "I'm sure he's loving and takes good care of her, but he isn't a mother. That's why I wanted to talk to you."

His eyes pierced into hers, as if he wanted to see into her brain and decipher what she was thinking. "I think that Yael suffers from a loss she isn't expressing. She'll keep getting headaches as long as she keeps her sadness to herself. As a woman"—he reached his hand and placed it on Ariella's—"even a young one like yourself, you may find a way to talk to her about your mother and your shared pain. You're feeling the pain, too, I'm sure. Maybe *you* have somebody outside of the family to talk to, but Yael needs *you*."

Ariella sat back in her chair. She wasn't even twenty years old yet. Her sister was twelve. How could she take care of her by talking? She felt frustrated.

That night after work, Ariella met Arik at Benny's apartment in Old Jaffa. It was just two weeks before her birthday. *Twenty*! She couldn't believe it herself.

They wasted little time, making their way to the bedroom. Arik patted her bare behind gently, and she felt as if she were melting; her neck turned to butter, her arms floating as if she were in a pool of water, her legs weightless, and her brain empty.

She felt euphoric. She moaned and twisted again, turning to face him. She arched her spine and dug her nails into his back. Sometimes she felt embarrassed by the strong desire she felt, as if she could never be satiated. Sex was so pleasing now, as if it helped her relieve some tension. The only thing she disliked was his withdrawing at the last moment, just before he came. She gently caressed the scar in his groin, wondering how intense his injury was. She remembered her first time, the throbbing pain and the bit of blood. It seemed so long ago.

But something bothered her, and she had to confront it. She had to ask Arik upfront. No more avoidance. No more pushing down her nagging thought.

One *Shabbat* morning when Ariella woke up, she found Arik sitting next to her in bed reading yesterday's paper. The clock read nine o'clock, and she wondered if her father would question her whereabouts, which he never did aloud. What would she say if he actually said something? She kept putting off telling him. It was easier that way.

Ariella took the cigarette from Arik's hand, and when he reached to get another one from his crumpled box on the nightstand, she said, "No, no. Here." She took one puff and handed it back to him. Then she lay back, pulling the soft snow-white sheet under her arms covering her breasts, still exposing her tanned shoulders.

"Good morning, *buba*." Arik kissed her forehead. She loved it when he called her doll.

Now was her chance to ask. "I have a question," Ariella said softly. Was she afraid of the answer?

"Yes?" Arik said, the paper up in front of him again. She felt like he wasn't taking her seriously.

"Why are we meeting only on Tuesdays and just some weekends?" she asked.

Arik put the paper down and turned to her. "Why're you asking, *motek*? Do you want to see me more often?" He winked at her.

"I'm not joking, Arik. And why are we meeting only here? What about seeing me on Thursdays at your place? And what's wrong with Wednesdays? Where do you live, by the way? Why don't we meet there?"

"Well, I don't live alone." He paused. Ariella sat up, feeling her eyes opening wide in surprise. "I have a roommate who has a son."

"So, you're three people in the apartment?"

"Yes. It would be very inconvenient for you to come there. You wouldn't feel comfortable, and neither would they. And we wouldn't be as free as we are here." He bent and kissed her lips, placing his hand on her stomach under the blanket.

"So why do we meet *here* only on Tuesdays?" Ariella didn't want to let it slide so easily.

Did he have a secret?

She had one, too.

She wouldn't tell him that she was busy on Monday and Thursday evenings at Berlitz. Even Abba didn't know about her English class, let alone Rachel and Eitan.

"That's another story," Arik said as a reply to her question. "With my travels and all, it's too complicated. But we also meet on Fridays, like yesterday, and we're together today, which brings me to my next plan." Arik got out of bed.

He walked naked to the kitchen and returned with two tiny cups of sweet, black Turkish coffee. He handed one to Ariella and lit two cigarettes, sitting next to her. Arik smoked and sipped his coffee, looking at Ariella over the rim of his small cup with puppy eyes, his face so handsome, his dimple so deep.

She still wasn't sure she could buy his reasoning, but before she could form her next question, Arik asked, "What are your plans for Saturday the thirteenth?" There was a mischievous look in his beautiful eyes.

"Why?" Ariella asked, feeling distracted; it was the day after her birthday, in two weeks, exactly.

"Would you tell your family that you'll be away on the twelfth *and* the thirteenth? I promise I'll get you back home by the fourteenth for Rosh Hashanah." He didn't wait for a reply but got up again and walked naked to the gramophone. His broad shoulders, muscular back, and firm round buttocks made her squeeze her knees together.

"Where are we going?" she asked, swallowing hard.

Arik turned his head to her and smiled.

Ariella wasn't sure how to return to the subject of his

apartment, and if she should really pursue it. At least this studio apartment was always available. Wasn't it? But wasn't he making a lot of money? Why did he need roommates?

She wasn't ready to push too hard. Her head throbbed from all that thinking; her words got stuck in her throat and refused to come out, and she was scared to say the wrong thing and lose it all. So she just stared again at his white buttocks, which made him look harmless and vulnerable, and sighed.

Arik placed Ricky Nelson's long-playing album on the gramophone, and his voice filled the air. Ariella wasn't a great fan and made a face. Arik quickly took the needle off and replaced the record with Louis Armstrong's "Kiss of Fire." She smiled; it was so much more to her taste and she really loved Arik's attentiveness to her needs.

She slipped out of bed and they joined in a steamy tango. Ariella wasn't sure if it was the late August heat—a humid month in Tel Aviv which made the air sticky even early in the morning—or Armstrong's thick voice, but before the song ended they fell onto the bed once again.

After another hour of tumbling, laughing, rolling, and crying out, Ariella got up and went into the shower, leaving Arik in bed reading the paper again, a new cigarette between his lips. When she stepped out and dried herself, she heard him in the kitchen. Was he making breakfast? Did he buy *challah*?

As she continued to dry her hair, she saw there was blood on the towel. Thank goodness she got her period. Only then did she realize the tension she had held lately. She was always very excited to see Arik and be with him, but lately she was petrified of becoming pregnant. She knew she had to talk with him about it.

Ariella used one of the pads she kept in the bathroom of the apartment. She was surprised to see that there were only four left in the package. Didn't I buy a new one? Maybe I don't remember. She went into the bedroom to dress. When she glided into the kitchen, Arik was ready with fried eggs and toast. No, no *challah*. She was famished, and it was late.

Ariella made more coffee, and she stood with her back to Arik, while pouring. "I just got my period, thank goodness," she said. "Shouldn't we use some birth control, Arik? It worries me sometimes."

"I should have known." He laughed. "Don't you worry your pretty little head, *motek*. I'm taking care of it."

"How?" She turned to him.

"I can assure you that I know what I'm doing." Arik sounded positive and confident, if slightly mysterious. She thought of the scar in his groin. Was he sterile? Did she want to get involved with a man who couldn't have children? But she loved him now and didn't want to think of the future.

They each took a section of the paper and read quietly at the kitchen table for a while.

Suddenly her cramps were too strong for her to move, and she doubled over in her seat.

"Do you have your pills?" Arik got up and brought her purse.

"Yes," she moaned. "Please take two Palgin from the box

in my purse." She suffered so much when she got her period that she didn't mind not being regular and not getting it every month; it was a relief.

Ariella went back to bed feeling very sorry for herself, and thoughts of Ima flooded her brain. She wanted her *now*; she was in such pain. She remembered how Ima took her to buy her first packet of small sanitary towels. She also gave her one Palgin when the cramps became overwhelming. *Oy*, Ima.

Ariella buried her face in the crumpled, expensive cotton pillowcases. Arik crawled into bed, too, and hugged her from behind. She tried to hide her face so he wouldn't see it scrunched up. She didn't care if he thought it was her period pains that made her cry.

"*Shh*...try to sleep, the pills will take effect soon and you'll feel better. I know, *motek*, I know that you're hurting." Arik rocked her while she cried silently in fitful whimpers, but it was Ima she wanted, and her mind went foggy. Didn't she have to return home to take care of Ima? She felt an empty space in her heart holding her mother's absence. Ima, we need you, Yael needs you, *I* need you. Ima.... She fell asleep.

Chapter Nineteen

AS Ariella entered the apartment after work on her twentieth birthday, Yael ran and hugged her, saying the customary Jewish greeting "May you live until-one-hundred-and-twenty!" which is wishing the birthday person to live as long as Moses lived, to a ripe old age. "You only have a hundred years left!" Her sister laughed at her own joke. She looked so much better in the past week; school and homework seemed to agree with her. She looked happier.

"Thank you again," Ariella said and smiled, patting her sister's head. She had to hurry and pack; she was leaving in an hour with Arik, going up north. How could she tell Yael and Abba? She wished she hadn't left the disclosure for the last minute.

"*Mazal tov*, Ariella. May you have a year of good health and happiness." Abba gave her a hug and handed her a bouquet of carnations.

"*Toda*, Abba," thanked Ariella. "I love pink carnations." As did Ima, she thought. Ariella kissed her father on his cheek and said in an apologetic tone, "I'm sorry, but I'm going to Haifa, to visit eh, Dina, from the base. I'll be back tomorrow night and will be going out with Eitan and Rachel. They're taking me out for coffee for my birthday." She said it all in one breath and turned to run to her room to pack, not wanting Abba to see the lie in her eyes.

She felt his eyes on her back. "Dina?" he called after her. "Have I met her? The one whose grandmother lives in Jerusalem?"

"Eh, um... Yes, that's the one," Ariella yelled from her room. She was caught off guard. She didn't expect him to remember and question her; he usually didn't. "I don't think you've met her." She hesitated. "No. You haven't." She thought of Arik as she said it.

"You're going out of town too often." Abba didn't seem satisfied with her reply. "You're needed here, Ella. Yael needs you and I need you. You can't just pack and go when the mood takes you." Abba stood by her door.

"Abba, it's only two days, and it's my *birthday*." Ariella felt like crying.

Abba walked away, but she was left with a bitter taste in her mouth and a hollow space in the pit of her stomach. Why was she lying so much?

An hour later she climbed into Arik's car and headed north to the *Kineret*, the Sea of Galilee. Ariella opened the car window to let the afternoon's hot wind blow her long hair. She inhaled deeply and smiled, her eyes closed. When she felt Arik's hand on her bare thigh, she thought it wasn't smart to wear shorts for the trip; she should have known it would turn him on, and he had to concentrate on driving. But she loved her new beige shorts and white cotton sleeveless blouse, showing off her summer tan. She placed her hand on his, stopping him from reaching under her shorts.

It was extremely hot in Tiberius, on the west coast of the deep and large freshwater lake. Ariella always wondered about these waters running all the way south through the Jordan River and collecting at the lowest point in the world, where the minerals turned them into the Salty Sea—the Dead Sea. From fresh and alive, to salty and dead.

Arik parked by a three-story whitewashed hotel and they walked into the restaurant. The light blue walls were welcoming, and the large fans hissed as the two of them sat down and ordered two tall glasses of iced coffee topped with vanilla ice cream. Ah, it felt so good! She drank it all and made a little sound with her straw. Then she took the long spoon and finished the ice cream that sat at the bottom of the tall glass.

"Come, let's get back in the car," Arik said suddenly. He got up, left some notes on the table, and grabbed her hand.

"Where are we going?" Ariella was mystified.

They walked hand in hand, and she heard the gravel crunching beneath her sandals. She didn't mind the heat, but the humidity was too much.

"Come, get in. It's a surprise, no more questions." Arik smiled and opened the car door for her. She didn't mind where they were going. Just being out in public with him was exhilarating.

In the car, Arik handed her his box of cigarettes and a lighter. Ariella lit two cigarettes and placed one between Arik's lips. She opened her window to get some air circulating and enjoyed feeling the warm wind on her face again as her hair flew back.

She noticed that he was driving west. "Are we going to Haifa?"

"You'll see," Arik replied.

On their way they passed Arab settlements, villages, and some vendors selling dark green watermelons—cut open, their blood-red flesh and black seeds exposed—and *sabres*—prickly pears—which they would be willing to peel for you. But Arik kept driving.

"Hey, why won't you tell me where we're going?" Ariella couldn't hold it in any longer.

"*Savlanoot.*" Patience. "You like surprises, don't you?"

At Sh'far-ahm, Arik continued northwest.

About twenty minutes later, Ariella saw the sparkling Mediterranean Sea with the sun hovering over it. It was an hour before sunset, but she knew the air wouldn't cool down anytime soon. It was low tide and Ariella could see the white sand exposed and shimmering, the soft waves and the white foam caressing the many shells lying in wait, desperate for cool water. But Ariella knew that the water wasn't cool. Even the sea was hot.

The small hotel on the north west side of the country in *Akko*, or Acre, was a delightful sight. Akko was an ancient city.

Ariella remembered that from the *Kineret* in the east to the Mediterranean in the west, it was less than sixty kilometers, and she had never ridden the width of the country but heard of people that had hiked it. Now, she was thirsty and tired; Tel Aviv to Tiberius and then across to Acre took the whole afternoon. But she was in Akko! For the first time!

When they entered their hotel room Ariella gasped. The high ceiling was painted with colorful flowers surrounding the fan; a typical spacious old Arab building with high ceilings.

After showering and changing, Ariella and Arik sat in a cozy Arab restaurant. She looked around at the red velvet-like wallpaper covering the walls, the gold wall lamps and the huge turning ceiling fans. White tablecloths gave the place a touch of elegance. So did the well-dressed people. Arabic music poured from the speakers and Ariella stared out through the large windows.

She looked over at the ancient seawall of the old city and remembered learning that it was first built in the twelfth century by the Crusaders and inhabited ever since by whomever invaded the country. Jews and Arabs lived there now side by side, all Israeli citizens since 1948.

"I have something for you, my Ella." Arik broke her thoughts.

Ariella loved it when he called her that. It usually happened in bed, when he would cry out, *Ella sheli,* my goddess, and hold her so tight it almost hurt. She looked at him and smiled. He was so good looking. So elegant in his dark suit and tie, even though it was hot and humid. He had dressed that way especially for her; it was her special day. Ariella smoothed out her green chiffon sleeveless dress, gathered under her bust. Empire style, it was called. The beautiful dress showed off her cleavage, and she had put a dab of perfume in between her breasts. Chills ran down her spine; she couldn't wait to get to their room. But she had to be patient; he had something for her.

She looked at him expectantly.

Arik placed a small black velvet box on the table and slowly moved it toward her, not moving his gaze from her eyes. "For you, my love. Happy twentieth birthday." He smiled warmly, his dimple deepening. "And may you have many more. I brought you something to go with your gold bangle. I've waited the whole day to give it to you."

The room swiveled. Ariella placed her hand on the box and waited, savoring the moment. She had to breathe deeply to calm herself. The candlelight in the center of their table shone in Arik's eyes. Were they damp?

She opened the box.

A pair of stunning gold earrings flashed in the candlelight. It was not the jewelry she'd hoped for, the kind that signaled a life-long commitment.

Every time Arik flew to Europe for three or four days, Ariella knew he'd come back with a gift. Always. A dress, a pair of shoes, an exquisite purse. He made her feel like a princess. Last time he brought her a suspender belt with silk stockings and insisted on showing her how to wear it.

"Thank you, Arik." She choked on her words before quickly regaining her composure, trying not to reveal her disappointment. "You spoil me so much. These are exquisite. I'm going to put them on right away."

She got up, took the box and her little purse, and went to the restroom. There she put the earrings in her pierced ears and looked in the mirror into her own eyes. Patience, Ariella, patience. *Savlanoot*, she thought. You've only known him for a few months and your father hasn't even met him.

What did you expect? Don't be a fool. Besides, where do you think you are, in the movies? In America? Scenes like this only happen in movies. Cheer up. You know he loves you; that should be enough for now. Don't ruin it all.

She straightened her dress, turned her head to and fro to move her new dangling gold earrings, re-applied her lipstick, fixed a smile on her face, and walked back to their table with a straight back as if she owned the place.

Chapter Twenty

ARIELLA knew that every Israeli man who completed serving in the army had to do *Milu'im*, an annual reserve duty, until the age of forty-five. Officers like Arik, though, had to continue until they were fifty. This was an annual training which lasted about a month. The army had to be ready at all times; all men well trained, in case Israel had to defend its borders. Arik was forty-five, so she wasn't surprised when he told her at the end of October that in mid-November he'd be going away for a month.

"In ten days?! How long have you known?"

"For two months already."

"And you never told me?"

"Well, I never found the right moment, sweetie. With all my travels I didn't want to burden you with that, too. You've had a tough year."

They were in his car on their way back from Haifa after spending *Shabbat* walking in the beautiful Baha'i Gardens, overlooking the Mediterranean Sea.

Ariella was sad that Arik would be away but knew one thing would keep her busy: her English class. Her secret escape.

Learning English was essential; her dream to move to America hadn't died. Yes, she loved Arik and hoped for a future with him, but she wasn't sure where or when it might happen. He traveled so frequently and worked in so many countries. She needed to take care of herself, be prepared for anything. She valued her independence, her freedom, in any country, and knew that she never wanted to feel trapped again, like she had felt in Argentina.

A faint memory of a journal entry nagged her. Her dream of escape when she was fifteen. She looked for it that night.

> **23 July 1953 – Buenos Aires**
> Dear Diary,
>
> How long do my parents think I'm going to stay here? In September when I turn 15, I plan to escape. I'll go to the Jewish Joint or the Zionist movement and tell them that I want to go back home. I'll tell them that my parents abandoned me here in Buenos Aires all by

> myself and I don't want to stay. I want to return to Israel and go to the army. That should convince them. I'm not sure they'll need my parents' permission. I hope not. If they do, I'll just run away. I'll find a way out. I have to!

And yet, she felt trapped. Sort of. She did love Yael. She truly did. But the headaches kept coming back, and her sister missed school more often than her teachers liked. Abba had to tell Yael's new teacher that her mother had passed away only six months previously, and she was still grieving and sad. That was what the doctor had said, and there was nothing to be done. Time would heal, they'd all said. There was nothing physically wrong with her. Ariella knew she had to talk to Yael about her feelings concerning Ima, but it was hard for her, too; she didn't know how.

The following *Shabbat* morning, Ariella decided to take her sister for a walk on the beach.

"Do you have any plans for today?" she asked Yael as soon as she noticed her sister's eyes were open.

"Ahhhhh," Yael yawned lazily. "Not for right now, maybe this afternoon." She sat up in bed. "Ouch, my head," she said and lay back down.

Ariella got out of bed and went to sit on the edge of Yael's bed.

"Listen, *motek*. I also have no plans for this morning, so why don't we make some?"

"What?" Yael's eyes were still closed, as if the morning light was too bright.

"Why don't we go for ice cream on the *tayelet*? I know it's November already, but it looks like a nice day," Ariella said and stood up. "I'll give you two Palgin, and we can go. What do you say?"

The sisters dressed up in long pants and light jackets and walked on Frishman Street to the Tel Aviv boardwalk. They both remained quiet. Ariella was contemplating what to say, and Yael seemed deep in thought, or nursing her headache. Ariella chose a corner café and they sat down. They ordered cheesecake for both, coffee for Ariella, and hot chocolate for Yael. It was too cold for ice cream.

Ariella put her fork down and placed her hand on Yael's.

"Yuli, we need to talk."

"About what?"

"About whatever is bothering you."

"Nothing is bothering me."

"Yael. We've seen two doctors and had tests done, and there is nothing wrong with you."

"So?"

"So, tell me what's going on." Ariella felt desperate; she really didn't know how to handle this.

Yael jumped off the lightweight chair so suddenly it fell backwards. "I don't know! What do you want from me? Do you think I'm pretending to have headaches?"

"Yael, sit down, be quiet." Ariella got up to pick up Yael's chair.

"I won't be quiet! And don't tell me what to do. You're not my mother!" Yael yelled, and tears came down her cheeks. She turned around and stormed out, swinging her arms in anger.

"Hey, wait for me!" Ariella yelled after her. She made eye contact with the waiter, who stared at them like the other patrons did. She left some notes on the table and ran after her sister but couldn't catch up to her. Yael raced toward their house, and Ariella gave up after five minutes of running.

She found Yael sitting in Ima's armchair, reading a book, as if nothing had happened. Yael didn't raise her head. Ariella sighed. Real communication was so hard in her family. She had promised the doctor to talk to Yael about Ima and their pain, their grief, but couldn't bring herself to do it; she just didn't know how. How did one start a conversation about the most painful thing in order to help somebody else, when one still needed to heal?

Chapter Twenty-One

A WEEK later, on the Saturday before Arik was supposed to leave town for a month, Ariella, Eitan, and Rachel walked out of the Esther Movie Theater by Dizengoff Square. They had just watched *The King and I* with Yul Brynner and Deborah Kerr. They all loved it, and broad smiles spread across everybody's faces. What a happy ending! Ariella thought as she tried to avoid the sunflower seeds' husks that dotted the theater floor. Some kids just spat out the peels as they cracked them noisily during the film. She found it disgusting.

"Ariella, I'm going to walk Rachel home, do you mind?" Eitan said as they stepped out into Zamenhoff Street. The evenings were getting cooler and Ariella pulled her sweater tight around her shoulders.

She was taken aback for a moment but quickly recovered and said, "No, no, I don't mind, go ahead." What else could she say? "It's late already. I'll take the bus home, no problem. See you later, Rachel." She waved and turned away, pretending she had no cares in the world, and made her way around Dizengoff Square to the bus stop.

But she felt distressed; Arik was leaving in two days, and Tuesday would be so sad and empty. She was lonely; since she met Arik she'd lost touch with friends her age. Rachel and Eitan were the only young people she associated with anymore, and they were so involved with each other that sometimes she felt like a third wheel in their company.

America! A thought flashed in her mind. I wish I could go to America. I wish I could go to Cousin Sonia! Even for a visit, to see what it's like. Where was that letter she'd sent me before Ima died? Ariella's energy rose. And then she remembered she'd torn it up before she ever opened it, thinking at that moment only of Ima and nothing else. That was six months ago.

* * *

Come early December, the phone rang in Goldberg's office. Ariella picked it up.

"*Shalom*, Ariella. This is Mira, Major Yom-Tov's secretary. Remember me?" Without pausing she continued. "I got your number from your Aunt Dalia—you left it with us when you were dismissed and said you had no phone at home. I hope it's all right to call you at work." The woman on the other side of the phone spoke in a rush, almost out of breath. "We're having a surprise party for Yom-Tov. He's retiring in two weeks. Would you like to come?"

"*Shalom*, Mira. Yes... I..."

"I have to be quick, before Yom-Tov returns," Mira said. "It's going to be at his friend's house, Arik Emmanuel's. The address is Eight Jeremiah Street, Ramat Chen. It's going to be on the seventh candle of Hanukah, on Saturday the thirteenth at seven o'clock sharp. Write it down. Yom-Tov's wife will bring him at seven thirty. It's a surprise, don't forget. He thinks that he is just going to visit Arik and his wife. Write it down now, Eight Jeremiah Street on the thirteenth, seven o'clock. See you there. Bye."

The blood drained from Ariella's face. She had to sit down. Did she hear her correctly? Arik and *his wife*? Did Mira say *his wife*? Arik? *Her* Arik?

The room began to spin. He had a wife! Not a roommate...

She grabbed the office phone book. She had never, ever, looked him up in the phone book. *Why?* Why hadn't she looked him up? Because she trusted him?

The liar! Because she didn't want to find out? What could she have found out? The phone book wouldn't have told her that he was married! *Arik and his wife, Arik and his wife, Arik and...*The words pounded in her temples; she couldn't think rationally. Mira's voice sounded mocking. Whom could she ask? Whom could she talk to? Who knew her *and* Arik besides Yom-Tov? She couldn't ask *him.* Her head felt light; she almost fainted. Oh, yes! Benny! She knew Benny. And he knew Arik!

If she took the bus to Jerusalem, she'd be there before it got dark. Forget the phone book; she needed to speak to Benny. Ariella walked into Goldberg's office.

"Mr. Goldberg, I just got a phone call," Ariella said, hearing her own heartbeat, and almost convinced her boss could hear it, too. She didn't know where the surge of energy came from, but her adrenaline was rushing, and she had to make up a story on the spot. "My friend in Jerusalem is very sick and her parents are...uh, overseas. She needs someone to help her, and she called me—go figure, calling me, in Tel Aviv—but she's a really good friend. May I take the afternoon off? I'll be back tomorrow morning, I promise, and I'll make up—"

"I really don't like these personal phone calls, Ariella," Goldberg interrupted. "I've hired you to work and not to run off to a friend in the middle of the day. She can find someone in Jerusalem. I'm sorry, but I need you to type some letters." Goldberg sounded annoyed. "Please don't give this number to anybody else besides your family." He got up and placed some files on his desk. "I need these letters to go out today."

Ariella had no choice. She'd have to wait until seven...and seven was so far away.

* * *

"*Shalom, ken*?" Hello, yes? A short and somewhat heavy woman in a dressing gown and shoulder length brown hair, maybe in her early forties, opened the door to Benny's home in Jerusalem. Must be Benny's wife, Ariella tried to guess.

"*Shalom*, my name is Ariella. I'm Arik's...eh... Arik's...friend. May I see Benny?" She had no time to waste.

The woman's blue piercing eyes stared into Ariella's and she averted her gaze. The woman took a step back, sized Ariella up, and motioned with her head to let her into the entrance hall, and yelled, "Benny, for you!"

"Ariella?" he called from the living room. "Come in, come in."

Sharp hearing, she thought, as she passed the woman and entered the living room; the woman followed her after closing the front door.

"Tzilla, this is Ariella, Arik's friend. Ariella, this is my wife, Tzilla." Benny sat in an armchair, the radio on a side table next to him, listening to the news.

"Nice to meet you," Ariella said, turning back to Tzilla. "Sorry for barging in like that... I know it's late..." She felt she owed Tzilla an apology.

Benny's wife nodded as she tightened the belt of her dressing gown. "I'll go back to the boys, excuse me. I was reading them a bedtime story. Please sit down and make yourself comfortable," she said and walked out.

Ariella sat opposite Benny and looked at him. He turned the volume of the radio down but didn't turn it off.

"*Nu, Meydele*." Well, girlie. Benny turned his face toward

Ariella. "This is such a nice surprise. But I have a feeling that it's not a happy occasion."

"Arik is married, right?"

"*Regah, Meydele.*" Just a minute, girlie. "I'm not sure it's my place to answer that. Did you ask him?"

The anger welled up again inside her, her eyes tearing. "Why are you both lying to me? I know he's married. I don't need to ask him."

"Well, maybe you should. Ask him, confront him. He'll explain."

"What's there to explain? What is he doing with me? Why are you letting him use your apartment in Old Jaffa?"

Benny turned his head toward the bedrooms, listening. Ariella tried to listen, too, but no sound came from that direction. It was late; maybe Tzilla had fallen asleep with the boys.

"The studio apartment is a complicated story." Benny lowered his voice. "I inherited it from my aunt. Tzilla said that we shouldn't sell it, just rent it out and keep it as our retirement plan. It's worth a small bundle." Benny fidgeted and looked uncomfortable. "What will you drink?"

Benny got up from his seat, went into the kitchen, and brought back a glass soda bottle. He poured himself some whisky and added a spritz from the bottle.

"Same for you?" he asked Ariella.

"No thanks, just some soda."

Benny spritzed some soda for Ariella, keeping a finger inside her glass to make sure he wasn't overfilling it. Ariella felt a bit disgusted but assumed that it was the way blind people did it.

"So I rented the apartment out to a painter to use as a studio, and after a year he came to me with a proposition." Benny paced the room. He intertwined his fingers, undid them, intertwined them again, undid them again, put his hands in his pants pockets, and stopped pacing. He stepped close to Ariella. "Four friends suggested to share the rent with him." Benny cleared his throat, looking toward the bedroom section again, and after sitting down, continued softly. "Each one wanted the apartment for just one day a week, every week. So one uses it every Monday, another every Tuesday..."

She jumped from her seat. "Tuesday!" she called out, forgetting Benny's family. "I meet Arik there on Tuesdays!"

Benny looked alarmed at her outburst but embarrassed, too, as if he had just divulged too much and regretted it. She noticed that his face had turned red, his breathing heavy, as if he were excited from whatever he could see in his mind's eye.

Ariella stood up and started pacing and talking quietly, as if to herself. "And they are all married, yes?" She didn't wait for a reply and concluded, "So this is an *apartment of sin.*" She was oblivious of Benny's presence, waving her arms in the air as she was talking. "Married men use it for affairs. Four disgusting husbands cheating on their wives."

"Five."

"Five?" Ariella turned to look at him. "And what about the weekend?" She couldn't believe that the logistics were what worried her at that moment. And now she understood why her sanitary pads had disappeared.

"They share Friday and *Shabbat*, I guess." He shrugged. "I don't dictate the rules." Benny's cheeks seemed flushed and sweaty. "But business is business."

"I never want to go there again! I never want to see the bastard...the pig...liar!"

"*Meydele*, please, talk to him, let him explain..." Benny seemed at a loss.

Suddenly, Ariella had no more stamina. Her arms fell. Her eyes were burned. She wanted to go home. She picked up the purse she had thrown on the floor when she stormed in. "It's very late, Benny. I have to take the bus back to Tel Aviv."

Benny stood up and walked around the coffee table, toward where Ariella stood. "Speak to him, Ariella. Give him a chance to explain. He is unhappy with..."

Ariella stared at him. She felt sorry for the blind man. "I have one more question, Benny. Why did you tell me all of this? Aren't you betraying your friend? You could have just said that it's not your business and I should just go home and confront Arik."

By now Benny was by her side. "It's complicated—Arik sells my paintings. We rely on him—but he may be cheating me—" He stopped abruptly.

Ariella looked at him for a second, and then walked out. She felt sick to her stomach and didn't have the energy to hear about more cheating; she had enough problems of her own.

Chapter Twenty-Two

ARIELLA took the Egged bus to the party in Ramat Chen. She was glad that Rachel hadn't mentioned Yom-Tov's surprise party. She probably wasn't invited. Did Arik know that *she* was?

Ariella wore a new turquoise-and-violet-striped taffeta dress, one she had bought with her own money; there was no chance she was going to wear anything Arik had bought her. The dress was narrow at the waist and ballooned out, emphasizing her petite figure. In the front, a narrow but deep V-neck opening revealed some cleavage.

She'd pinned her hair up, exposing her long neck, and wore Ima's pearl earrings. To top the outfit off, she borrowed a warm, black jacket from her stylish next-door neighbor Rita, put on her black heels, and placed deep-red lipstick in her small, black clutch bag after applying it onto her lips.

The bus ride over was torturous. Ariella clenched her fists and opened her hands several times. She felt cold sweat dripping down her back under the dress. She didn't want to think, but couldn't help seeing Arik in her mind's eye, hugging and kissing a voluptuous blonde. Tears stung her eyes.

As Ariella arrived at the semi-detached house, she noticed a figure by the front door, huddled in a coat.

"Mira...?" Ariella wasn't sure; the only time she saw her replacement was at Yom-Tov's office, and in uniform.

"Ariella? You look so nice I almost didn't recognize you. You're late. It's almost seven thirty. Let's go in. Everybody is here already."

"Sorry. What are you doing outside?"

"I'm guiding people in. I think you're the last one. Come, come, let's go in."

Ariella's body shook, and not from the cold December wind. Her hands were sweating and she felt clammy. What would she say to Arik? What would he do when he saw her? Would he act surprised? Pretend he didn't know her?

There was only one small light on in the entrance hall, which threw long shadows into the living room. She couldn't see how many people there were, but the room seemed full, judging by the silhouettes and the whispered voices. As she stepped in and her eyes adjusted to the semidarkness, Ariella saw that some men were in uniform. She thought she'd recognized one or two.

People continued to speak softly, not wanting to disclose their presence when Yom-Tov arrived. She couldn't see Arik; it was too packed and dark.

When the doorbell rang, someone said *Shh* and everybody stopped talking.

Somebody, Ariella first couldn't see who, opened the front door. Then she saw. It was Arik. He stood right under the entrance hall light fixture. Yom-Tov walked in with a tall brunette woman behind him and shouts of *mazal tov* were heard from every corner. The lights flicked on, and Arik turned to face the crowd.

That was when he saw her; she knew it when their eyes met. He looked frozen.

She stood on the first step of a staircase, so she'd be taller, holding her jacket and purse in one hand and a round, long-stem champagne glass, which somebody had handed her, in the other. Everybody lifted their glasses, and together they yelled, *Le'haim!* Cheers!

Everybody, but her and Arik.

A short woman in a black dress and shoulder-length black hair approached Arik and the guests of honor. Ariella couldn't see her face, as much as she tried. The short woman hugged Yom-Tov and the woman by his side. Those must be the wives, Ariella thought. People rushed to greet the newcomers and Ariella lost sight of them.

She tried again to get a good look at Arik's wife, but a tall man stepped in front of her and obscured her view. She stood on the second stair leading to the upper floor to get a better view. It didn't help; in a minute the room was like a train station, people shifting in different directions. The short woman disappeared from Ariella's view.

Waiters carrying large, round trays pushed their way in between drinking guests. Ariella stepped back down the stairs and froze. She wasn't sure what to do next. Should she look for Arik? Talk to him here? She was being pushed from all directions, but her shoes felt stuck to the marble tiles, her legs immobilized. She wasn't tall enough to see Arik anywhere, nor the short woman in the black dress. She searched for Yom-Tov but couldn't find him either. What am I doing here? she thought. Her hands trembled, spilling champagne on her dress and onto the floor.

A waiter passing with a tray asked her something, but she couldn't make out his words. She handed him the glass with the remaining champagne. Somebody bumped into her, and she almost fell. She turned around and saw it was Benny.

"*Sliha,*" Sorry, he said. She never uttered a word, but her feet became unglued. She walked to the door and in a minute was out.

Oh, wait. She stopped. I should have gone upstairs and looked around. Find their bedroom and—and what? She wasn't a snooper. And what if the wife would have come in and enquired as to what she was doing? Would she have confronted her? Before even speaking to Arik?

Arik. The pain gripped her body, and she almost doubled over. How could he? Pretending to love her, only her! And she envisioned a future with him! How can one un-love someone one adores? Somebody who says that he loves you, brings you gifts, treats you like a princess—

Ariella walked in the street crying.

What an idiot she'd been! What now? What was she going to do now? She felt stuck... she couldn't leave Abba and Yael to go to America... it was too selfish; Yael wasn't well. Besides, she had no money. Eitan and Rachel were so involved with each other... she wouldn't be surprised if they got married... married—

Arik was married. What was she doing with him? I hate him, I hate him!

Ariella jumped as a passing white car honked at her. She looked up and realized she had walked farther than the bus stop and was almost at the next stop. The streets were deserted in this new wealthy neighborhood. All the little semi-detached homes had gardens, she noticed. What a nice place to raise children. Children! Did he have children?

When the bus arrived, there were only five people on it, and she found a seat in the front behind the driver. Wiping her face, she decided she wouldn't see him again. No matter how badly she wanted to. She was done with Arik.

* * *

The following day, Sunday—the beginning of the

working week—the phone in the office wouldn't stop ringing. Ariella got tired of answering it, listening to someone breathe and then disconnect. On Monday it happened almost every hour, like somebody was obsessed. She didn't want to think it might be Arik.

Goldberg approached Ariella's desk, a questioning look on his face and his glasses down at the edge of his nose. "What's going on?" He raised his eyebrows and his glasses almost fell off. "How come the phone is ringing off the hook for two days already? Who is it?"

She felt her cheeks burn and her hands sweat. "I'm sorry. I have no idea who it is. Nobody answers when I say hello."

"Is it for you or for the office?"

"I can't tell, Mr. Goldberg. The person won't talk." She hated his questions.

"You know, I don't like these interruptions. I asked you not to give this number to anyone. Could it be your friend from Jerusalem or an old boyfriend?" He sounded sarcastic.

Ariella looked at him in surprise. She was worried she was going to lose her job, but she bravely stared Goldberg in the eye; she wasn't going to repeat "I don't know who it is."

"Maybe it's one or the other." Goldberg continued to annoy her. "Not many men are good with words, you know." He walked back to his desk.

I know a man who is very good *with words,* Ariella wanted to say. *But* only *with words.* And then she thought of the gifts. And the weekends. And the restaurants. And the lovemaking. This was what she missed most: the lovemaking. Tomorrow would be the first Tuesday she wouldn't be meeting him in almost a year, aside from when he was out of the country. Or maybe he wasn't even overseas; maybe he was home with his family, his wife and children? She missed him; she really did, and she wanted to talk with him. Ask him. She couldn't envision life without him. The phone rang again.

"*Shalom,* Goldberg Accounting office." Ariella's voice quivered.

Silence.

"Arik?" She had to know.

"*Metukah sheli.*" My sweet. She heard a hoarse whisper, full of anguish and longing.

"Arik..." Ariella didn't know why she was whispering back.

"Can I see you tonight? I need to explain." Arik's voice was clearer now, but still low.

"Yes, you need to explain." Ariella found her voice as her anger reared its head again, and suddenly she didn't care if Goldberg could hear her. "But it will have to wait 'til tomorrow. Tomorrow is Tuesday, remember?" Ariella didn't know where the sarcastic tone came from. "But not in the usual place." She had to think of an alternative.

Then she had an idea. "No, not tomorrow, next week Tuesday, and we'll meet in a public place, in a restaurant that you and *your wife* frequent." She almost hissed the words. She'd make him wait now, let him suffer; she knew he was longing for her as much as she was longing for him.

There was a long pause. She knew she had given him an

ultimatum and feared the outcome, but she wouldn't relent. Her throat felt dry when she heard Goldberg get up from his chair.

"Ariella....*motek*," Arik almost begged, "Can we meet in Old Jaffa at Mustafa's?"

"I need to go now. Next Tuesday at Mustafa's. But I won't be going to Benny's afterwards." Her hands were wet, and she almost dropped the receiver.

"Okay."

Ariella put the phone down. Goldberg was watching her from his doorway, and she felt as though her insides had just slid down and lay at her feet.

Chapter Twenty-Three

ARIELLA couldn't sleep. She would toss and turn, trying to visualize life without Arik. She would wake up in a cold sweat. During the days at work, she jumped every time the phone rang.

Tuesday came, and Ariella once again took the bus to Old Jaffa after work. Mustafa's restaurant was almost empty. Arik was already there when she arrived at seven thirty, and she sat down, ignoring Mustafa's sweet talk and warm greetings.

Arik looked tired; his eyes were droopy, and the corners of his mouth kept turning down. "I'm married, yes, and I never told you, yes. I'm sorry, but I'm suffering, Ariella. I need you to understand."

Ariella didn't know what was wrong with her. She knew she should have been screaming at him, *hitting* him. But suddenly she felt more pity than anger.

"My wife is sick, Ariella," he continued, when she didn't say a word. "She is schizophrenic." It was as if he were continuing a conversation they had just stopped. But she didn't mind; she needed answers; she'd been waiting for them since Mira had first called.

"She acts strangely sometimes." Arik kept looking at his clasped hands on the table, not making eye contact with Ariella. "She is irrational and moody, and constantly fatigued. It's very hard to live with her. She either stays up half the night cleaning the kitchen or she lays in bed, crying. The doctors don't know what to do." He looked around nervously. "I think we need to hospitalize her, but I need to find a suitable institution I can trust."

"Institution?" Ariella finally found her voice but was confused. "She looked totally normal to me at Yom-Tov's party," she hissed, bringing her face closer to his, across the table.

"Yes, for an hour or so she was fine. Then she went to bed and cried and cried and kept saying that she hated everybody and wanted to die."

Ariella didn't know what to say to that; she never knew that anxiety and depression could be an illness. She was hearing it now for the first time. Institutionalized? Could it be true? Ima used to get depressed sometimes, but this sounded extreme.

Mustafa had brought menus to the table, but they both set

them aside. Next, he carried two glasses of hot tea and remembered to put *nahna,* mint, in Ariella's.

"*Baklava,*" Arik snapped at Mustafa, his eyes still cast down.

Mustafa nodded and went to bring the dessert.

"So what's your plan once you find a suitable institution for her?" Ariella asked, wishing he'd look at her; she needed to see his eyes. She needed to believe him.

"*Then* I can file for divorce."

Her anger rose again. "Why did you lie to me, Arik?" Ariella knew she was taking a chance but couldn't contain herself. She was much too upset, her head pounding. "Why didn't you tell me you were married? Why did you say that you were living with a roommate and a son?"

Arik smiled awkwardly and looked at her sadly. "It wasn't a complete lie." He sighed and scratched his nose. "My wife is alienated from me, really more like a roommate. And she does have a son—our son." He looked her in the eye now.

"You have a *son*?" She almost shouted. "Arik! You never told me you had a child!" Ariella felt confused and hopeful at the same time. "How could you hide it from me? Where is he? How old is he?" Was *she* going to be the cause of a family's breakup?

"I'm not hiding anything anymore. Enough, it's all in the open now. My son Boaz is in London studying art. He completed his army service and left for England."

He's older than me! Ariella realized in shock. Then she had another thought. "You have only one child?" She couldn't understand why she was softening, but she wasn't ready to let him go.

"Remember my groin injury? I think it took care of that. We never had more children afterwards. That's the reason I told you not to worry about getting pregnant, but I take extra precautions, as you know. We want to be completely safe, no?" He looked apologetic.

Ariella wasn't sure if this was good news or bad. But now she needed to find out more about the wife and decide if she was a threat and an obstacle, or not.

"Was this confirmed by a doctor?" She felt stupid. Wasn't she supposed to be angry?

"Not really. It never came up in checkups after the war, and babies just never happened again, so I know I'm safe."

Ariella was so confused. Sometimes, when he pulled back just before he climaxed, she felt regret and emptiness. She so wanted him to stay inside her, to hug him tight, to stay like that forever, being one. But now she was hurt and felt cheated, betrayed again.

If she married him, she may never have children. Still, she didn't want to let go, to lose him. She still loved him. Her head felt like it was going to explode, and she felt drained, until he put his hand on hers and looked directly into her eyes. Ariella saw a look of contrition in them. That was all it took.

They arrived late at the small hotel by the clock in Old Jaffa; Ariella refused to go back to Benny's apartment.

Now she stretched out in an unfamiliar bed with unfamiliar sheets. But it was Tuesday night, and she was exactly where she wanted to be—in Arik's arms.

As Arik stopped the car to let her off, she turned around to face him, seizing the moment.

"You're leaving your wife, yes?" Ariella asked. "In an institution, of course."

Arik buried his face in the side of her neck and mumbled something.

"Arik. You promise?"

"I promise," he said plainly.

Ariella got out of the car, not sure if she felt triumphant of defeated. How stupid she had been, thinking that he cared for her good name when he'd dropped her around the corner from her house. He worried about his *own* name! She should have known then that something wasn't kosher. But his wife was sick...right? The poor woman. A good institution would be just the right place for her.

Chapter Twenty-Four

"ARIK!" Ariella yelled out as Arik almost hit an oncoming army jeep before swerving back quickly.

It was late on the last Saturday of March 1959 and Ariella and Arik were making their way back north after spending two days in Kibbutz Ein Gedi in the Negev desert.

"Are you all right?" Arik asked Ariella, keeping his eyes on the road. It was pitch black out in the desert. Only his headlights showed him the way; there was no moon to be seen.

"Oy, that was close. Yes, I'm fine. Are you okay?" Ariella opened the car window and let the wind blow through her long hair. The scent of the desert flowers was faint, but she could smell spring approaching.

"Yes, it's so dark out here...I didn't see that pothole, nor the car that blinded me."

Ariella started to relax again.

They were almost to the outskirts of Tel Aviv when Ariella knew it was time to ask.

"You know what?" she said, stretching her arms and twisting her torso, stiff after sitting in the car for hours. "I would like you to meet my friend Rachel and my brother Eitan." She decided to be bold. This seemed to be the right moment to say it.

"Sure," Arik replied easily, shrugging his shoulder. "We can meet, but not in Tel Aviv. I don't want to bump into anybody I know and give them a reason to gossip. You understand, right?"

That gave Ariella a weird feeling, like secrets were something dirty. She understood now that Arik avoided public places not for her sake, but for his own.

"Well, maybe they can come with us to Tivon in the Galilee next month?" She knew Arik could pay for them and decided to test him. "I'm so excited, Arik. I'm getting three days off this coming Passover, and we can celebrate with them. They're engaged, did I tell you?" Ariella yawned loudly. "They want to get married next year, in June, right after Eitan graduates. Isn't that great? My best friend will become my sister-in-law!"

She felt she was rambling, so she closed her mouth and shut her eyes.

Arik didn't say a word.

They listened to the radio, and Ariella hoped he was wide awake after their near miss with the army vehicle, so she leaned her head on the car's window. Marriage, she thought. Marriage and divorce, that's all I think about lately.

And that brought her to think of her aunt who lived in South Africa. Poor Aunt Pearl, her marriage didn't last long.

A letter had arrived two days ago telling them that she and Uncle Irwin were separating.

Since her return to South Africa from Israel about ten months ago, after Ima had died, Aunt Pearl had lived through hell, she'd written, but hadn't shared the truth earlier because of their loss, which was hers too. She'd been busy with lawyers. Irwin was arrested, twice, for having intimate relations with a Bantu prostitute—a Black woman—which was against the law.

Irwin was detained in jail for one night each time, and she had to bail him out. To make Aunt Pearl feel better, or so he had thought, he confessed all his crimes and admitted to having a year-long affair with his dental nurse. He'd impregnated her, and had to marry her, or her parents would make a scandal and take him to the cleaners. He'd be ruined.

"Well," she had written, "God must be showing me the way back home. Good riddance! I just need to make sure I don't leave here penniless, so I've hired a good lawyer."

Could she stay with them until she got a job, and found her own apartment or rented a room?

Arik stopped the car, jolting Ariella; she didn't realize that she had dozed off. As she awoke, her mind slowly cleared, and she wasn't sure if Aunt Pearl's letter was a reality or just a dream. She looked around and noticed that Arik had arrived at her father's apartment building and was sitting and watching her.

"What's the time?" she felt a bit disoriented.

"Hey, sleeping beauty, it's after midnight. Just as well I had the radio on; you were lousy company on the way back." Arik smiled, but she noticed that he looked exhausted, too. He was pale and must have been chain smoking to keep awake. It wasn't easy driving for so many hours.

She felt guilty, and her neck was sore from the way she had been sitting. "I'm sorry, Arik. Thank you for a lovely weekend in Ein Gedi. I'm sorry I fell asleep, but I'm so tired. I'm sure you're finished, too."

Arik pulled her to him and kissed her passionately, but all she wanted was to get inside her home and get into bed; she had to be up early for work.

Arik released her reluctantly. "I'll see you on Tuesday, my Ella!"

Ariella was sleepy, her head empty of thoughts and her limbs heavy. She wasn't sure how she felt, so she didn't reply, and slammed the car door.

Chapter Twenty-Five

ON Sunday when Ariella was at work and Goldberg was out, she called Pihl, the kids' shoe store where Rachel worked. But Rachel wasn't there. Ariella was told that she hadn't been at work on Friday either.

After work, Ariella took the bus to Rachel's home, but her mom said that she was sick and couldn't see anybody and that Ariella should try to come tomorrow. Ariella was shocked; she felt that Rachel was avoiding her. In the kibbutz where they met, Ariella and Rachel used to get into each other's bed when one of them got sick; they would comfort each other, sing to each other, tell jokes, and were never worried about catching whatever illness or germs the other one had. So what was wrong now? Ariella felt rejected and puzzled when she took the bus home.

"Eitan, what's going on with Rachel?" Ariella asked her brother as soon as he got back home from university. She noticed that he wouldn't make eye contact with her.

"Eitan? Talk to me," she whispered, almost hissing, bending and tilting her head, trying to catch his eye. "I stopped by her house and her mother said Rachel wasn't feeling well."

Abba and Yael sat at the kitchen table; Abba reading the paper and Yael doing homework. Eitan motioned with his head toward Ariella's bedroom. She walked there first, and he followed.

Secrets. Everybody had secrets. When Ima got sick, she and Abba had kept it a secret. Ariella had her own secret. What was Rachel hiding?

Ariella sat on her bed and Eitan sat on Yael's. They faced each other, their knees almost touching. He got up again and closed the door. They had never closed a bedroom door in their home, not since Ima got sick. Eitan sat down again.

"Rachel had surgery late Friday." He looked at the floor. "She had an abortion."

Ariella gasped and placed her hand on her mouth. She stared at her brother wide-eyed. "Late Friday? Is she okay? Do her parents know? How far along was she? Who did the..." Her head was on fire, and she realized that she was shooting questions out as fast as her brain produced them, with no filters, and stopped.

"She's doing fine. She's recovering. Yes, her parents know. They paid for it. We went to see Dr. Levy last week. She's a gynecologist, a very nice lady, and she confirmed that Rachel was pregnant and said we should take a week to think it over." Eitan caught his breath; he seemed to be struggling to speak calmly. "We want to get married, Ariella, you know that, but not until I graduate next May. We have no money. We can't raise a child now." Eitan placed his elbows on his thighs and his head in his hands. Ariella stood up and went to sit next to her brother, hugging his shoulders.

"So she had it three days ago, and you've known for at least ten days." She tried to calculate, more for herself than for him. "But why doesn't she want to see me?" Ariella felt hurt that they had known but didn't tell her.

"She's very sad. Me too." His face twisted as if he wanted to cry but stopped himself.

Ariella had never seen Eitan cry. Not even when Ima died. "Don't cry, Eitan. You did the best for now." She felt overwhelmed but had to calm herself and him. "Once you're married, you'll have lots of children." She was looking for comforting words.

Eitan didn't reply.

A new thought crossed Ariella's mind. "How did you even know where to go? Where did you hear of this doctor?"

Eitan took a deep breath again. "Mania, the woman Rachel works with at Pihl, caught Rachel vomiting and knew immediately. She recommended that Rachel see Dr. Levy.

Mania has four grown children and had needed her services too."

"When are you going to see Rachel?"

"I'm going to eat something and then go to see her." He got up.

"Let's make salad together. Abba made soup and schnitzel for dinner. Will you tell Rachel that you told me, and that she and I don't have to talk about it if she doesn't want to? But I must see her, please." Ariella said quietly. "Ask if I can come and see her tomorrow after work, *beseder*?" Okay?

Eitan nodded.

Ariella got up and opened her bedroom door. The familiar aroma of chicken soup filled the house. Abba had reheated it, and Yael was already placing plates and silverware on the table. Ariella noticed that Yael had five forks and five tablespoons in her hands. She watched as Yael placed four of each on the table, went back to the silverware drawer and slowly, very slowly, and reluctantly, returned the fifth set. How long had she been doing that? Tears filled her eyes as she watched her little sister.

As Ariella cut the small cucumbers into tiny pieces for the salad, she thought of her own secret. How could she be surprised that Rachel kept such a secret from her, when she had a secret she couldn't tell anybody? The tightness in her chest wouldn't let go.

The next day Ariella got a call at work from Eitan. "Rachel said to come after work," he said. Ariella quickly placed the receiver back before Goldberg could say anything.

When Ariella rang the doorbell, Rachel's father, who was hard of hearing, shouted from behind the closed door, "*Mee zeh*?" Who is that?

After she declared her name, he opened the door and hugged her. She followed him to the kitchen where Rachel sat drinking hot tea with her mother. Rachel's face looked drawn, but she wasn't as pale as Ariella expected.

"*Erev tov*, Rachel." Good evening. Ariella wasn't sure what to say next. "*Shalom*, Mrs. Bernstein," she added.

Rachel's mother got up, hugged Ariella, and left the kitchen.

"*Shalom*, thanks for coming." Rachel didn't look her in the eye.

"How are you feeling? When are you returning to work?" Ariella asked.

"Tomorrow. I'm much better. I really miss the shop, you know? How is your work?" Rachel asked.

It seemed like they were both avoiding what was on their minds.

"Work is fine. I just miss our lunches together." Ariella felt great sorrow for her sweet Rachel, seeing her in her worn dressing gown and old slippers, her red hair in disarray and her eyes filling up. Ariella couldn't help herself and gathered her friend in her arms.

Rachel didn't resist. She melted into Ariella's body, placed her cheek on Ariella's shoulder, and cried, but not for long.

Rachel's mother must have heard the sobs and came to the kitchen. Together, they both held Rachel's elbows and led her to her bedroom. As Rachel got into bed, her mother left the room.

Ariella tucked the blanket around Rachel, bent to kiss her cheek, and tiptoed out.

She had to leave before she started crying, so she bid goodbye to Rachel's parents and left. She was going to take the bus home but decided against it; she wanted to walk and think.

Arik. What was going to happen to her and Arik? What if she became pregnant, would she opt for an abortion, like Rachel? No way, she thought. Arik would divorce his wife and marry her on the spot. Or would he? Oy, Ima, what would you have done? She wished her mother were there. But if Ima were alive, would she have told her?

Alone and confused, Ariella slept fitfully that night.

* * *

The phone rang in Ariella's office.

"Want to get falafel for lunch?" It was Rachel.

"Yes! Where are you?" Ariella missed Rachel and needed cheering up.

"I'm back at work. Want to meet at Shuk Bezalel at one thirty?"

"All right, see you then."

They met at the corner of Allenby and Nachalat Benjamin, bought their falafel at Shuk Bezalel, and walked to

Gan Meir to sit on a bench in the park, eat and talk.

They entered the small park off King George Street and found an unoccupied bench. There were some grandmothers with children who were playing in the sandpit and swinging noisily on some wooden swings. They knew their conversation wouldn't be completely private, but they had no alternative.

Rachel wiped her mouth. "I'm sorry I couldn't see you for a while."

"Yes," Ariella decided to be straightforward. "I was surprised and somewhat hurt. I felt like you shut me out."

"I know. I'm sorry. It was a very difficult time. When I found out, I was shocked. Then Mania sent me and Eitan to that Dr. Levy. A very nice lady but," Rachel lowered her voice, "she asked if we were married, and when we said no, she was quiet for a very long time. Then she said that it was good that we came together, and we should have a week to think it over and then call her. That was very nice, but what was there to think about? It was agony making the decision." Rachel's eyes filled up. "I was scared out of my mind to have the baby but afraid to get rid of it. She sighed. "Do you understand?"

"Yes." Cold chills ran down Ariella's back; she couldn't even picture what *she* would have done in the same situation. She felt her stomach heave, and the falafel almost came back up.

A bird was chirping, and Ariella, not wanting to dwell on her thoughts, quickly looked at her watch. "Oh, it's almost time to get back to work. Want to get some juice or *gazoz* on our way back?" She loved the red raspberry syrup in soda water.

Ariella stood up from the bench. "The falafel was very salty."

As they stood and drank their sodas, Ariella said out of nowhere, "It's *Pesach* next month. Do you have any plans?" Ariella regretted her question as soon as it left her lips.

"Plans? Besides the *Seder*? No, why?"

Ariella wasn't sure how to continue. She wanted Rachel and Eitan to meet Arik but maybe the time wasn't right? Could she assume that Arik would pay for her brother and friend to stay at a hotel in Tivon? Well, *Pesach* was a month away.

"I'm just asking," she blurted, suddenly wanting to get away. "I have to go back to work." Ariella looked nervously at her watch several times, not registering the time she was seeing.

Rachel frowned but said nothing.

The girls hugged, and Ariella walked to the bus stop. She could smell the spring air and looked at her watch again, realizing that she actually needn't hurry. Soon enough it would be too hot to walk in the streets, so she decided to walk and think; she had some time.

It had been a year since she and Arik started seeing each other. She had been very secretive since she met him. Somewhere deep inside she knew that she wasn't doing the right thing.

Yes, he was wonderful to her, and she loved him. Maybe she was overreacting? She loved the tender moments, the passionate lovemaking, the luxuries, and the excitement. But why didn't he tell her that he'd been married? Was he scared she'd leave him? How could she if he was suffering, living with a schizophrenic woman? He must be going through hell. She didn't know much about the disease, but from what he'd described, the woman should be in a caring and professional home that would keep her comfortable.

Ariella's heart filled with compassion for Arik and his wife, for Rachel and Eitan, and for the baby who never had a chance.

Chapter Twenty-Six

THERE was a cold spell in early April when Eitan and Ariella picked up Rachel at her parents' apartment to go to the movies.

"Nice dress," Rachel remarked as she locked the door behind her. "And shoes."

It was wonderful to see Rachel fully recovered. Like Yael, Rachel also noticed Ariella's new things. Ariella had new leather gloves for the past winter and a new pair of Audrey Hepburn sunglasses for the coming spring, which she placed on top of her head, like a hairband.

"Thank you." Ariella smiled, smoothing the front of the new dress Arik had brought her from...she couldn't remember. Probably Dusseldorf.

It was her favorite dress. A cotton-mix in bold plaid, blending black with purples and pinks. The top was fitted down to the waist, and the skirt was full and whirly. Ariella wore it with a thin black patent leather belt, patent shoes, and a matching clutch bag. Her expensive, navy blue coat, which she wore open that night, flowed from the shoulders down with a high collar and one large button in the front. She didn't need to borrow her next-door neighbor Rita's coat anymore.

"I bought it in a small store on Dizengoff Street." She waved her purse as they walked down the stairs of the apartment building. "Do you like it? And the shoes?"

"Yes. But the dress? And the coat?"

"Well, the dress is from Dusseldorf, in Germany, I think, you know." Ariella was stalling, trying to explain without giving too many details. "And the coat is from Paris. My boyfriend...uh...the guy I'm going out with bought it on his last trip." She knew that she stood out but didn't care; she was basking in luxuries.

"Your *boyfriend*?" Rachel exclaimed, stopping on the staircase ledge. "What do you mean boyfriend? You have a boyfriend?! And he goes to Germany? And Paris? What's going on, Ariella? Eitan?" She turned to her own boyfriend, who stopped just behind her.

Eitan shrugged.

They were walking down the stairs of the apartment building where Rachel lived, and Ariella got to the building's entrance first. She didn't turn around and didn't reply, as she felt trapped. By her own confession. Like a thief who wanted to be caught? The thought crossed her mind.

"Come on, Ariella." Rachel stepped onto the sidewalk; Ariella could hear her run to catch up with her. "Who *is* he? When are we going to meet this mysterious guy? I knew you've been with somebody but avoided telling us. How long have you been seeing him?"

It's been over a year, Ariella thought, but how could I tell you...

"You once claimed that you've been seeing someone, but that he was always away, out of town, or out of the country. So when did *you* see him? Ariella, why can't we meet him?" They all walked side by side, Ariella slowing down but unable to respond to Rachel's outburst.

If you only knew, she thought.

"Eitan, aren't you curious to meet Ariella's boyfriend?" Rachel asked, as if looking for reinforcement. "This is so weird you two siblings don't seem to be living on the same planet."

Again, Eitan didn't reply. Ariella knew her brother's philosophy: *live and let live.* He never asked too many questions; Ariella was used to it. She knew him too well to worry about his silence, and to be honest, she preferred it that way.

But Ariella felt the need to tell them the truth. They'd earned it; they'd been honest with her and were her closest allies.

"It's true," she began. "He does travel a lot." Ariella was protecting Arik and tried to justify the delay in them meeting him. "Can we sit somewhere and talk instead of going to the movies?"

Rachel and Eitan stopped in their tracks. Ariella stopped walking, too, and looked at them. Eitan stared at his watch, at his sister, and then at his girlfriend, as if waiting for a decision. Ariella knew she looked nervous, and her brother's stare confirmed it. They were just turning from King Solomon Street to Zamenhoff Street on their way to the Esther Movie Theater.

"Let's sit," Eitan said. "There are plenty of coffee places on Dizengoff Street."

They walked into Café Roval. It was too cold to sit outside, although some square tables and plastic chairs were placed on the sidewalk. Roval was frequented by actors and artists, writers and intellectuals. It wasn't an everyday occurrence that three very young Israelis walked into this bohemian coffee house. Ariella didn't mind; it was going to be her treat, a special occasion. She was nervous but excited, too; she was ready to unload this burden.

She looked around and noticed that most women wore open jackets with white-collared shirts underneath. She detested the masculine look this gave women, like on the kibbutz, khaki pants and white shirts, all with collars and buttons. The noise was deafening from the lively chatter, and she was grateful when they found a corner table, although people lifted their heads to stare at her.

They sat down, and a waiter in black pants and a white apron tied to his waist appeared at their side. Eitan looked a bit nervous and out of place and frowned when he scanned the menu, but after they ordered three black teas and three slices of cheesecake, Ariella got right to the point.

"I met this man, who is a bit older, when I was in the service. His name is Arik. He's General Yom-Tov's friend and was an officer in the army." She looked at Rachel, who opened her mouth in surprise and quickly shut it. "I met him just before Ima died, but I wasn't really interested. I was planning to go to America then." It was Eitan's turn to look at his sister in surprise, but he quickly recovered, too.

"My world—our world—shattered when Ima died." Ariella took a deep breath. "Abba and Yael were so vulnerable. Yael is still young and suffering from those awful headaches we can't explain." Eitan frowned as he looked at Ariella talking. "Once Aunt Pearl left, I felt it was all on my shoulders."

"But I'm here too, Ariella. I thought that Yael's headaches were due to the extreme summer heat, maybe a sunstroke she once had at camp." Eitan played nervously with the cake fork as he talked, turning it with his fingers as if rolling a cigarette.

"No, Eitan. Abba and I took her to a neurologist, and he claimed it wasn't physiological." She didn't want to continue and tell him that he was too busy lately to pay attention to his little sister.

Eitan placed the fork on the white tablecloth and looked down at his intertwined fingers resting on the table. He said nothing.

"So I decided to put my plans on hold," Ariella continued, not wanting to lose the momentum; she may regret it in a minute. "It was no time to be selfish. I decided to stay until we all found our footing and Yael got better. And then Arik appeared again." She looked at Eitan. "He's a prominent businessman working in exports and imports. Problem is..." Her mouth went dry. Where was that tea? "Problem is... that he's still married, but he is planning to get a divorce soon. I still have to keep our relationship secret, of course."

Ariella said it all in one breath, in monotone, knowing she sounded emotionless, as if reporting about somebody else. It was surreal for her to hear her own voice saying it all out loud, at long last. Thank goodness the place was noisy, and only Eitan and Rachel could hear her.

"He also has a son one year older than me," she added quickly, putting all her cards on the table.

She saw Rachel stifle a gasp as she placed her hand on her mouth.

Eitan and Rachel looked at her with wide eyes, not even trying to conceal their shock.

"Do you love him?" Rachel recovered first, although it took her the best part of two minutes.

"Yes, very much. He's a wonderful man."

"And here I thought he was either an Arab, a Christian, or *Mossad*," Israeli intelligence, Eitan muttered as if to himself. He averted his eyes and started playing with the fork again.

"But he's...he's...he's *married*?" Rachel said it as if it was a dirty word, her eyebrows raised in surprise.

"Yes, he is, but he's going to divorce his wife," Ariella repeated, but could hear the doubt in her own voice. It sounded more like she was trying to convince herself more than them.

"When?" Rachel wouldn't let go, her tone skeptical. "It's been how long now, Ariella? What's keeping him?" An image of a bull terrier flashed in Ariella's mind. Rachel was holding on.

Eitan played with his wristwatch, turning it around and around.

"As soon as he finds a reliable place for her. She's sick." Ariella found herself defending Arik again. She had to. She ended with, "He's really a good man. He cares for her. That proves that he is a good man, doesn't it?" Was she losing her confidence?

Nobody said a word.

Ariella swallowed hard. "I want you both to meet him. He is ready, he said, but not in Tel Aviv. I know you'll love him."

Rachel had been trying to stop Eitan from fiddling nervously with his wristwatch. Now she pulled her hand away from his and took Ariella's hand in hers. "He has a son one year older than *you*? How old *is* this Arik?"

"Forty-five."

Rachel and Eitan exchanged a look that Ariella couldn't miss. "Are you sure he's willing to meet us?" Rachel asked. "Is it okay that you've told us?" Sweet Rachel was back.

"Yes."

"What do *you* think?" Rachel looked at Eitan sideways.

"Arik wants to invite you both to join us on a trip to Tivon during *Pesach*," Ariella interjected quickly, before Eitan could respond. "The *Seder* is on Wednesday night, and we can leave the next morning. We don't work Thursday...it's a holiday, and with Friday being a bridge and then Saturday, we have three days off." She felt the excitement engulf her, although she knew she was assuming Arik's agreement to the plan. "We'll return Saturday night, so we can all be back at work Sunday morning."

"Do you think it's right for him to invite us?" Rachel asked Eitan. "We don't even know him!"

Eitan shook his head but said nothing.

"That's the point; you'll both meet him and get to know him." Ariella knew she was taking a chance. Arik had extended no such invitation, but once she'd started, she had no option but to continue confidently, "The *Galil* is beautiful in spring."

"I'm not sure we'll get a bridge day on Friday. I'll need to ask at work," Eitan said eventually. "And why not meet in Tel Aviv?"

"He doesn't want a scandal, Eitan. He's an important business man. If he happens to bump into somebody who knows him, and sees him with a young woman, what would they think?"

"And you're okay with that?" Eitan surprised her.

Ariella had to search inside for a true answer. "Yes, for the time being," she took a breath. "I'm being patient. He's worth it, you'll see."

Yes, she thought, he *is* worth it.

Chapter Twenty-Seven

"I NEED to talk with you all," Abba announced at dinner one night, as they sat at the kitchen table. That was his thing; 'I need to talk with you,' always meant that something serious had to be discussed. Ariella pricked up her ears. "We received another letter from Aunt Pearl today with the exact date of her arrival."

Did Ariella hear some excitement in his voice? She looked at Eitan to see if he noticed something, too, but he sported his usual poker face.

Yael looked at Abba in anticipation. "*Nu?*" Well?

"We need you all to empty the small, enclosed balcony and clean it out, so we can turn it into a bedroom for her," Abba said. "I'll borrow a bed from my brother."

"Is she really coming to live here?" It seemed that Yael had to make sure she understood completely before she got too excited.

"Yes, *motek*, she'll stay here for a little while, until she gets her own place." Abba looked almost as happy as Yael but still didn't divulge the date.

"So *when* is Aunt Pearl arriving?" Yael couldn't wait and interrupted Ariella's thoughts.

"In four weeks. On June seventh. She'll be here for the placing of the tombstone on Ima's grave on the eighth," Abba continued. "For the one-year anniversary." His mood changed suddenly.

"That's cutting it close," Ariella said somewhat unsympathetically; she wasn't sure how she felt about having Aunt Pearl living with them. Her jubilation of somebody to help her take care of Yael and Abba was mingled with fear her aunt would find out about Arik. But she had to react to Abba's announcement and said, "We have the whole of May to clean and prepare." She said assertively. "We can do it after *Pesach*. I don't have time before." Now was as good a time as any to tell her father, "I'm going away for three days on *Pesach*, the day after the *Seder*." She looked at Eitan, but he just nodded and walked out of the kitchen. Ariella wondered why he didn't say that he and Rachel were going, too.

"Where are you going?" Abba wanted to know.

"My friend, uh, is taking me to the Galilee. It's so pretty at the beginning of spring." She was searching for words. "Maybe Eitan and Rachel will come, too."

"A friend? Which friend?" Abba frowned. "Did I meet him?"

"Uh, no, not yet," the hair on her neck stood up. "Eitan and Rachel will meet him first...you know, guys are shy to meet the parents..."

"Well, if he's taking you out on a trip to the Galil, somebody should meet this shy boy." Abba smiled good-heartedly. "I trust Eitan's judgment, and I'm sure you'll make wise decisions."

The hair on her neck stood up again.

* * *

Arik raised his eyebrows, looking surprised, when Ariella asked him if he would invite her brother and almost-sister-in-law for the weekend, and pay all their expenses.

"Oh, uh, sure," Arik stammered, kissing her lips, moving his naked body closer to hers.

"You said that you're willing to meet them but not in town." She tried to move her face away.

"Yes, yes." He didn't seem to care much for talking as he was caressing her naked body.

Did he feel guilty that he lied to her about his wife?

It feels like I can ask him for anything now, she thought. Especially when making love.

* * *

Ariella returned home from work at half past one on *Erev Pesach,* the eve of Passover. She placed Elvis Presley's record on the turntable, and music filled the room as she sang along to "One Night With You" while folding her lingerie and placing it in her suitcase for her trip. She felt positive Eitan and Rachel would absolutely fall in love with Arik, like she had.

Eitan entered the apartment; his office closed at two o'clock.

"I feel very uncomfortable, Ariella." Eitan shook his head as he looked her in the eye. "I gave it a lot of thought. I don't know this man, and he is paying for me to stay in a hotel for two nights? And paying for my food? I can't afford such a vacation, but I don't want a handout."

"But Arik is rich, Eitan. He doesn't mind spending the money. You can come out to the car with me tomorrow morning, and I'll introduce you. Then we'll all pick up Rachel and drive somewhere for coffee and sit and talk. It will be wonderful, you'll see. Come on, Eitan, don't spoil it. I need you to meet him. He's great."

Eitan didn't argue farther but he also didn't start packing.

Dressed in their best, they made their way to Uncle Gabriel's house, a mile away, for the *Seder*. There they met with Rachel and her parents, who were also invited. Around midnight, they stayed to help clean up while Yael slept on the couch. Ariella and Abba woke her up to walk back home, and she didn't stop moaning. They walked because Abba wouldn't drive to his Orthodox brother on a Jewish holiday, out of respect.

* * *

The loud alarm beep woke Ariella at eight the next morning. She jumped out of bed.

Eitan wasn't there. For a moment she wondered why, but then she remembered that after the *Seder*, he had gone to Rachel's house with her and her parents.

Arik was to be around the corner by nine. It was daylight, and he wouldn't park right in front of her building for all the neighbors to see her drag a suitcase into his car.

She got ready and kissed Yael's sleepy head as her sister turned in her bed. Abba sat in the kitchen reading the paper. He got up, offered her a cup of coffee, and sat down again.

"*Toda*, Abba. I'm leaving in five minutes." Ariella bent down to kiss his cheek.

"Where exactly are you going?" Abba asked, looking at her.

"To Tivon." Ariella was glad she didn't have to lie.

"So can we clean out the balcony when you get back?" Abba seemed fixated on Aunt Pearl's arrival, thank goodness. "I'll be on vacation and I can help you."

He sounded cheerful. The bakery usually closed for the eight days of the holiday, due to the flour and leavened food that was not to be touched or consumed during Passover. It was Abba's only annual vacation, and now he had something exciting to fill it with. They never had money to go away on vacation, and this year was no different. Ariella was glad she could get away with Arik.

"*Betach,*" sure, she replied, and picked up her little red suitcase and walked outside.

Arik was waiting in his car, his face grim. He reached over to unlock the car door and pushed it open for Ariella. She quickly slid in and sat down, looking at him, her little red suitcase on her lap. The car stank of cigarette smoke because all the windows were closed.

"*Shalom*, sweetie," he said.

"*Hahg Same'ach.*" Happy Holidays. She couldn't understand his frown. "What's wrong?"

"I'm sorry, Ariella, but I can't go to Tivon today," Arik said quickly in a hoarse voice.

Ariella was stunned. The abruptness, the cold way he said it made her stomach tighten. Was he leaving her?

"Why? What happened? And what about Eitan and Rachel?" She couldn't breathe.

Arik was staring ahead, his windshield covered with smoke. "I received a call only an hour ago. I have to fly to London tonight, I'm sorry."

Ariella just sat there; suddenly she didn't care which of the passersby saw them. She needed air, so she opened the car door.

Arik turned the ignition on. "I'm afraid I have to go home now, Ariella, but why don't you all go without me and have a good time?" He opened his door, flicked his cigarette out, closed the car door, and turned to kiss her. "I'll pay for it."

Hot tears of anger rolled down her cheeks. "The whole

idea was for you to meet my brother and Rachel and get to know each other. It's silly. What would we do there without you? We won't go." She choked on her words. "Why didn't you tell me sooner you were cancelling on me?"

"You don't have a phone, *motek*. I couldn't call you," he said, and she had to admit it was true. "I really have to go now. I'm so sorry. I'll make it up to you, I promise. In June, we can all go away on *Shavuot*," Arik continued, referring to the next Jewish holiday. "Please apologize for me to Eitan and Rachel, will you, sweetie? I love you. I really do, but this is an emergency. I have to run and get ready." Arik stretched to kiss Ariella but only reached her ear as she turned her face away.

Ariella shot out of the car in a rage, her little red suitcase in one hand and a white purse in the other. She dropped the suitcase on the sidewalk and slammed the car door. Arik drove away. She shook with anger and disappointment, her eyes red and her face wet. She felt abandoned and betrayed, and even worse...humiliated.

This is it, she thought. I won't see him again.

Somebody pushed her. Ariella looked up. An elderly woman had bumped into her and continued walking without apologizing. It woke Ariella up from her thinking. *Eitan*! She stared at her watch. He must have been waiting with Rachel, wondering where she was.

She grabbed her little red suitcase, which looked ridiculous now on the gray, dirty sidewalk, and rushed back home. Abba picked up his head from the newspaper he was reading and looked at Ariella over his reading glasses.

"What happened?" he asked, surprised.

"I'm not...we're not going." She felt distraught and ashamed, and it was hard covering it up. "My friend has an emergency and can't go," Ariella said with a broken heart. "He was supposed to meet Eitan and Rachel..." She jumped from her seat. "They must be waiting for us now...at Rachel's parents." She looked at Abba. "I have no way of telling them. Rachel has a phone, but we don't, and all the stores are closed. What am I going to do?"

Abba put his glasses down on the table, got up, and said quietly, "Come, I'll take you there with my van." He got up and took his keys.

"You will? On a *hahg?* You don't mind people seeing you driving your van during a holiday?"

"Since when do I care about the *hahg*? Or about what people think? You know I'm not religious. Besides, you're more important, and so are Eitan and Rachel. Come on, let's go."

Yael called out from her perch in bed. "Where are you going?" Clearly, she didn't understand what was going on.

"Stay in bed and read, Yulinka. I'm just taking Ariella to Rachel, and I'll be right back."

Ariella saw the look of surprise on Rachel's and Eitan's faces when she arrived with Abba in the gray van. They stood on the sidewalk outside the apartment building, two small suitcases at their feet. Ariella was angry with Arik, but for some unexplained reason, she also felt relieved.

As she climbed out of the van, Ariella said, "*Shalom,*

Hevre." Hello, guys. "I'm so sorry, but Arik can't make it. He has to fly to London tonight, family emergency."

They all looked from one to the other. Abba was silent in the car.

"What do you think we should do?" Eitan seemed at a loss.

"Are the rooms at the hotel in Tivon paid for?" Rachel was always the one who found her bearings first.

"I don't know, but Arik said he will pay if we stay there."

"So why don't we take your car and drive up north?" Rachel looked at Eitan.

"Tivon? Drive to the Galilee? With my little Fiat 600? It'll never make it up there."

Ariella and Rachel looked at each other.

"Never mind, let's just leave it." Ariella gave up. "Let's think of something else."

"I know that you're disappointed, Ella, so am I. I really wanted to meet Arik, but if he has an emergency, we need to understand. There'll be other times," Rachel reassured her.

"I guess so," Ariella said.

"Will your car make it to Tel-Yitzhak?" Abba asked Eitan from inside the van. "Why don't you all visit your old friends in the kibbutz? It's *hahg*, so nobody's working, and I'm sure they'll be delighted to see you all."

"What a great idea, Abba!" Ariella crawled back in to hug him. "Let's go, Eitan." She stepped back out, working hard at cheering herself up. "It would be so much fun showing you around. Let's get out of town...it's not far...we can have a super day with our old friends and show them we didn't really forget them." Her spirits rose, and Rachel's eyes shone, too.

"Okay, now can you move away from my van so I can return to Yael," Abba said, and he was off.

Ariella and Rachel stood on the sidewalk, waiting for Eitan to return with his car keys, when Ariella lifted her chin and said, "It's spring, and I was so excited to go up north and see the beautiful flowers blooming." A sense of nostalgia washed over her. "Remember the fields on the kibbutz? We may see new flowers there now." She was determined not to think of Arik, at least not until she saw him again and questioned him about the details of his emergency.

Chapter Twenty-Eight

THE following Tuesday, Ariella was surprised to see Arik leaning on his white Opel outside her office building and not around the corner. He'd apparently replaced the canary-yellow one that could be spotted from afar. Ariella figured he did it so she wouldn't have to sneak around street corners to meet with him; people didn't pay as much attention to him now.

Just the same, as soon as she saw him, her anger, which had slightly dissipated with the passing of time, rose again. Her trip to the kibbutz had been a bit of a disappointment, most of her former friends had moved away, and besides that, she was supposed to have been on a luxury vacation finally introducing her boyfriend to her brother and best friend.

She frowned at him, trying to hold on to her fury. His looks still took her breath away. His dark tan and muscular arms, his well-ironed khaki pants with a crease right in the middle of each leg, his new haircut, his deep dimple, and that handsome head of his, tilted to one side—it all rendered her helpless to his charm.

A cigarette dangled from the corner of his mouth, and his hands were pushed into his pockets. He leaned on his car, facing her and smiling. He looked just like Cary Grant.

"Hi, *motek*, I'm sorry about the weekend," Arik said, crushing his cigarette on the sidewalk and opening the car door for Ariella. She hurried in, sat erect, and waited.

Arik walked around his car, got into his seat, turned the ignition on, and started driving.

"Look, Ariella." Arik sounded like he had a speech prepared. "My son needed me in London on an urgent matter, and they don't care about *Pesach* at this college. Jewish holiday or not, we had to go. I couldn't get around it. I'm sorry I disappointed you."

"*We*?" She was mad.

"Well, yes, you don't think my wife would have let me go to our son and not come with me, do you?" He held out his box of cigarettes to her as if to calm her down. She ignored it. She didn't want to smoke; she wanted to stay focused. She was also not going to light one for him this time. He put the pack down between their seats.

"Instead of going with me to Tivon, you went with your wife to London?" Ariella had to do something with her hands, so she uncrumpled the cigarette box now, lit a cigarette, and puffed on it. "And she was fine?" Sarcasm crept into her voice. "Not too many unpleasant episodes? Suddenly, she was well?"

"Well, yes, she was fine." Arik either didn't hear her tone or decided to ignore it; she wasn't sure which, so she kept on smoking. "But let's forget it now, sweetie. I bought you something beautiful in London, a silver evening purse and sandals to match—"

"Wait a minute, Arik." Ariella was in no mood for distractions or bribes. She had to take a deep breath to calm herself down. "I can't let it go yet. I'm still really mad at you." She closed her eyes, noticing her fists were clenched.

"I'm so sorry, *motek*...I really am, but it isn't easy." He shifted in his seat as if agitated and impatient. "I need to maneuver so many things in my life. But I need you to know one thing: I promise I'll never let you down again." He reached for the cigarettes and pulled one out, holding on to the steering wheel with the other hand.

Ariella didn't offer to help. She was stewing in her anger; she wanted to hit him, but it took a lot of energy to stay mad. The truth was, just being with him, in his presence, had a calming and comforting effect on her. She tried to stay focused on her anger, remind herself that he couldn't be trusted even if he'd just promised not to do this again.

She knew she had to be patient. He was married after all; she couldn't make his wife disappear just by willing her away. That was a fact. In the meantime, she thought, she needed to enjoy her time with him. She loved him, his attention and enthusiasm, his love of life and energy.

Ariella shook her head as if to make room for other thoughts.

"I'd like to take you to Europe," Arik continued. His eyes sparkled when he turned to look at her. "I have to go to Italy, to Roma and Napoli for five days. Will you come with me? I promise I'll make it up to you." He was pleading now.

Italy, Napoli. Her rapid pulse told her that she hadn't forgotten Giovanni, the Italian sailor.

"I'll have to ask Goldberg," was the first thing that came out of her mouth. "He wants to take in a partner and another clerk...his office is expanding. I also have to tell my father."

"Your father? Tell him what?" Arik's voice was almost a whisper.

She looked out at the sea, noticing he was driving to Old Jaffa on the familiar route. "That I'm going to Italy with the same man-friend who let me and my brother down." Again, her anger surfaced. "He was very concerned last week that my plans to go to Tivon were cancelled at the last minute." She knew she was taking a chance of him dropping her, but she decided to be bold. She *had* to let him know how she felt.

Arik was unusually quiet now and looked sternly ahead.

Ariella's chest tightened. She knew that mentioning Abba always made him nervous. So, she tried another angle. "I need you to meet Eitan and Rachel real soon. I think we owe them a face-to-face apology. It was an awful disappointment for them, too."

"Yes, I'm really sorry. I'll make it up to them, too, I promise."

* * *

Ariella sat on the couch in Benny's apartment in Old Jaffa,

while Arik made coffee and sandwiches. She was tired from the emotional turbulence she was experiencing. Her stomach growled. The cheese-and-tomato sandwich was delicious, as was the Turkish coffee.

Arik put on a record with her favorite song by Louis Armstrong, and the music of "The Kiss of Fire" filled the room. She felt more like crying than making out; her body refused to react to the music like she usually did. Arik tried The Platters, and the lyrics of "The Great Pretender" spilled from the big, black vinyl record and into her heart. She shuddered.

For the first time since she'd met Arik, she didn't want to make love to him. Her hurt was larger than her love.

"Can you please take me home?" she almost whispered. She didn't want to fight, but it was too hard to forgive. Right now, she was exhausted.

Arik stood by the window and looked at her. He shook his head. Without saying a word, he took his keys from the top of the kitchen counter, opened the front door, and waited for her to come through, looking at her with a sad expression. They drove in silence for a while.

"I'm not sure how to convince you, Ella, but I feel bad about what I've done to you and your brother. I need you to believe me; it was an emergency. I couldn't help it. I was torn. Please forgive me, my love. I'll do everything from now on to prove to you how much I love you."

"I need time," she said as she got out of the car. "Good night, Arik."

Chapter Twenty-Nine

WHEN Ariella got into bed, thoughts of Naples and Italy flooded her head. She remembered every detail of what had happened four years ago, but that night, when Yael was asleep, she still had to take out her diary and read, again, about Giovanni, the Italian sailor.

December 1954 – Tel Aviv
Dear Diary,

We're back in Israel now, and I haven't written in a long time, so here is what happened on our way back.

Again, we were on a half-cargo, half-passenger ship. I was bored to death.

Every night we watched a movie, and every time the celluloid tore, I turned around to see if the electrician was fixing it. The first time, I saw a pair of tanned, strong, muscular arms, and then I dreamed about them at night, craving that they would hug me.

One evening after the movie, I got up and walked to find out who those arms belonged to and saw a gorgeous Italian man, about thirty years old, with pitch black hair falling over one eye. He had dark blue eyes, a strong jaw, and muscular, tanned shoulders. He was wearing white shorts and a white tank top; the projection room must have been hot.

I kept going up to him almost every night. Couldn't help myself; like a magnet. One night after the movie, he asked me in Italian if I wanted to go up to the top deck. I understood, thanks to my Spanish, and because he pointed up. So I said *si*, yes.

As we walked up the stairs to the open deck, our hands touched. Soon his fingers interlaced with mine. His hands were rough, but I didn't mind. They felt manly and foreign, and exciting. Even the scent of his sweat was appealing. We sat on a metal bench and first he patted my arms, then he started kissing my shoulder and I let him feel my breasts.

Oh my God! I never let any boyfriend in Argentina do this.

"*Bella, bellissima,*" he kept whispering into my ear, and the hair on my neck would stand up. He spoke Italian, and I spoke Spanish, so we got along quite well, but mostly, our hands spoke.

When we got to Napoli, he wanted to show me around the city, but my father wouldn't let me go. He said I might never come back and under no circumstances would I be allowed off the ship. I was shocked. I knew the ship was going to continue to Haifa in Israel, but the crew was changing, and I would never see Giovanni again. We were going to dock in Napoli in the morning for only one day. One day in Napoli! I cried the whole night. My father sat next to me and tried to explain why I couldn't get off and go with Giovanni, but I didn't want to listen. "You're only sixteen, Ariella," my father said as he got hold of my arm, maybe to shake me, and my sleeve got caught in his watch. I didn't realize it until I pulled my arm away, and my sleeve tore. I yelled at him, "See, you tore my pajamas."

I cried and cried until I fell asleep. I hated Abba then.

> The next morning, I saw Giovanni get off the ship. As he walked on the gangplank, I saw he held his suitcase in one hand, the other hand was on the railing, a cigarette dangled from the corner of his mouth, and his hair fell over one eye. He stopped, looked at me, and continued walking. He never came for me. Maybe because Abba was standing behind me, like a guard. He never claimed me; he just gave up. I could hardly sleep that night; I'm not sure if it was from disappointment or relief. I can't explain.

Ariella turned her lights off, put the journal on her chest, and closed her eyes. Giovanni. Beautiful Giovanni the sailor. She loved handsome men by her side. She loved being part of a good-looking couple.

Arik and me in Italy, she smiled in the dark, feeling better. We'll cause heads to turn. Just as she felt sleep engulf her, she forced herself to get up and hide the journal back in its box.

"Abba, where is my passport?" Ariella asked him the following evening. They sat in the kitchen, eating a slice of the warm chocolate babka he'd brought home from the bakery, and drinking a glass of cold milk. Her appetite had returned, and this comfort food was always there. It was one thing she could trust completely.

"Why? Where are you going now?" he asked, letting go of the paper he was reading and taking his glasses off.

"I'm going to Italy with a friend, to Roma and Napoli. I

haven't been there, really been there. I need to look at my passport; I may need to renew it."

"When are you going?" He sounded worried. "And is this the same 'friend'? What's his name? Arik? Are you sure you're going this time?"

"How do you know his name?" Ariella felt alarmed.

"You mentioned his name to Eitan and Rachel. When can I meet him?"

To her surprise, Abba fired questions at her. He didn't usually do this; he sounded anxious now. Why was he asking? She was twenty, for goodness sake! Was it because he had disturbing memories of Naples and Giovanni? Or because Aunt Pearl was coming soon, and he was becoming nervous?

"You'll meet him soon, Abba, I promise. I don't think he is ready to meet you yet." She was caught by surprise and had to think fast. "You know how it is with...with some men." Her throat felt dry. She was getting quite nervous now.

"I don't know, Ella." Abba placed his glasses on the table and rubbed his eyes with the palms of his hands. "All I know about him is bad stuff." He lifted his head to look at her.

"What do you mean, bad stuff?" She began to sweat.

"I know that he is shy and doesn't want to meet me." Abba put his thumb up. "I know that you disappear every Tuesday night and meet with him and sleep out..." His index finger came up, like he was counting. "I know that he was supposed to take you and your brother and Rachel on a short vacation and canceled at the last minute." His middle finger followed, "and all of this is adding up to a very negative impression." He put his hand down and looked her in the eye.

"But Abba, Yom-Tov knows him," she said, the idea suddenly coming to her. She hoped it could satisfy him. Lucky, she didn't say they were friends.

"Oh, a boy soldier." Abba seemed pacified, but only for a moment. "How can he afford it? He's paying for both of you? You have no money to go to Europe!"

"He was an officer, Abba, but he is not in the army anymore. He...he is in business now and can afford it...yes, he is paying for me, too."

"Napoli, not a safe place. He better take good care of you there."

Ariella knew that her father was concerned for her safety but didn't know what to say.

"He better come to see me when you both get back. This is it. No more avoidance." Abba sounded angry. "Do you hear?"

She knew that she had to confront Arik.

Chapter Thirty

ARIELLA stood alone in the airport's departure hall, her hands sweating. *Airplane*! She was getting on a plane for the first time! How could she be sure it would stay up? What if it fell out of the sky into the Mediterranean Sea? Ships were so much safer; she'd been on several. She wasn't sure she liked the idea of flying. Where was Arik?

It was mid-June and very warm. Large fans stood in different corners of the stuffy hall where she handed in her renewed passport before going to sit and wait for Arik.

He had asked her to take a taxi to the airport and said he'd be somewhere in the departure hall, but she was not to come toward him once she saw him; there might be somebody there who knew him. The ground crew did, he'd said.

Ariella sat and looked at the beautifully dressed Alitalia air-hostesses. With their dark green knee-length pencil skirts, their white short-sleeved shirts, their little dark green round hats with the Alitalia emblem, their small dark green scarves tied around their necks, and their tans, they looked gorgeous. Whom did Arik know? Probably all of them.

She felt a pang of jealousy and looked around to see if he was coming. What if he'd decided he had another emergency? Oy, no! He wouldn't do that again, would he? She heard flights being announced and listened for her name. Would they call her if he had phoned and said he wasn't coming?

And if she did see him, he had warned her, she couldn't talk to him until they were seated on the plane. They'd be sitting next to each other and pretending they'd just met.

Ariella felt awkward sitting all by herself in a big hall with strangers, looking for a man she couldn't even talk to. She opened and closed the magazine she had bought especially for the trip and kept raising her head to scan the faces. She didn't see him anywhere. She tried to read but couldn't concentrate.

A strange thought crossed her mind: what if she were on her way to America now, all by herself? She decided she needed to act more confident, resilient, sure of herself. So she sat up straight and pulled her shoulders back. Ima, she said to herself, I'm getting on an airplane.

She thought of Aunt Pearl, who had flown by herself a few days ago. All the way from South Africa to Israel, via Tehran. She admired her aunt's courage and resilience. Ariella remembered how she had stood with her father and sister in Lod Airport, watching Aunt Pearl deboard her plane and walk down the stairs to the tarmac—

Just then Ariella's flight was called.

She picked up the gray vanity case and the black purse she had borrowed from her aunt and strode erect to the stairs of the Alitalia plane, which was waiting on the tarmac. She still didn't see Arik. Where was he? Ariella started to perspire as she walked in line up the stairs to her seat on the plane.

A smiling air-hostess showed her to a middle seat, next to a very thin, blonde woman with rosy cheeks. British? Ariella sat down, a vacant aisle seat to her right.

As people walked down the plane aisle, Ariella became more agitated and could feel the heat in her cheeks. Where was Arik? The British woman looked out the window, not making eye contact with Ariella, which made her uncomfortable. She felt so alone and still couldn't see Arik. It seemed like everybody was seated and the little overhead cabins were all being locked. Ariella saw some people fasten their seat belts, but she held hers in both her hands, ready to jump off the plane at a second's notice. If she didn't see Arik, she'd run out.

And then she saw him. He stood by the open door of the cockpit, coming out laughing, a cigarette in his hand.

"I'll take you to your seat now, Mr. Emmanuel." The air-hostess smiled shyly as she said it, walking in front of Arik and pointing to the seat right next to Ariella.

"Hello," Arik said to Ariella, smiling, as he took his seat. "*Grazie, bella,*" he said to the pretty air-hostess who rushed to show everybody how to fasten their seat belts.

Arik fastened his, and squeezed Ariella's fingers, which were resting on the armrest between them. The British lady kept looking outside her window, thank goodness.

Chapter Thirty-One

IN the spacious, high-ceiling room in the hotel in Roma, Arik caressed Ariella's naked body with large, soft, demanding hands. Her skin was always hot, his hands cool, but they grew warmer.

When they became one in their passion, their rhythm, and in their final gasp, crying out together, Arik hugged her tightly and whispered, "You're mine, you're mine, only mine."

Ariella smiled; she never thought of Arik as a jealous and possessive man before, and it pleased her.

When they awoke from their afternoon nap, they looked

for a nice place to have coffee and relax. They walked hand in hand on the sidewalk to the square and passed a row of colorful Vespas parked side by side as if for display. There must have been about twenty scooters there.

The small streets around the piazza buttled with people walking, talking, laughing. A sailor in white uniform leaned on the wall of a building kissing a girl in a black and white striped dress. Arik squeezed Ariella's fingers. She laughed and pecked him on the cheek.

They were fortunate to find a vacant table along the sidewalk, in the shade under a green and red umbrella, at a café near the *Fontana di Trevi.* Arik ordered two espressos. Ariella added a bit of cream and a cube of sugar to hers. She wasn't sure what she was supposed to do with the twist of lemon rind she had found on the little saucer. Lemon in coffee? Not just in tea?

She *loved* Rome. Men turned their heads to look at her, and some even whistled in appreciation, but when she smiled back, Arik's eyes narrowed, and a crease appeared in between his eyebrows. The Italian men were extremely good-looking; she got an eyeful of them.

It was perfect being away from home, being out on the street with Arik, and she couldn't stop smiling, as though she had no worries in the world. They could sit in a street café in public, without Arik being anxious he might run into an acquaintance. Ariella felt euphoric, attractive, and desirable. She forgot the time of day, didn't think of her father or her sister. Blank. She felt blessed.

Sipping her coffee and staring at her lover over the rim of

her tiny cup, Ariella sighed. "I wish we were on our honeymoon now. It's so perfect here. I wish you were free and this was real life, not a fantasy."

"But this *is* real, *ahuvati,* my beloved. You are here and I'm here. We're sitting together in this beautiful piazza. What else do we need?" He took her hand in his and gazed into her eyes.

Ariella smiled at him lovingly and patted his cheek with her other hand, the one with the ruby ring he had given her last night. He took both her hands in his and kissed them. She didn't want to start a row and decided the moment was too precious to spoil.

* * *

Arik hired a tour guide by the name of Umberto, who spent half of the next day with them. Short and chubby, the elderly man had lived in Britain as a child, and spoke perfect English, although some Italian words crept into it. Ariella found it charming. She knew that Arik wouldn't have hired a young man, just in case he took a fancy to her. Arik's jealousy was new and surprising; he suddenly wanted her all to himself, as if he was scared to lose her. She had never felt it in Israel; they were seldom in public.

Umberto took them to visit the gigantic Colosseum and the Arch of Titus on the *Forum Romanum.* Seeing the embossed *menorah* carried by the Romans from the Second Temple in Jerusalem sent shivers down Ariella's spine. Like an ancient fear.

By two o'clock they said goodbye to Umberto.

The almost-four-hour drive from Roma to Napoli that afternoon, in the little two-door yellow Fiat convertible Arik had rented, was a dream. Arik had a thing for yellow cars; she laughed. She felt so happy. Her hair was blowing, and she put a pink scarf on top of her head and tied it back on her neck, below her hair.

The view of the whitewashed houses on the mountainside, traveling all the way down to the blue bay of Napoli, took her breath away. Sown in between beige buildings were white and yellow houses with red roofs, which looked like toy homes. She couldn't believe the red colors of the bougainvillea, the blue skies with a few little white clouds, the blue Mediterranean Sea with its foaming surf, and in between, mature olive trees, green bushes, and glorious flowers in a multitude of species. It was an image to savor. The air was full of the scent of roses mixed with the gas from the cars and vespas that passed them. She wished they could stay parked by the side of the winding road looking down at the bay forever.

Italy was the most romantic place in the world, Ariella concluded with some sadness, as the trip came closer to the end. She wasn't going to tell Arik that Abba wanted to meet him. She'd find an excuse; she was scared that Abba would put a stop to her romance.

On the flight back home, Ariella worried that Aunt Pearl was going to question her about this trip. Her aunt arrived a day before Ima's tombstone unveiling, and there was no room for talk of anything else. It had been such a sad day. The devastating memorial service they had held for Ima at the cemetery had taken her back to where she hadn't wanted to go; deep inside her soul, where Ima had been missing for a year. Unveiling the white marble with the black inscription had been a stabbing moment. It read:

Ophelia Paz nee Silverstein
Beloved Wife, Mother, and Sister
Left this world much too soon
We will always love you
1910 – 1958

When the plane landed back in Tel Aviv, Arik squeezed Ariella's fingers again on the armrest. "Tuesday, *amore mio*," my love, he mouthed.

He put Ariella in a taxi to go home, paid the driver ahead of time, and looked around, no doubt to make sure he didn't know anybody. Arik leaned in for a quick peck goodbye before shutting her door and hailing another taxi for himself.

Chapter Thirty-Two

ARIELLA was extremely surprised to find Abba sitting in the living room with Uncle Rafael and Aunt Pearl when she returned home late that Saturday night.

She set the black purse and gray vanity case down and, somewhat embarrassed, stared at the three adults and her sister, who stopped talking abruptly as she walked in. She also noticed that Yael just let go of Aunt Pearl's hand and looked innocently at the ceiling.

"*Shalom*," she said as she stood by the door. "Where is Dalia?" Ariella couldn't seem to think of anything better to say, trying to overcome the feeling of dread as they all quietly stared at her. What was going on?

"Come sit down, Ella," Uncle Rafael said. "Dalia is at home with the girls. Come, come, we have some news, good news, I think."

Ariella exhaled.

"Welcome back, Ariella," Abba said just as she sat down beside him. "How was Italy?" He seemed to look at her strangely.

"It was phenomenal!" she said, ignoring her father's look. "But what's going on here?"

"I was offered to work in Zurich, Switzerland," her uncle began. "The bank is sending me for one year for professional development. I'll be working with other banks there before we open our own branch back here. That means that Dalia and the girls are coming with me, of course, and our apartment will be standing empty. I've just asked Pearl to move in and take care of our home. She'll be free to look for a job and won't be bothered with rent. Sounds good, no?"

Ariella was stunned; it had come out of nowhere. She looked from one to the other, her brain like a train station, running in different directions. Uncle Rafael and Dalia were leaving? For Switzerland? For a whole year? Aunt Pearl would be staying in their apartment? She'd only been here one week. They'd prepared a room especially for her. Well, one couldn't compare the little enclosed balcony, which looked like a small sunroom, to a whole apartment: two bedrooms and a living room, a kitchen and a bathroom *all to herself.*

"Thank you for preparing such a cozy nest for me, Ariella. I didn't even have a chance to thank you properly before you flew away." Aunt Pearl blew her a kiss. But was there a hint of sarcasm in her tone?

"You're welcome, Auntie. *Regah*, wait a minute, this is a lot to absorb." Still, it felt like Ariella was thinking aloud. "You're going to Europe." She pointed at Uncle Rafael, "and *you've* just returned from Africa." She looked from her uncle to her aunt. "What an international family," she said. "Eitan is planning to get married next year June, so he'll be leaving, too..." Ariella didn't know why she felt left out and couldn't rejoice in their excitement. Everything she wanted was happening to everybody else. Was the universe telling her it was time to move on, too? Should she confront Arik and tell him he had to decide?

They all stared at her as she talked, her temples throbbing, her tongue dry and moving slowly. "When are you leaving, Uncle Rafi?" Ariella retreated to the name she had called him as a toddler, when "Rafael" was too hard to say. She missed him already.

"At the end of this month. We have two weeks to get organized and have to be in Zurich on the first of July."

Eitan walked in. They all smiled at him, and he looked surprised. Now they had to repeat it all for him.

As they finished telling him, he turned to his uncle and said. "I'll miss you, Rafael." Eitan never called him Uncle Rafael; being only four years younger than his uncle, he never had, and their parents didn't insist, like they did with the girls. "Are you planning to return in a year?"

"Yes, my contract is until the end of next June, but I can

return earlier if I need to. When is your wedding planned for?"

"We were thinking of June thirtieth. I graduate on May twentieth."

"Oy, I'm sorry I won't be here for your graduation, but I'll make sure we'll make it for your wedding. Congratulations, such milestones in your life—graduation and marriage!" Uncle Rafael smiled as he got up. "All right, my little sister, enjoy your enclave for another two and a half weeks. I love you all, but I must leave now."

As he stood by the door, he looked at the coffee table and said, "I almost forgot, *hevre.*" Guys. He returned and picked up a parcel wrapped in brown paper that lay on the table. "I brought you a gift you can all share. It's a new book. It has just been translated into Hebrew. It's called *Exodus* and was written by Leon Uris. I read it in English, really excellent." And he left.

He read it in English! I need to be fluent in English, too, Ariella thought when she got into bed that night. She started reading the Hebrew translation of the new book, but changed her mind and placed it on the nightstand. She'd let Eitan read it first, or Abba. She wanted to read it in English, too, and was going to ask Uncle Rafael to lend her his book before he left for Switzerland.

Chapter Thirty-Three

IT wasn't simple to find a cab late on the October eve of *Sukkot*, but eventually, after searching in quiet Tel Aviv for a while, Ariella managed to find a lone taxi which took her to Benny's apartment in Old Jaffa. According to Arik, she'd have to wait for him for about an hour before he joined her. Ariella wasn't happy to go back to the apartment, but where else could she meet him?

Ariella had just had the evening meal in the *sukkah*, the traditional holiday hut, with her extended family on the large flat roof of Uncle Gabriel's big house.

Earlier that week, Arik had turned to her in bed and said,

"Let's take Eitan and Rachel to Nahariya with us next weekend, what do you think?" They could all meet up the morning after *Sukkoth* in front of Rachel's apartment building and go together to Nahariya in the north, almost by the border with Lebanon.

Ariella's eyes had sparkled, and she hugged him tightly. She'd waited patiently for months to hear those words. After the last disappointment, she wasn't going to bring the subject up again. It made her so happy that a tide of love rose in her heart.

But as the minutes ticked by, her joy unraveled. The wait was agonizing. She sat curled up on the sofa in Benny's apartment, legs folded underneath her, a glass of grapefruit juice in her hand, and her thoughts racing. What was Arik doing at that moment? Was he kissing his sick wife goodbye before he left the house? What was he telling her, where did he say he was going?

He must have lied. Did the wife cook the holiday dinner? And if she didn't, then who did?

Ariella knew that she was torturing herself with all her questions, so she closed her eyes and almost fell asleep by the time Arik walked in.

"*Shalom, motek.*" Arik bent down to kiss her. "I missed you. Have you been waiting long? Oh, my God, it's so late. Sorry I couldn't get here earlier. I had to pick a fight with my wife so I could have an excuse to storm out of the house with a suitcase. It's in the car. Where is yours?" He looked around the room.

"Hi," Ariella said sleepily. "Eitan took it to Rachel's." She yawned, talking as if in her sleep and not sure she understood everything he was saying.

Arik hugged and supported her as they made their way to bed. Ariella felt she was drifting off again as Arik undressed her and snuggled close to her body.

When they arrived at Rachel's the following morning, Arik got out of the car and shook hands with Eitan, patting him on the shoulder like he wanted to hug him. Ariella got out, too, and stood watching. She held her breath when Arik took Rachel's hand in both his hands, and with a warm smile, told them both how pleased he was to meet them at long last. Ariella smiled broadly; she'd been waiting so long for them to meet. She offered Eitan her seat next to Arik and went to sit by Rachel in the back.

"I need to apologize for last time," Arik said as he drove. "I'm really sorry. I travel for business so often, and so far, I really don't have much time to have fun with friends. I hope you both forgive me." Ariella noticed that he looked through the rearview mirror to catch Rachel's eye. "I'll try to make it up to you all." He smiled his most charming smile.

"Oh, no problem," Eitan was quick to respond. "What business are you in?"

Ariella knew that Eitan was trying to make conversation; she had already told him what Arik was doing. She smiled; Eitan, the quiet guy, seemed really interested in Arik.

And so the conversation began; Arik talked about his business, and Eitan about his studies. The girls sat in the back, listening. Ariella saw Arik's smiling eyes through the rearview mirror.

They arrived at a four-story, sparkling white building on the beach of Nahariya. The *Pension*, a guesthouse, included prepaid three meals a day. They hurried to change their clothes and met again by the crowded, shining pool. The girls tucked their hair into swim caps and they all jumped in, splashing other guests. The pool was so packed that nobody could swim, so they decided to get out and head for the beach. It was a perfect October day.

Leaving their sandals by their towels, they walked on the warm sand, talking and smoking.

Ariella could see that Eitan was charmed by Arik. The two men walked shoulder to shoulder, their feet deep in the soft, golden sand; their heads tilted toward each other, Arik's taller than Eitan's.

For almost two hours, Eitan listened to Arik talk about the galleries in Europe's largest cities, about the ploughs he bought for the *kibbutzim*, about the Israeli oranges competing with the Spanish ones, and on and on. Ariella and Rachel either walked beside them, listening, or ran holding hands at the edge of the water splashing each other.

When they got back to the hotel and decided to rinse off before lunch, Rachel said she'd rather go to her room to shower; she wasn't fond of public showers, she said. She'd had enough of those on the kibbutz.

Ariella felt Rachel's reluctance to be alone with her. So she also went to her room to shower and change. They both happened to walk into the dining room at the same time to meet the guys for lunch, the main meal of the day.

"Rachel, what's going on? I feel like you're trying to avoid me," Ariella complained.

"Eh, why? I spent the whole morning by your side." Rachel picked up speed as she walked.

"I don't know, just a feeling. So? What do you *think*?"

"About *what?*" Rachel neared the dining room door.

"Rachel! About Arik." Ariella flicked her hair behind her shoulder, knowing Rachel well enough to sense that she was stalling.

"Oh," Rachel said and pulled opened the door, "here, here are the men." She rushed to Eitan's side.

Ariella hesitated. Rachel didn't like him! She might even hate him; she didn't say one nice word about him. Rachel, *her* Rachel, didn't like Arik! What was she going to do?

Arik waved to her from a large table, and she had to move. They sat at a table of twelve, and everybody talked with everybody. Some couples sat alone at other tables, but their table was lively with conversation and laughter.

Ariella didn't talk much; she was hurt by her best friend's rejection. She observed Arik giving business advice to some young men who sat across the table from him, completely oblivious of Rachel's indifference—almost hostility—toward him. Rachel talked to the girl next to her, and Eitan kept quiet as usual.

After the heavy lunch, they all went to rest and met again for coffee at five o'clock.

"Can we take our coffee to the pool?" Ariella asked.

"*Betach,*" Sure. Arik said, agreeing. "Would you like ice cream in your iced coffee?" he asked.

"But of course," Ariella laughed, "what is iced coffee if not cold coffee and ice cream?" She took Rachel by the hand and pulled her to the pool, ignoring Rachel's attitude. Eitan waited by Arik to help carry the four tall glasses the waiter was preparing.

"Rachel, you can't keep avoiding me. What's the matter? Don't you like him?" Ariella was direct. Rachel's reply was important, and she had to hear it spelled out. They both set at the pool's edge, dangling their feet in the water.

"Well," Rachel sighed. "I don't know, Ella. I really don't know what to say. He's a *shvitzer*...he boasts a lot. About his business, about helping what's his name, the painter?"

"Benny," Ariella said.

"Yes, Benny Sarkowski...like he is some kind of savior, the Messiah. Benny is so dependent on him, I feel sorry for him. Arik has an air of arrogance, and the worst is..." Rachel looked Ariella in the eye. "He's a cheater."

Ariella gasped, and her hand flew to cover her mouth. She jumped up, just as Arik and Eitan arrived with the coffees, the ice cream dripping on their hands, and placed their glasses on a side table.

"Let's jump right in, what do you say, Eitan?" And without waiting for a reply, Arik dove into the water, gliding like a dolphin in the small hotel pool which was almost empty now; most of the guests rested in their rooms after the heavy main meal.

By seven o'clock Ariella's tummy was rumbling again. The sun was about to set, and her body was hot from absorbing as much sun as it could. "I'm going in to shower and change. Should we grab something to eat in the dining room?"

"Let's go," Arik said. He extended his hand to help Rachel get up. Rachel hesitated for a second and then stretched her arm toward Eitan, who stood by Arik. Arik raised his eyebrows and dropped his hand.

"Come, let's go," Ariella grabbed Arik's hand and pulled him to their room. She hoped he wasn't hurt by Rachel's behavior.

Arik didn't say anything and got straight into the shower. Ariella peeled off her wet bathing suit and joined him.

Pacified and smiling, they joined everybody in the dining hall for light salads and cheeses, hummus and olives. The pita bread was still warm and fragrant.

"Let's dance." Ariella's hunger dissipated as the live band began playing. She wanted to enjoy every moment; there was enough heartache in her daily life—Yael's sporadic headaches, Abba waiting to be introduced to Arik, and now Rachel? She missed a step, and Arik stepped on her foot by mistake. She cried out, and he apologized, leading her to a chair.

"I'm just tired," she said and leaned her head on his

shoulder.

"No problem." Arik kissed the top of her head. "Let's sit this one out."

Ariella sighed. He was sweet and understanding and very apologetic. She adored him.

The following two days flew by as they spent their time on the beach or by the pool. Ariella stuck by Arik, and Rachel by Eitan. The girls didn't talk much to each other, only exchanging pleasantries in front of the guys. Ariella noticed that Rachel talked to Eitan in a lowered voice and wondered what she was saying. Was she poisoning him against Arik?

"Thank you for a wonderful weekend, Arik," Eitan said on the drive back to Tel Aviv on Saturday night. The air in the car lay thick with tension, and Ariella tried to doze off as to escape the heavy feeling.

"My pleasure, Eitan. I'm glad we had the chance to meet and spend some time together." Arik was as polite as could be. A champion, Ariella thought.

It went quiet again.

"Yes," Eitan tried again, awkwardly. "It was very interesting to hear about your business."

"Toda," thanks, was all that Arik said.

He dropped Rachel off first. She muttered "thank you" and "*shalom,*" quietly, not making eye contact with Ariella, nor Arik. They waited for Eitan to see her to the entrance of her building and return to the car, and then Arik took Ariella and Eitan home.

When Arik got out of the car to say goodbye, Eitan hugged him and thanked him again.

Arik kissed Ariella lightly on the cheek, winked at her, and left.

"He's really a nice guy." Eitan turned to Ariella as soon as they entered the apartment. "I like him a lot. He's interesting, polite, generous. But Rachel is dubious. She claims that a cheater is a cheater, and she's scared that if Arik is cheating on his wife, he might cheat on you too one day." That was a long speech for Eitan. But he wasn't done. "To be honest, I doubt it. Arik told me that life at home was very difficult for their son, Boaz, and no wonder he preferred to live in London. I appreciate his honesty and can't understand Rachel's reservations."

Ariella was elated. It gave her the feeling that what she was doing was right, justified, and she was hopeful. They'd all prove Rachel wrong.

* * *

"Are you free today at one thirty?" Ariella was astounded to get a call from Rachel the next morning.

"Yes. Hot dog machine?" Ariella was short; Goldberg was listening.

"*Le'hitraot,*" See you later, Rachel said and put the phone down.

The girls met by the American hot dog machine just across from Rachel's work.

"I'm really not sure how to word this, Ella," Rachel said once Ariella was seated on the round metal chair, a hot dog in one hand and a mixed-flavored *gazoz* in the other. Rachel preferred the lemon-raspberry syrup in her soda water. "But I don't have a good feeling about this."

"About Arik?" Ariella asked, knowing precisely what Rachel meant.

"Yes. About Arik and you." Rachel sounded unusually impatient.

"Why, Rachel? Why don't you like him? Eitan loves him, and—"

"Yes," Rachel said. "I know that Eitan has fallen under his spell, like you have, but I see another side to Arik, a dark side, and I think I should warn you, as a friend, as your future sister-in-law, as someone—"

"Warn me?!" Ariella almost spat out a piece of her hot dog. She swallowed. "Rachel, I can't believe what I'm hearing. You've just met him, and you're judging him already. Not everybody is as lucky as you are, to find a wonderful young guy like Eitan. But Arik is a successful business man. He travels the world and is well respected wherever he goes. He is kind, considerate, and generous. I think I'm lucky that he treats me like a princess." She panted on the cusp of running out of breath. "What else could I wish for?" Ariella stood up, her unfinished hot dog on the table and her drink still full.

"That he wasn't married?" Rachel suggested quietly.

Ariella sat down, as if a lightning bolt had just hit her. She'd felt so good the night before after talking with Eitan. She had tried to forget Rachel's attitude, and now this? Sweet Rachel, who loved everybody, had a bad feeling about Arik? Ariella felt a lump in her throat. She wanted to scream but knew that she wouldn't dare. Not in public.

Chapter Thirty-Four

"ARIELLA, can you come in for a moment?" Goldberg asked her one Thursday evening in mid-December. She held in a sigh and glanced at her watch; it was forty minutes before her English class at Berlitz—she had ten minutes to spare. Her teacher didn't like the students to be late.

She rushed into his office wondering what was coming next and wasn't at all prepared for what he had to say.

"You remember that my new partner, Yossi Lupo, is joining us on January first, yes?" Goldberg looked at his calendar. "January first. Can you believe it's almost 1960? Where did the time fly?" He scratched his head and continued. "His office assistant, Shoshana—or Shosh for short—will set up their offices. I'm so glad the space next door was standing empty for these last few months. I was able to negotiate a good price for its rental." Goldberg seemed pleased with himself. Ariella nodded and gave her watch another quick look.

"The thing is that you and Shosh will need a third person, a typist who can help you both with the correspondence and the phone. So I need you to place an ad in the paper and interview applicants for this position, please." He looked at her fondly now and cleared his throat before he continued formally. "You're now the office manager, Ariella." Goldberg paused, and Ariella felt her eyebrows rise involuntarily. Was he offering her a promotion? "As you've proven yourself so capable these past eighteen months, you'll oversee everything that happens here." He sounded like a radio announcer. "Both Shosh and the new typist will be under your supervision. *Mazal tov* on your promotion, Ariella!" He smiled broadly and got up, leaning over his desk and reaching out his hand to her.

Ariella shook his hand and mumbled a surprised "thank you." She stood still for a moment to absorb the news, nodded to him, and smiled nervously as she walked out.

Then she stopped and returned.

"Thank you, Mr. Goldberg," she said cheerfully. "I'm really happy, and I appreciate it very much. You just caught me by surprise. I don't know what to say. Thank you." She didn't ask about a raise but hoped that it would follow.

On her way to Berlitz, she felt like she was walking on air. Promotion. And not because she had served long enough, like in the army when she became a sergeant, but because she'd proven herself! Her thoughts raced as she hurried, her head buzzing, and with every step she took the realization set in slowly.

A promotion. She never saw it coming; she had thought that Goldberg and his new junior accountant would work in parallel, as would she and Shoshana. She never expected a hierarchy to be formed, and *she* had to interview and choose an *employee*! Ariella found she was almost skipping now; it was hard to restrain herself.

The next day, Friday, Ariella asked Goldberg if she could leave at twelve thirty, half an hour early, to go to the bank. She promised him she'd make it up on Sunday.

"I'd like to open a savings account," she told the clerk, "locked-in for six months for a higher rate. When I deposit my paycheck, I'd like half of it to go into my checking account and half into my savings. Can I do that?"

She had to sign some papers and completed setting everything up just in time for closing. It was almost one o'clock.

* * *

The following week as English class ended, and Ariella collected her books, she noticed a commotion by the blackboard.

"Listen up, everybody." One of Ariella's classmates, a young man in army uniform, stood by the door with his hand raised, prepared for an announcement. "I write notice—is this correct, teacher?" He turned to their English teacher who corrected him, "I wrote a notice...please carry on." He started over. "I wrote a notice on the board. Please all copy my address. You all invited to party in my house on thirty one December. Yes? You all come." He looked at the teacher proudly. She smiled.

The students cheered, and Ariella wrote down the address, not knowing what she was going to be doing next week on New Year's Eve. Arik was going to be in Zurich the whole week working, and Eitan was taking Rachel to his office party.

"You'll come, right?" The young soldier surprised Ariella.

"Yes. Thank you, I think I will."

"My name is Oded. A pleasure to meet you," he extended his hand to shake hers.

"I'm Ariella. Very pleased to make your acquaintance."

Sitting on the bus on her way to Oded's place, all dressed up and with a new lipstick, Ariella wondered if she was the only one Oded had approached when he announced the invitation. She had noticed that he was always standing by her when she was asking the English teacher something she hadn't understood in class. She didn't pay much attention to him before, but he seemed polite and reserved, maybe even shy. She brushed it off.

When she rang the doorbell, Oded opened the door and a wave of music poured into the street. Laughter and shouting followed. He took her hand and said something she couldn't hear. He yanked her purse and threw it on the couch, closed the door behind her, and pulled her to the middle of the living room, which served as a dance floor. Elvis Presley's "Blue Suede Shoes" was blaring, and everybody was doing the Rock 'n Roll. Once the song "Love Me Tender" began, Oded held Ariella close.

After dancing several slow songs with Oded, other guys invited Ariella to dance, but Oded stayed close. She wasn't sure how she felt about that.

When she got tired, she went to the kitchen for some juice and there she saw Oded kissing a girl. She slowly retraced her steps and returned to the living room, hoping he didn't see her.

What did you expect? She thought. Did you really think—

"—5,4,3,2,1 – Happy New Year!" Everyone shouted.

Ariella found herself standing by her English teacher and her husband, who both hugged her and wished her Happy New Year.

Without saying goodbye to anybody, Ariella walked out. She was twenty years old, and her boyfriend was away. Wasn't his place right by her side? Where was he right now? Was he celebrating in Zurich? Didn't she deserve to have a man by her side, if she so desired? A man, no matter what age, who *loved* her and *wanted* to be with her?

The buses had stopped running that late at night, and Ariella felt the wind on her face as she walked. A taxi-sharing service, *Sherut*, which ran the same route as the bus, waited at the next bus stop, not far from Oded's home. It was almost full, and Ariella was fortunate enough to have the last seat.

She got home just before one in the morning. Tomorrow was a regular work day.

* * *

When Ariella got to work at eight o'clock, she saw two people she didn't recognize moving cardboard boxes from a van outside into the new offices. "Good morning, I'm Ariella," she called out.

A short and plump young Yemenite woman about Ariella's age, with a mop of black curls and huge brown, smiling eyes, placed a box on the floor and rushed to extend her hand to Ariella.

"*Shalom*, Ariella, I'm Shoshana. Please call me Shosh, everybody does." Her smile was huge and her teeth very white. She was wearing a wide floral dress in blues and greens.

"*Shalom*, Shosh, welcome to our company." Ariella stopped. A tall, thin, bald man appeared behind Shosh. This must be Lupo, Yossi Lupo, Ariella thought. She had to keep herself from laughing. Lupo was at least a head taller than Shosh. He was very pale while Shosh had chocolate-colored skin. He possessed blue bulging eyes under heavy dark eyebrows that looked like they'd stolen all the hair from his head. He must have been around thirty. What a comic pair they made!

"You must be Yossi Lupo." Ariella smiled broadly and extended her arm. "I'm Ariella, Mr. Goldberg's secr...assis...I'm the office manager," Ariella stammered, not being used to her new title. Lupo nodded in acknowledgement, but never tried to shake her hand, so she dropped her arm. He turned and went back to his office. Shosh shrugged and followed him.

It was Friday, a short work day, and Ariella had to interview three women who came in after answering her ad in the paper. She offered the job to one of them, a woman in her forties called Etty.

"I have my recommendations right here," Etty said in her raspy voice. She handed Ariella an envelope with a steady hand that sported two yellowing fingers, maybe from nicotine, Ariella guessed. Her shoulder length brown hair and clothes also smelled of cigarette smoke, but she had twenty-two years' experience as a typist, great recommendations, and green eyes that reminded Ariella of her siblings.

* * *

Tuesday felt like a holiday. At seven in the evening Arik picked Ariella up outside the office building. She noticed that Shosh and Etty stared at him through the open car window as they passed by it, mumbling their goodbyes before walking down the street to take their respective buses home.

Etty turned back for a second look, squinting her green eyes and biting her thin lower lip. Ariella wondered what she was thinking. Did she disapprove of Ariella climbing into a car with an older man? Did Etty suspect Arik wasn't Ariella's father? Ariella flicked her hair over her shoulder and took a deep breath, reminding herself that it shouldn't matter what Etty, or anyone else, thought. Still, she waited for the women to be far away before she turned to look at Arik.

"I missed you," she said simply, reaching to kiss him.

"I missed you more, but let's drive away," Arik said and peeled out.

Ariella was surprised to see a small black suitcase on the kitchen counter in the apartment in Old Jaffa. Arik picked it up with one hand, pulling Ariella's hand by the other toward the bedroom. He threw the case on the bed and grabbed Ariella by the waist, hugging her tightly.

"I...I can't breathe." Ariella gasped, not able to respond to him, as she kept seeing the black suitcase on the bed and was wondering if he was going away again.

Arik let go of her. "Happy New Year, my sweetness," Arik said and emptied the suitcase on the bed.

There was a small black dress made of pure wool with a small bolero to match, a pair of brown boots wrapped in tissue paper, a brown leather jacket, a pink silk scarf with lilac and purple leaves drawn faintly in one corner, and a pair of soft, pink leather gloves. She smiled and wondered, where on earth would she wear those? But it didn't matter.

Arik pulled her into a warm and gentle embrace. "You're the best thing that's ever happened to me in my whole life."

She hugged him back. That mattered. How he felt about her and how he treated her, mattered.

Chapter Thirty-Five

ON the last Friday of a cold February, Arik surprised Ariella with a phone call. They had a new switchboard in their small but growing firm, and when the phone rang and Etty put the call through to Ariella, she saw a small, red light flickering.

"I'm sorry to call you at work, Ella," he said and paused, making her pulse quicken. "I have some bad news." Ariella held her breath. "Yom-Tov died last night. He had a heart attack in his sleep."

Ariella gasped, realizing she wasn't breathing, and quickly put her hand on her mouth.

Arik sounded upset and angry; he was loud and agitated, almost scared. "This man fought in three wars and was as strong as an ox, God help me." He was lashing out although she wasn't sure at whom. "How could this happen?! To Yom-Tov, of all people! I don't know the details, but I'm heading to Jerusalem now. The funeral will be at around two thirty in the afternoon at Mount Herzl, and it's going to be dark by four thirty, when Shabbat comes in. Many officers and generals will be there and some government officials, I think. What a mess. Yom-Tov gone. Can you believe it?"

Ariella held the receiver, listening, unable to say a word, her heart sinking and her brain racing. She wanted to go to the funeral. Should she ask him to pick her up on his way? Would he? But there would be so many people who knew him there. Should she take the bus to Jerusalem? Oh no, it was Friday; how would she get back? She'd have to find a ride. Could he...

"Arik..." she wanted to ask him about a ride but hesitated a minute too long. Would he be taking his wife with him?

"I have to get into my car and go now. I just thought you should know, but you don't need to come. It will be crazy there, such a rush before Shabbat." Arik continued in a hurry, as if he could read her thoughts, "I didn't want you to find out on the evening news or in the papers on Sunday. Will you be okay?" She still couldn't talk. "I have to go. Bye, sweetie," he said, not waiting for her reply, and she heard the phone disconnect.

Ariella stayed seated, her hands shaking now. Yom-Tov was gone. Her beloved army-boss. *Make wise choices,* his words still haunted her. Hadn't Abba used the same words? Yom-Tov'd been a father figure to her, caring and gentle. Had he been trying to warn her? Like Rachel? She'd never asked him, and it was too late now. Like Ima. So young. A heart attack in his mid forties.

Ariella felt a sudden ache for Rachel. She wished they could talk; she needed someone's shoulder to cry on. She placed her elbows on her desk and pressed the base of her palms hard into her eyes. Don't cry here, not here.

It was almost one o'clock, the end of the working day, and Ariella was still sitting and pressing her hands into her eyes when she heard, "Are you okay?" The raspy voice was full of concern.

Ariella quickly put her elbows down and looked up into Etty's eyes as Shosh entered her office, too, to say goodbye.

"Ariella, your eyes are red. Were you crying?" Shosh came closer while Etty stood by the door, waiting.

"I'm sorry..." Ariella tried to find her voice. "I just got a phone call from my...from my army boss's friend." She looked down. "My former boss just died. Yom-Tov is dead." She said out loud, as if to convince herself. Her eyes filled with fresh tears as she looked up again.

"Major Yom-Tov is dead? You worked for Amos Yom-Tov?" Etty asked in surprise.

"Yes, why?" Ariella asked, surprised, too.

"I went to school with his wife Edna. Oh my God, Amos is dead? When? What happened? I'll have to go visit Edna. I haven't seen her in such a long time—" It seemed like Etty was thinking out loud. Ariella and Shosh watched her in amazement; Etty wasn't usually a talker. "We were three inseparable friends in high school, Edna, Sara, and me." Etty bit her lower lip. "Sara was older. I think she landed up in medical school, and Edna...? Oh, I don't remember." She shook her head. "But I went to their weddings. That was many years ago," she said, her voice tired and far away. "Poor Edna, she must be devastated: he was still young."

"Are you going to the funeral?" Shosh asked Ariella.

"I wish, but it's on Mount Herzl in Jerusalem, and I don't know anybody who's going. Plus, I'd need a ride back. It's Friday..." She couldn't mention Arik, could she? Tears filled her eyes again.

"Yeah, no more buses after three..." Shosh said sympathetically.

"What about the friend that just called to tell you?" Etty asked.

Ariella didn't know what to say; she had to think quickly. "He, he is in Jerusalem already..." She lowered her eyes. So much lying.

"Don't worry," Etty said empathically, "You can come with me next week to visit Edna if you'd like, and convey your condolences."

"Yes? All right, thank you." Ariella nodded.

They wished each other "*Shabbat shalom*," and Shosh added, "See you Sunday."

Ariella walked slowly to the bus stop to go home, trying to imagine lively Yom-Tov dead. His smile, his kindness, and his concern when Ima was sick were so vivid in her mind. She couldn't believe he was gone.

Ariella wished she could talk with Rachel. But Rachel hadn't called or asked her to go for lunch in the past two months. Why couldn't Rachel understand that Ariella was deeply in love with Arik? After all, Rachel was in love, too. It was *her* life; *her* choice. Why was Rachel so judgmental? Ariella felt angry and disappointed, but still, she longed for her sweet friend. Ariella needed to speak to Eitan, ask him to get the two of them together, but she was scared to be rejected.

She had no other friends. Keeping her relationship with Arik a secret had made her keep to herself. Whom could she talk to? Maybe Aunt Pearl? Since her aunt had moved to Uncle Rafael's apartment six months ago, Ariella hadn't really seen much of her, especially since she took a job working in a flower shop. Yael often dropped by there for lunch after school when the shop was closed. Ariella thought that maybe she should do the same. Yes, Aunt Pearl was family; she could talk to her.

It was one thirty when Ariella arrived at Uncle Rafael's apartment building. She was surprised to see that her father's gray van was parked on the street. Was Abba there? Where? All the shops were closed already for Shabbat, and he'd have finished his deliveries earlier that day. Was he at Aunt Pearl's? Ariella wasn't in the mood for a family gathering. She wanted her aunt all to herself; she wanted to tell her about Yom-Tov.

Ariella didn't feel like going upstairs to her aunt anymore, so she sat on the bench by the abandoned bus stop, not far from the building, and thought about what to do. About ten minutes later, she saw Abba walk out of the building alone and get into his van. Where was Yael? Ariella was surprised; her little sister loved Aunt Pearl and came to visit often.

She heard the ignition turn on and saw her father's van pull away. He didn't seem to have noticed her, and she felt strange hiding from him. She entered the building, walking the two stories up the stairs, still wondering what her father was doing there at that hour. She rang the doorbell.

"Oh, *Shalom*, Ariella, what a nice surprise. I thought you were your fa—uh, never mind," Aunt Pearl said as soon as she opened the door. She was wearing a lilac dressing gown and matching slippers, her hair a mess.

"Did I wake you up? Were you resting?" Ariella was shocked to see her elegant aunt so disheveled. She frowned.

"No, eh, yes. Come in, come in," Aunt Pearl said.

"I received a very sad phone call today," Ariella said, still standing by the door, her eyes welling up. For a moment her mind didn't connect...until her aunt tightened her robe and smiled...two minutes after Abba had left.... She shook her head.

"Oh, you did? I'm sorry, what happened?" Aunt Pearl grabbed Ariella by her wrist and pulled her into the apartment, closing the door behind her.

Ariella's own loneliness and sadness overwhelmed her again. "My army boss died last night, Major Yom-Tov," she said. She sat at the kitchen table and started crying. "His funeral...will be taking place...very soon on Mount Herzl," she managed to say in between sobs.

"Oy, *motek*, I'm so sorry. Yes, he was a nice man, I remember. He let you visit Ima in the hospital. I'm sorry. What happened to him? And how did you find out?" Aunt Pearl placed two bowls of chicken soup with thin egg noodles and two spoons on the kitchen table and sat down.

"He...he had a heart attack last night, Arik had told me. And...and he was Arik's good friend. And Benny's. The three of them were in the army together. They fought the wars together." Ariella forgot for a moment to whom she was talking, the names just rolling off her tongue. "And I met Arik while I was working for Yom-Tov. He came to the office one day. It's been two years already, but his wife is crazy, and he can't divorce her, and he won't leave her." She couldn't stop the landslide. "Oh, my God, what am I going to do if he dies, too? If he has a heart attack? I'm twenty-one already. I'll be an old maid soon." By now she was sobbing hysterically.

Aunt Pearl stood up.

Slowly Ariella calmed down and realized what she'd done; what she'd just spoken *out loud.* She looked up at Aunt Pearl in horror. Her aunt stared back at her.

"Arik? Is this his name? The guy you've been seeing?" Aunt Pearl asked, her face contorted slightly. "The one you go on vacations with to Europe?" Aunt Pearl asked and looked at Ariella with big eyes, as if trying to absorb what she'd just heard. "Did you say *his wife*?"

Ariella looked down at her untouched soup and saw blobs of fat floating on top, like tiny gold coins. It's done; I've said it, she thought. I told my secret.

Now her aunt stood with both hands on her hips, yelling, "How could you sleep with a married man? Like the...the...the whore *my* husband slept with!"

Ariella stood up, too, shocked. Did she just call her a whore?

"Ariella!" Aunt Pearl waved a finger at her face. "I was suspicious, and I've told your father to talk with you. I've said there must be something wrong with you dating a man for so long, gallivanting with him to God knows where, which means that he has a lot of money, maybe even an older man, and you're not bringing him home to meet us. I've—"

"Us?" Ariella exclaimed. "Meet *us*? What about Ima?" Tears flooded her eyes again. She shook from grief, a sense of betrayal, and anger.

"Well." Her aunt raked her hands through her hair. "He was my beloved sister's husband, but I was madly in love with him since I was a little girl. His gentleness, his quiet demeanor, his wisdom and intelligence. He is brilliant, Ariella." Aunt Pearl stopped yelling and tucked her hands in her gown's pockets. "You must know by now that...that...that your father and I are...are seeing each other very often. I feel like I'm part of him, of you, of his life, Ariella, part of your whole family. I've always loved him. I was devastated when you all left for Argentina. I thought I'd never see him again, or my sister Ophelia. I loved her. Don't you think even for one minute that I didn't." She waved her finger at Ariella again, her mood changing and her voice rising. "And it was terrible when she died. She was my oldest sister and the only one left after bloody Hitler. What could I do? I fell in love with her husband when I was little, and it never went away. He was my first love and I thought I'd get over him, but I didn't. I thought that marrying Irwin and moving far away to South Africa would cure me, but it didn't. And I did nothing...nothing...you hear? *Nothing* while he was married." She was crying now. "So now, yes, he and I are one. I know it. I feel it. And he feels it, too. At long last." Her crying subsided, but her face remained contorted in anguish.

She took a deep breath and continued slowly, deliberately. "But I did *nothing* while he was married to my sister. You must believe me. You can ask him. But now that he's a widower and I'm a divorceé..." Aunt Pearl stopped and placed both her hands on her chest. "We're *us*."

Ariella wasn't sure if she was relieved that the subject had diverted from her and Arik to Abba and Aunt Pearl, but she felt nauseated. Her legs shook. She snatched her purse and ran out, feeling quite disgusted, with herself and with the image of Abba taking the lilac robe off Aunt Pearl and—tears streamed down her cheecks as she ran down the building stairwell.

"Wait! Ariella! Where are you going?" her aunt yelled after her, standing at the top of the building staircase looking down, leaning over the metal railing. Ariella fled, two stairs at a time, out of the building.

She'd implied I was a whore, Ariella thought. I'm not a whore. Maybe I'm his lover now, but this is only temporary, until we get married.

Ariella walked fast, not sure where to. All she knew was that she was headed west, toward the setting sun. Her steps echoed in her head in rhythm to her thoughts. Abba had known—or at least suspected—that Arik was married. Her temples were thumping by the time she arrived at the Tel Aviv boardwalk and sat on a bench, exhausted. She wasn't sure how long she sat there, but as the sun set into the Mediterranean, sadness enveloped her as the chill in the air increased. Her world was collapsing; Rachel, Aunt Pearl. Even Ima wasn't there to talk to.

As she stared at the sinking sun, she made a promise to herself, and to her dead former boss who had just been buried: Arik had to get a divorce and propose to her by the time she turned twenty-two in September or she'd leave him.

Chapter Thirty-Six

ARIELLA was sure that Aunt Pearl would relay their encounter to Abba and was willing to explain if he came forward. But he didn't.

The following Wednesday at seven o'clock, Etty said to Ariella, "I'm going to visit Edna Yom-Tov tonight. Are you interested in coming with me?"

Ariella was caught by surprise; she had to think fast. "Is she...is she still sitting *Shiva*?"

"Yes, I think tomorrow is the last day. Or maybe Friday. I didn't have a moment to spare this week, but I must go. Would you come with me?"

Ariella was surprised. She'd never met Yom-Tov's wife.

Was it appropriate for her to go?

"He was your boss." Etty seemed to read Ariella's mind. "I think it would be respectful of you to visit her, considering you couldn't go to the funeral." She tilted her head to one side, questioningly. "We can take the bus together or a *Sherut* taxi." She sounded persuasive, willing to take the shared-taxi minivan, although it was more expensive than a bus.

"Yes, all right," Ariella said hesitantly. "I'll come with you, although you know, I've never really met her before." She shivered at the thought of meeting Arik there, by coincidence.

Ariella fixed her hair, re-applied lipstick, and joined Etty as she walked out of the office, waving to Shosh.

As they walked to the bus stop to take a *Sherut* taxi to Ramat-Chen, Ariella started feeling anxious. Etty had the address and it was a twenty-minute ride. Ariella felt the sweat building up on her upper lip and in her armpits. Just don't let him and his wife be there. She shuddered. But her curiosity to meet Edna and genuinely wanting to convey her condolences got the better of her. The risk excited her.

The *Sherut* taxi stopped at the bus stop, on the corner of the main road and Rakefet Street, and Etty and Ariella stepped outside. The small, tightly built white houses featured matching tiny front yards flowing with shrubs and flowers. Ariella would have loved to switch their apartment with one, but she preferred the city and this neighborhood was too far out.

They arrived at Yom-Tov's house and Etty knocked on the door. A small woman, with dark hair pulled up into a bun, opened it.

"Good evening," she said politely, seemingly not recognizing her guests.

"*Shalom*, Edna," Etty said in her unmistakably husky voice, "You don't recognize me?"

"Etty! Oh, my goodness!" The woman's eyes lit up. "I never expected you! What a surprise! How long has it been? Ten years? More?" She seemed happy to see her old friend. "Come in, come in, is this your daughter?" She smiled at Ariella.

"No, this is Ariella." Etty moved aside and let her go in first. "She's my boss." Etty laughed and coughed.

Edna Yom-Tov smiled, not comprehending, and shook hands with Ariella. "Nice to meet you."

"And you too, Mrs. Yom-Tov." Ariella took the outstretched hand in both of hers. "I worked with Major Yom-Tov when I did my military service. He was like a father to me." Her eyes teared up. "I'm so sorry for your loss. I wish you'll never know sorrow again."

"Oh, thank you, uh, what was your name?"

"Ariella."

"Yes, Ariella. So, you knew Amos well if you worked with him. Did you come to the funeral? Wasn't it something? So many people, and generals."

"I'm so sorry, but I couldn't come. It was on Friday afternoon, and I had no transportation."

"Oh, we had buses full of soldiers who came from the base and took them all back to Tel Aviv afterwards." She sounded pleased. "Well, if you had been in the service still, you would have come, I'm sure. But it's very kind of you to visit me." Edna walked to the living room and kept a hand on Ariella's shoulder. "Please, sit down, eat something." Edna turned to Etty now. "And you, my dear friend, tell me about yourself." She took Etty's hand in hers and added, "So nice of you to have come."

"I also have to apologize, Edna. By the time I'd heard from Ariella, it was too late to get to Jerusalem," Etty said.

"I understand. Being Friday and all. But you're here now, good of you to come. I'm really glad to see you."

Ariella sat down on a worn blue velvet sofa, nodded to some people, and observed the women. Could one of them be Arik's wife? She stared hard at each and every woman in the room, but Etty didn't seem to have recognized anybody.

With a shaky hand, Ariella helped herself to a cookie from the coffee table. She remembered the amount of food family members and neighbors had brought to their house when Ima had died. She looked around.

There, on a long brown wooden table, lay a white tablecloth with and ten or twenty different dishes heaped on it. She got up and scanned the food. There was gefilte fish, egg salad, chopped liver, herring, eggplant salad, chopped Israeli salad, cut up fruit, pickles of all sizes, olives, *Challah* and cookies, a cheesecake and an apple strudel—every woman must have brought her specialty.

Ariella took a slice of *Challah* and smeared some chopped liver on it. Once she returned to her seat she looked around and noticed the love and attention that surrounded Edna, who remained engaged with her new guest. Ariella knew that Edna hadn't fully realized yet what had happened to her. Poor woman. She seemed much too happy to see all her visitors.

"...and you should see Sara," she heard Edna tell Etty excitedly, "as young-looking as she was ten years ago. I'm sorry she isn't here now. She visited this morning. Her husband really takes good care of her. He brings her face creams from Europe—only the best of course—takes her to spas and short vacations, especially to visit their son in London. She had said once that she was glad they only had the one child—she couldn't have handled more. She's very busy in her—"

The doorbell rang. Ariella gagged.

"—wait, I need to get it," Edna said, stopping mid-sentence to get up and open the door for more guests, leaving Etty standing alone.

Before Ariella could comprehend what she'd just heard, Etty took her by the hand and pulled her off the sofa. "Come. Let's go. More and more people will be coming now. The house will be packed in a few minutes." She stretched over the table, snatched an olive with her hand, and popped it into her mouth.

They had to push their way toward Edna to say their goodbyes. Edna hugged them both and thanked them for coming, tears in her eyes. "I'll speak with Sara, Etty. The three of us must get together again, soon. It was so nice of you to come."

"I'm sorry it's under these circumstances, Edna. I promise to keep in touch."

On their way to the bus stop, Ariella asked Etty, "Who is that Sara she was talking about?" Was her voice quivering?

"Oh. Sara, Edna, and I were inseparable at school. I think I told you. She was one bright cookie. I haven't seen her in over ten years, but I know she is an—oh, here is my bus. I'll see you tomorrow, Ariella. Thanks for coming with me. She was really touched by our visit, wasn't she? *Le'hitraot.*" See you. Etty hopped on her bus.

The soot and scent of gas almost choked Ariella as the bus chugged away. She wasn't sure if it was the smoke or what she'd heard in Yom-Tov's house that made her eyes water. A cool wind chilled her to the bone. As she waited for her bus, she thought: Sara...could *Sara* be Arik's wife? Sara Emmanuel? Did Edna and Etty know of her mental health problems? No, couldn't be. Edna would have mentioned it, wouldn't she? *Her husband* brings her face creams, takes her on vacations, spas—there was no mention of illness. Very odd. Ariella pulled her coat tightly around her neck. And what if it was her, and Etty discovered Ariella's affair with Arik? She almost threw up the chopped liver.

The next day Oded took a seat next to Ariella in English class. "You want to do conversation with me?"

Ariella smiled at Oded's attempt to speak English. He wasn't in military uniform, so she asked him, "Have you been discharged?"

"Not yet," he grimaced and retreated to speaking Hebrew. "My sister is getting married, so I got a few days' vacation. The wedding is next Tuesday, and I thought you may want to join me. What do you think? Free food and lots of dancing. And I know you love to dance," he smiled broadly.

"What happened to your girlfriend?" Ariella remembered the girl he'd kissed in his kitchen on New Year's Eve.

"My girlfriend...? Oh, eh, I don't have a girlfriend."

"I'm sorry, but thank you for the invitation, Oded. I'm busy on Tuesdays and —"

The English teacher stood by the board, tapping it with her ruler, waiting for silence.

Ariella smiled at Oded apologetically.

When she returned home from English class Eitan asked her, "Ariella, would you like to come to the movies with us on Saturday?"

"With us? You and Rachel? Does she know?" Abba had told her that Rachel and Eitan visited Aunt Pearl quite often, and sometimes even took her out to the movies. Just like they used to do with Ariella. The loneliness and jealousy hurt her soul.

"Of course she does, silly," Eitan said. "It was *her* idea." And just before Ariella got all excited, he added, "Aunt Pearl and Abba want to see the movie, too, so we can all go together."

"What movie?" She didn't really care; she was just buying time to think. She ached to see Rachel but didn't want to go out with Abba and Aunt Pearl.

"*The Bridge on the River Kwai,*" Eitan said. "Everybody's raving about it. Yael will come, too. We'll celebrate her birthday. Can you believe our baby sister is fourteen already?"

Ariella wanted to see Rachel so badly, to talk to her, to pour her heart out, that she almost forgot her sister's birthday was coming up. What was she to do? Go out with all of them? She had to.

She also had to pack for Sunday.

Chapter Thirty-Seven

"*SHALOM.* Are you Ruth?" Ariella said, walking into the travel agent's office on Friday after work. "I'm Ariella Paz."

"Oh, *shalom* Ariella!" Ruth said warmly, as she got up to shake Ariella's hand. "Yes, I am. And I recognize you from your passport photo." She was a heavy woman with short brown hair, small brown eyes, and a broad smile.

Although Ariella had just met Ruth in person for the first time, she'd spoken to her on the phone several times during the past year, and Ruth was always polite and professional, but she could never picture her. For over a year she'd issued airline tickets for Arik and Ariella and never shown any interest in her clients' personal business. A real professional. But now was the first time Ariella was flying on her own and had come to pick up her ticket; Arik was usually the one to pick them up.

"It's nice to meet you face-to-face after such a long time," Ruth said as she opened a drawer and handed Ariella her airline ticket. "Here, Mr. Emmanuel said you'd come for it."

"*Toda.*" Thanks. Ariella opened and looked at it, surprised to see a return ticket to Paris. Didn't Arik say London? She had been so excited she was going to meet his son Boaz at long last. Wasn't that a good sign? Arik was willing to meet Abba, when they got back from London, so he'd said. Should she confront him about what she'd learned in Edna's house? Should she give him the ultimatum she'd promised herself as soon as she saw him? Her birthday was four months away.

Maybe she shouldn't say anything. It might be out of place, too aggressive and pushy if he was willing to meet her father. It was all so confusing.

Ariella frowned at her tickets. Besides meeting Arik's son, she'd been looking forward to seeing Buckingham Palace and the changing of the guards, the Crown Jewels, Big Ben, London Bridge—and so much more! The list of what she wanted to see went on and on; she'd read all about it. It would also be very exciting to visit the two galleries that exhibited Benny's paintings.

Now, *Paris*? The ticket said *Orly, France*. There was no way she could contact Arik before she left. He left for London two days ago, and he said he'd pick her up at the airport on Sunday afternoon.

"There must be some mistake here, Ruth," Ariella said, her

voice a bit high pitched. "I'm supposed to fly to *London* to meet Arik, not Paris."

"Seems like he wants to surprise you this time."

Ariella felt uncomfortable; she wished she could call Arik and find out where the mistake was. Why would he say London if he meant Paris? And what about Boaz? Their plan was to meet Arik's twenty-three-year-old son at a philharmonic orchestra concert followed by a late dinner. Just the three of them: Arik, Boaz, and her. The plan had felt so right, and she'd so looked forward to it.

Would he be in Paris, too?

"When did Arik book my ticket?" Ariella didn't really want Ruth involved but had nobody else to ask.

"Oh, when he booked his own. First, he said London and gave me the dates, but he called the next day and changed *his* ticket to Zurich and *yours* to Paris. If he didn't tell you of the change, I guess he wanted to keep it a surprise as long as possible." Ruth smiled and cocked her head. "He'll be flying to Paris on Sunday from Zurich."

Ariella still felt uneasy; Arik had never done this before.

Confused, she took the ticket and examined it. The dates were correct. Did he want to surprise her with a romantic long weekend in Paris? The truth was, as long as she got to meet his son, it didn't really matter where. Ariella had heard that Paris was beautiful in spring. Maybe he was going to surprise her in romantic Paris. Perhaps he'd found a suitable place for his wife. She was afraid to dream.

That evening, as soon as Eitan came home from work, Ariella called out to him, "*Shalom* Eitan. Are you still all going to see that movie tomorrow night?" She came out of her bedroom with a hanger in one hand and a cream raincoat in the other. Was it going to rain in Paris in April? She was sorting out her clothes, choosing what to take with on her trip.

"Yes, Rachel and I are going," he replied. "Aunt Pearl and Abba are going to see something else...I'm not sure what. I think *Dancing in the Rain* or something like that, more suitable for Yael."

"Well, maybe we can all take her out for cake and ice cream beforehand, and then Abba and Aunt Pearl can take her to see *Singing in the Rain*, and we can see *The Bridge*-whatever."

"Sounds good," Eitan agreed.

She decided to come out with it. "I'm leaving for Paris on Sunday." She showed him the raincoat, as if this would explain why she held it.

Eitan looked surprised. "Paris?" He lowered his voice. "With Arik?"

"Yes."

"I wish we could all meet again. I really like him," he said, "but Rachel won't hear of it. She said it will only encourage you." Eitan looked away.

"Well, I don't need encouragement or discouragement," Ariella said, waving the hanger as if threatening an invisible foe. "I know what I'm doing. But if Rachel can get over it, it would be nice to see her again." Ariella resented her friend's attitude and turned her back to return to her room.

"How long, Ariella?" Eitan asked.

Ariella turned around to face him again.

He looked his sister in the eye. "How long will you wait for him to commit to you?"

Ariella's arms dropped, the raincoat dragging on the floor. This was the closest she had ever felt to her brother, and she loved him for asking. Her reply was ready; it was only Passover now, and Arik had five months to come to a decision. She'd decided she was going to give him the ultimatum in London, after all—oh, Paris.

"Until my birthday, Eitan. My twenty-first birthday." Ariella wanted to sound confident, reassured by her own words, but instead, her voice came out weak.

Eitan stared back at her and said nothing.

Ariella and Rachel smiled politely at each other across the ice cream parlor, over the children's heads, when they met at Whitman's Ice Cream on Alenby Street. Voices echoed with so many children and adults calling out orders over one another's heads in effort to avoid standing in line.

Yael stood in front of the huge refrigerator, choosing the flavors she favored.

Ariella searched around for a table. Sitting down was more expensive than taking a cone and walking out, but it was her sister's birthday celebration and she would share the expense with Abba and Eitan, if needed.

She found a small table and started gathering chairs; they were six and each table had only four. She sat down, waiting and looking for her family to join her. Rachel and Eitan, Abba and Aunt Pearl, the world was made of couples, she concluded; even Abba wasn't alone anymore. Well, she was going to Paris the next day. That was good enough for the time being. Oh, she still had to tell Abba.

Ariella stared at her father. His eyes had a shine to them that she hadn't seen in a long time, and his smile stretched wider and warmer. For the first time since they returned from Argentina, Abba looked relaxed and content. He suffered with Ima's illness and death, Ariella knew, but now, since Aunt Pearl returned home, he seemed to have renewed energy and serenity.

Still, his dead wife's little sister? She'd been so rude to Ariella; she'd called her a horrible name. Was Abba falling in love with Aunt Pearl? Yes, Ariella wanted her father to be happy, but she was still hurt by Aunt Pearl and couldn't forget it. How could they ever be close again?

"What flavor ice cream are you going to get, Yuli?" Abba asked Yael. She chose chocolate and strawberry, and then he went around and asked everybody for their choice, just as the waiter arrived. They all laughed and repeated what they wanted.

Ariella noticed Aunt Pearl kept touching Abba's hand as they spoke softly to each other in an intimate manner. She missed Arik. She wished he could have been sitting with them now, eating ice cream and laughing. Ariella couldn't wait to escape the ice cream parlor's glaring lights and disappear into the darkness of the movie theater.

"Bye, children," Abba said cheerfully when they finished their treats and got up to leave. "Enjoy your movie. We're going to see Gene Kelly now, and we're going to sing and dance with him." He took Yael's hand in one hand and Aunt Pearl's in the other, and they strolled out of the parlor, a happy family.

Aunt Pearl looks like his daughter, too, Ariella thought in a flash, as she, Eitan, and Rachel also got up. They had to walk to the Migdalor movie theater, a little bit further than the Mugrabi, where Abba had gone with Yael and Aunt Pearl.

Coming out of the movie felt like old times. Both Rachel and Ariella were revved up and ready to discuss it, forgetting they hadn't spoken to each other in two months.

"Don't you think the officers should have worked shoulder-to-shoulder with their soldiers?" Ariella asked as they walked to the bus stop.

"No way!" Rachel exclaimed, stopped walking and turned to look at Ariella. "Officers give orders and see that the work is done properly."

"But do you think the bridge should have been destroyed? I don't think so." Ariella continued walking between Rachel and Eitan.

"I agree. That was bad. A really bad idea," Rachel said.

It seemed like the ice had melted in the heat of the discussion, and Eitan smiled.

"Do you both want to come to my place for coffee?" Rachel asked, and Ariella jumped at the opportunity, although she still had to pack.

It felt so good to be in Rachel's company, to have a stimulating conversation with her and to just enjoy her pleasantness. Ariella loved Rachel, it couldn't be denied, but she also knew that she had to be careful not to mention anything about Arik or the upcoming trip.

Ariella wasn't sure if Eitan had told Rachel of her decision to confront Arik; Rachel hadn't mentioned him.

* * *

"You're packing again?" Abba said as he stood by the door to Ariella's bedroom late that night.

She spun to face him, fear gripping her. Yael was asleep by the time Ariella had returned home, and Abba's bedroom door was closed. She had turned on only her reading light and started quietly packing her suitcase. Abba stood in the hallway, the light from the kitchen behind him illuminating his silhouette. She couldn't see his face.

"I'm going to Paris tomorrow for just a few days," she said quietly, not wanting to wake Yael. Or was it because she felt ashamed she didn't keep her promise of bringing Arik to meet Abba before the trip?

Abba motioned 'follow me' with his hand.

She walked behind him to the kitchen, her head bent.

"With Arik?" Abba turned to face her.

"Yes."

"What's his last name?"

"Emmanuel."

"Where does he live?"

She never expected to be questioned like that and felt cornered. Anything was better than telling Abba the whole truth about Arik.

"Ramat-Chen."

"And what's his line of business?"

"Import-export." Ariella thought she knew now where Abba was going with his line of questioning.

"Oh, so he must be wealthy. Galloping all over the globe with a pretty, young girl. He's also not that young. How come he hasn't gotten married yet?"

Ariella felt as if she'd been slapped in the face. She had to hold on to the edge of the kitchen table so as not to fall over.

"I...I don't know, Abba. I guess he hadn't found the right woman yet...uh, I mean...until he met me." A taste of sour ice cream came to her mouth.

"Don't be naïve, Ariella. He's taking advantage of you. You're young and beautiful. You should put him in his place or I will."

"Abba!"

Yael stirred in the next room.

"I'm serious. Are you sure he isn't married? A man his age and position?" Abba hadn't moved an inch.

"Abba, please." Ariella was on the verge of collapse. She wanted to cry on his shoulder, tell him everything. She wanted Abba to hug her and say that everything would be all right. But she knew it wouldn't happen. He'd make her stop seeing Arik, and she didn't want to do that.

"You have to give him an ultimatum, Ariella. Don't be careless. It's your life you're playing with," Abba said. "Promise me you'll make wise decisions."

Chills ran down her spine. Again. She hesitated.

"Ella, please promise me."

She trembled as she looked at the floor. "I promise," she whispered.

Abba went to his room, closing his bedroom door behind him.

Ariella's legs shook as she walked back to her bedroom and collapsed onto the bed. She almost cried out when her head knocked the edge of her suitcase.

Her promise hung in the air.

Chapter Thirty-Eight

ARIELLA got off the plane at Orly in Paris and spotted him immediately. Arik hadn't aged a bit in the past two years, she thought with pride, as if she were the one who kept him young. Goldberg had developed a little belly pouch and so had Abba, but Arik remained trim and fit, and she noticed the glances some French women threw his way. In an instant, she was in his arms. This was Paris. She knew they could stand in the middle of the airport hall and kiss passionately; nobody stared or cared.

"Were you surprised, my love?" Arik's eyes twinkled like a child who had succeeded in tricking his parents. "I had to be in Zurich on Friday and Saturday and flew to Paris this morning.

So now I have no more business to attend to, and I'm all yours!"

Ariella was excited to see him and to learn why he'd changed their destination. She looked around and saw women in small hats and lightweight coats of all colors, hanging on to men's arms. The men wore suits and ties and all wore hats. Many had porters following them with their suitcases on a cart.

Ariella felt anxious and didn't reply, but Arik didn't seem to notice. They retrieved her elegant beige suitcase from the carousel and walked out of the airport building to hail a cab.

When they sat at the back of the taxi, Arik nuzzled her ear and whispered, "Oh, my darling, I missed you so much!" He hugged her shoulders and squeezed it with one hand, and her knee with the other, working his fingers up her skirt.

"Arik!" She tapped his hand to stop him, looking at the rearview mirror; the driver didn't even look up. "Why didn't you tell me about the change? I thought we were meeting in London and meeting Boaz. I felt like an idiot standing in front of Ruth and not knowing where I was going." Her anger rose. "Did you change your mind about me meeting Boaz? Or were you planning to surprise me with Paris all along?" Was he going to propose to her in Paris? What about his wife's hospitalization? Was it really happening?

"Of course I meant it as a surprise," Arik said as he drew his hands back and lit a cigarette. "I thought you'd be happy; this is the most romantic city in the world!" He looked outside the cab window. Did she hear an accusatory tone in his voice?

"Will Boaz be coming here, too?" Ariella asked hopefully.

"Not this time." Arik puffed on his cigarette and continued staring out. "He wanted to go to Israel to visit his mother on his spring vacation. She isn't well, you know."

"Oh, has she taken a turn for the worse?" Ariella tried not to sound happy. She didn't know why he wasn't looking at her. Did she sound ungrateful?

"Her usual craziness. But Boaz couldn't come home for Passover, so he arrived as I left."

Ariella bit her lip in disappointment. Not meeting Boaz felt like a bad omen. "When am I going to meet him, Arik? You promised." When should she present her ultimatum? Her armpits felt damp. Maybe he had never *really* planned for her to meet his son? How would he have introduced her? His secretary? An acquaintance? A business colleague?

She was in Paris. She decided to relax and make the best of it. After all, it was *Paris in springtime*! She took a deep breath and looked out the cab window. She thought she saw the top of the Eiffel Tower far away, then black cabs zoomed right by them, and she gazed at the women in heels and colorful raincoats who walked the cobbled streets with poodles on leashes.

"Look." Arik pointed out. "Aren't the little dogs in their raincoats cute?"

Was he trying to lighten her mood? Her heart wasn't in it yet.

She saw small round tables and chairs on the opposite sidewalk, and people sitting, talking, eating, and drinking. She took another deep breath and tried to smile. Tomorrow she also could be sitting in one of those cafes; what was so bad about it? You're in Paris, Ariella! she thought, trying to cheer herself up.

The hotel on Rue du Sommerard in the Latin Quarter on the left bank of the Seine looked new, or at least recently renovated. As they passed the Sorbonne Ariella felt her chest clenching; she still dreamed of attending a foreign university.

The sun hid behind heavy rain clouds gathering in the sky, but their room was warm. The bed was covered with a red velvet bedspread and it had matching curtains. The French doors led to a tiny balcony that couldn't even accommodate one person. That made Ariella laugh. Her attitude had changed, and so had her mood. Arik paced impatiently, most probably waiting for the bell boy to bring her suitcase up. Once it was delivered, he tipped the man and closed the door. She flew into his arms.

His kisses were hot and demanding, and she messed up his hair with both her hands.

Ripples of orgasm shook her body, again and again. He was relentless, as if he had been in prison for a year. He was on top of her again, inside her, and cried out as he came, moaning, "You're mine, mine, only mine." She felt the same. He was hers. They were one. She knew why she loved him, needed him, forgave him.

He kissed her face again and again, until it was completely wet. She wasn't sure if it was sweat, saliva, or tears. His or hers. But it didn't matter. Maybe those were the tears that had been collecting there from longing, desire, and happiness, and were released at last. The clouds must have felt the same; soft April rain pitter-pattered on the windows.

* * *

Ariella always craved food after making love, so they strolled to a little bistro near the hotel. The rain fell in heavy sheets, and she was glad the restaurant had a corner table available, even if it was too close to the restrooms.

She sat down and looked around. The place was packed and the noise deafening. The tables were so small that Ariella thought their food would never fit on it. There were about five inches between their table and the tables on either side. She could feel the knee of the man sitting next to her touching her knee periodically. Colorful plates, full wine glasses, bread baskets, and silverware adorned the starched, white tablecloths.

She felt exhilarated. Paris was beautiful; alive, happy.

Ariella looked outside through the bistro's large glass window. The rain had stopped, and the round tables with black-and-beige rattan chairs on the sidewalks looked inviting after the waiters had dried them and people started occupying them again.

"I love the air after it rains," Ariella said in a dreamy voice when they left the bistro. "It's so fresh and romantic."

"Romantic?" Arik asked and smiled, hugging her shoulders.

"Yes. I don't know why. Rain makes me think of a soft bed and fluffy cushions. The smell of hot chocolate and a lit fireplace..."

"Yes, you're a romantic. It's written all over your face," Arik said as he stroked her cheek and looked at her tenderly. "And I can arrange for a soft bed and some fluffy cushions—"

They shared a laugh and continued walking.

The next morning Ariella had to have hot chocolate and a warm croissant. She fell in love with the hot chocolate in Paris; it tasted just like a bar of melted chocolate in cold cream. Good food always pacified her, and she felt content. She must have had some chocolate left at the corner of her mouth because Arik stretched over their little round table and licked it off. Nobody looked at them; Parisians were used to public displays of affection.

After breakfast Arik suggested they go look for a dress for her to wear to Eitan and Rachel's wedding. Ariella clapped her hands in joy. They were greeted with "*Bonjour, madame et monsieur!*" and a smile in the stores, and were offered coffee in some, which they declined. They much preferred the hot chocolate.

And then there it was. A green, silk shantung sleeveless number with a boat collar stared at them. Ariella stood mesmerized at the shop window and then noticed Arik looking at her with a big smile.

"You have to try it on," he said.

"But we don't know the price."

"Don't worry. You'll look beautiful with your hair up. I have a feeling this dress only needs long earrings, and you'll look breathtaking."

They entered. The shop was small and didn't have many items, but the colors and designs were breathtaking.

The dress fit perfectly around her waist and small bust; all they had to do was shorten it an inch.

"We can do it right away, *madam.* Would you like to return in a half hour?" the old tailor asked in English with a French accent, which Ariella loved. "Oh, *madam* has her shoes with her?"

Ariella looked at Arik. "It would look beautiful with the silver, high-heeled sandals you brought me from London. And the purse." Now she looked down at the kneeling tailor with pins sticking out of his mouth and a white chalk to mark the hem in his hand. "Sorry, I don't have my sandals here, but I know the size of the heel." She stood on her toes on the little, round raised platform, turning slowly around as he pinned the hem.

They left the store promising to return in half an hour.

"You'll be an eye-catcher, my love." Arik kissed the tip of her nose.

They walked into a jewelry store, and Ariella's excitement rose. It was the first time she's stepped inside a jewelry store with Arik. But it wasn't happening. She knew it when he'd asked to see earrings. *Earrings*...again. He didn't even glance at the ring cases.

The next day was surprisingly warm and humid, and they welcomed the cool air at the Louvre. Ariella had never seen such huge paintings; so much sadness and beauty that overwhelmed her. Three hours later, Arik wanted to go out for a cigarette, and she agreed to leave.

After lunch they decided to walk by the *Seine*. They crossed over on the *Pont Neuf,* marveling at the difference between both sides of the river. Ariella loved the hundreds-of-years-old ornate buildings, the palatial museums and the elegant shops and small *brasseries*—nothing like Tel Aviv. She had her portrait drawn at the Montmartre and sat restless while posing.

However, something was amiss. She wished Arik could at least come with her to Eitan and Rachel's wedding. Maybe that would prompt him to propose, but she knew better than to bring it up. He wouldn't be seen as her date at her brother's wedding, even if he'd met Abba beforehand.

She couldn't bring herself to say anything negative to him; her words stuck in her throat. After all, he was doing his best to please her, buying her expensive gifts, showing his love every moment of the day and night. Why couldn't she just enjoy the lavish life he was bestowing upon her?

Ariella decided she had to delay giving him her little speech. It didn't seem fair to pressure him while they were on vacation.

Chapter Thirty-Nine

THE day after Ariella returned from Paris, Eitan told her that he and Rachel were going to the rabbinate to register for their marriage. Ariella witnessed their excitement with a mixture of joy and envy. The following day Rachel started looking for a wedding dress.

First with Eitan, then with her mother, then with Ariella, and finally, with Eitan again. Together they decided on an ivory satin dress. Ariella thought it was too plain but didn't say so. Rachel had said that she didn't want a pure white dress; it wasn't right with red hair, freckles, and fair skin. But secretly she'd told Ariella that she was no hypocrite; she knew she wasn't pure. Tears filled Rachel's eyes, and Ariella knew she was thinking of the baby. She just nodded in agreement.

Ariella thought of the dress she'd buy for her wedding with Arik. It would be puffy, she knew, tight at the waist and flowing like a princess's gown. Definitely white. She would have it heart-shaped at her bust and she—she had to stop. The image burnt into her brain and felt like it left a scar. Jealousy and anxiety throbbed at her temples. Would that day *ever* come?

* * *

"*Mazal Tov*," Ariella hugged Eitan. "You did it!"

They all stood hugging each other in the university hall in Abu Kabir in Jaffa after the exciting but modest graduation ceremony.

Ariella watched her handsome brother in a suit and a tie, his red hair shining and his green eyes sparkling, hugging Rachel's parents. When Abba turned to hug Eitan, Ariella was surprised by Aunt Pearl's hug. It was hard for Ariella to return her aunt's hug; she still couldn't look her in the eye after the insult. But she decided to forgive her, if not forget. After all, she thought, next month Eitan and Rachel would be getting married, and she wasn't willing to be the one to spoil the atmosphere.

* * *

The sun was still high in the sky when Ariella got dressed

for her brother's wedding. She stared at herself in the bedroom mirror, and suddenly saw her sister's reflection, too.

"You look beautiful." Ariella said as she looked at Yael's reflection twirling in a pale-pink chiffon dress, her red curls bouncing. She knew that Yael bought the dress with Aunt Pearl while Ariella was in Paris. Pink? Ima wouldn't have approved, she thought sadly.

"Thanks. And you look like a princess." Yael smiled at Ariella.

"Thank you." Ariella liked how the long diamante earrings looked above her shiny silk shantung green dress from Paris. She decided to splurge that morning, and had her hair done up by a professional hairdresser. She thought she looked like a Hollywood actress, and smiled.

Abba hailed a taxi for the groom, himself, and his daughters.

Ariella knew that Aunt Pearl would come to the wedding with Uncle Rafael and Dalia and their little girls. It was wonderful to have them back in Israel.

Aunt Dalia, dressed in an elegant midnight-blue taffeta dress that came below her knees, kissed Ariella on her cheek as they met at the reception hall. "Soon by you, my dear," she said. This was the customary blessing for a single person at a Jewish wedding.

Aunt Pearl wore a purple velvet dress with a deep but narrow front cut, one large diamond on a thin chain just above her cleavage, and diamond earrings. Her brown hair was cut in a bob.

Rachel's red hair was up in soft curls, and her lipstick matched her flushed cheeks. Her nails were painted silvery-white just like her shoes that peeped out from beneath her dress. She wore pearl earrings, a gift from Eitan when they got engaged.

Aunt Bronka kissed Ariella and said, "Soon by you." Then she pinched Yael's cheek, saying to her with a smile, "and then by you, sweetie." Yael frowned and stepped back.

Eitan stood on the other side of the hall with a nervous smile, handsome in his dark suit and black hat. Abba, a head shorter, and Uncle Rafael, a head taller, stood on either side of Eitan, ready to lead him toward Rachel. Ariella was pleased that Eitan had chosen Uncle Rafael, and not Aunt Pearl, to join Abba in leading him to his bride; this was much more appropriate. No woman should take Ima's place.

Ima. Was anybody thinking of Ima? Yes, Ariella was sure they were. Ima was missed daily, but today her absence was so pronounced; her son—her firstborn—was getting married, and she was bitterly missed.

The band began playing. Abba and Uncle Rafael led Eitan to the canopy and stood underneath it, waiting beside the rabbi. Rachel got up and, accompanied by her parents, was led to the *Huppa,* the wedding canopy, and stood by Eitan. The rabbi began the ceremony. After blessings and wine sipping, the groom placed the ring on the bride's finger, announcing that he was marrying her, and kissed her. Then Eitan stomped on a glass wrapped in paper, for all to remember the destruction of the two ancient temples in Jerusalem.

"*Mazal tov, mazal tov*!" Everybody cheered and clapped.

Two chairs stood now in the center of the dance floor, and the bride and groom went to sit in them. Male friends and family lifted them up in the air and everybody cheered as the band played "*Simahn Tov U'mazel Tov.*" Hand in hand, a large circle was formed around the raised couple, and guests danced the *hora.* As people joined the circle and it grew bigger, the couple was put back on the ground, and the chairs were whisked away. Ariella took Rachel's hand in her own and Eitan's in her other and walked them to the center where they formed an inner circle of three. Soon enough, Yael, Abba, Dalia, Uncle Rafael, and Aunt Pearl joined in the inner circle, followed by Rachel's parents. With the music blaring and a new larger circle forming, it seemed like the whole of Israel was dancing.

Ariella snuck out of the circle and took a seat, poured herself a glass of cold water, and sipped. Her two cousins collapsed on the seats next to hers.

After a while they both got up to join one of the circles again, and when they tried to pull Ariella by her hands, she said, "In a minute. Go, go, I'll join you in a minute."

Although she didn't. She kept sitting and thinking of Arik. What would the family have said if they saw him? What would Abba have said? Would he have welcomed him to his son's wedding with open arms? And Aunt Pearl? And Uncle Rafael? Would it have upset Rachel? No, she couldn't do it to Rachel on her wedding day; maybe it was better he hadn't come.

The band started playing the bride and groom's waltz. Eitan and Rachel danced shyly as everybody watched, clapping. Uncle Rafael was the first one to get up and invite his wife Dalia to dance. Ariella watched when Abba did the same with Aunt Pearl and flinched. When her cousin Yonatan came to invite her to dance, her throat was in a knot. She shook her head and ran to the restroom.

She missed Ima, and Arik. The loneliness felt suffocating. Ariella sat on the toilet and couldn't stop the tears.

Chapter Forty

IT was the last week of a hot and humid June when Ariella began packing. She was flying alone. Again. She was going to meet Arik in Athens, Greece.

Arik had to attend to business in Switzerland, but Ariella couldn't join him there and take too many days off from work. Not again. Yossie Lupo was a real pain; he kept complaining about her accumulating short vacations.

The night before her trip, Ariella plopped on Yael's bed.

"What?" Yael asked as she put her book down.

Ariella pulled her hair into a quick bun, to relieve her neck from the overwhelming heat and humidity. "Nothing. I just wanted to tell you that I love you."

"So? I love you, too. We both know that." Yael seemed impatient to get back to her book, but then her facial expression softened, and she asked, "Are you all right?"

Ariella's eyes welled up. "I don't know what's wrong with me. Everything makes me cry lately."

"Why? What's wrong?"

"I don't know. I think the heat is getting to me this year. I usually don't mind it."

"That shouldn't make you cry."

"I know. Forget it." Ariella tried to smile. "How are *you* feeling?"

"I'm fine. I don't get those awful headaches any more, and the heat doesn't bother me. I'm okay."

"Yes. It's been a while now. Since around the time that Aunt Pearl came to live in Israel you haven't complained about headaches. Do you think there's a connection?"

"What an odd thought. Why should it be connected?"

"I don't know. Just a coincidence, I guess," Ariella said. "By the way, I noticed that the Palgin bottle in the bathroom is almost full."

"I don't know. I haven't used any in a long while. Are you checking on me?"

"No, I've just noticed because I've packed some to take with me to Athens just in case I need it. I may be getting my period."

Ariella felt bloated during the flight. Was it time for her period? Not good timing to have the period while on vacation, she tried to smile. Not being regular had its downfalls, she concluded.

She took a taxi from Athens airport to the hotel and fell into Arik's arms as she entered their room. He didn't come to pick her up this time; she'd become an experienced traveler.

"Ooph." She kicked off her sandals and fell onto the soft bed. Thank goodness for the ceiling fan. "The heat in Athens is terrible; just like Tel Aviv."

"Should I order some cold coffee?"

"Not coffee." She grimaced. "Maybe lemonade? With ice?"

She never got to drink it, because by the time room service arrived, she must have fallen asleep. Toward evening Arik woke her gently, and it took her a minute to figure out where she was.

They went out for dinner, hoping it would be cooler, but it wasn't.

When they got into bed and Arik fondled her, her breasts felt sore and tender.

"I hope I'm not getting sick." Oh my God, it's not cancer, is it? How did Ima's cancer begin? Ariella felt the pulse in her neck, constricting her throat with fear.

The next day they attempted to venture out, but it was almost 40 degrees Celsius, 103 degrees Fahrenheit. Arik ordered breakfast in their room.

"I may be getting my period," she moaned.

"Oh, no!" Arik frowned and got out of bed, looking for his cigarettes.

"Maybe it's something I ate on the plane." She said apologetically.

She must have picked up a germ just before she'd left Israel, she thought, or maybe it was a stomach bug. She discarded any other thought.

In hot and humid Tel Aviv, she knew what to do; she would close all the windows, wrap a wet towel over her head to cool her down, and throw cold water on the tile floors to cool the rooms.

"My hair is too long. I feel hot. I want to cut it in a bob. Like my Aunt Pearl's."

"Cut your beautiful long hair?" Arik sounded surprised. "Here in Athens?"

"Why not? What difference does it make, Athens or Tel Aviv?" The heat made her irritable. "We can't go anywhere, it's too hot to visit the Acropolis, and the fan in this room just twirls around and mixes the hot air but doesn't really cool it. Until I feel better, I just want to stay cool. Maybe the hair salon is cooler." She felt moody and restless. She couldn't sit still, so she walked around the room in her underwear and a bra, picked up a book, and put it back down again. Eventually she threw on a white cotton dress, took her purse, and walked to the door. "I'm going to look for a hair salon."

"All right, sweetie, do you mind if I go to the hotel pool? Will you join me afterwards? Maybe the water will cool you down." He was trying to help, she knew, but all she wanted now was to have her long hair cut off. She was hot and miserable.

* * *

"Oh, my Lord!" Arik said when Ariella appeared by the pool about an hour or two later. He looked around to see if other men were looking, too. They were. Ariella smiled at his jealousy. She felt a bit better, lighter, not so nauseated.

She took off her see-through, white organza gown and stood by him in her yellow bikini. She knew her skin was smooth and brown, and the oil she'd used for tanning made her shiny. She could see in his eyes how beautiful she looked; she needed no mirror. And her hair! She'd made a good choice. She'd cut her hair in a bob with bangs, which emphasized her big brown eyes. When she had looked into the mirror at the hair salon, she froze; it was as if Aunt Pearl was staring back at her.

"Ariella! You look like you're made of gold! Cleopatra! My goodness, you're so beautiful!" Arik said it loud and in Hebrew, and many heads turned in curiosity. People smiled, and someone wolf whistled. She felt so much better.

"Maybe you should put your gown back on?" Arik said in a hoarse voice.

"Why? It's so hot. I'd like to have some iced coffee now, please, with vanilla ice cream and fresh cream on top," she announced as she yanked the striped towel Arik had stretched on the lounge chair next to him, spread it on the edge of the pool, and plopped onto it, dangling her feet in the water. "Do you think they have cherries?"

Arik motioned nervously to the waiter.

Ariella had decided to stop complaining and enjoy the pool, to try to have a good time; it was a vacation after all. But her lighter mood didn't last long.

"Do you need a doctor, or do you want to go back home?" Arik asked the next morning, as the nausea returned. Ariella was so disappointed. What was wrong with her? Her period wasn't coming. She couldn't be pregnant, could she? Arik was always so careful. And he was sterile.

All she really wanted was to go home and told him so.

"I'm sorry, *motek,* it wasn't a good idea to go to Athens in June. I should have known better, but I so wanted to be with you for a few days. I go crazy when I don't get to be with you."

They took the short flight back to Tel Aviv.

A big surprise awaited Ariella when she got into her apartment.

A telephone.

A rarity in Israel in 1960. A technician from the post office must have installed it in their living room while she was away. Ariella figured Abba or Uncle Rafael knew somebody in the right places to be able to move to the top of the list of people waiting to get a telephone line.

It held a place of honor on a small, round side table, which Abba must have bought in a secondhand store, right by Ima's favorite armchair. When Ariella saw the new black addition, she almost cried out. Ima! She could picture her mother sitting on her favorite armchair, talking to her friends, or her siblings, or Abba at work. She felt like crying. But she had to pull herself together, so she took out her little black address and telephone book. She dialed.

"Yes, Hello. This is Ariella Paz. I need to make an appointment with Doctor Cohen."

She listened then said, "Yes, tomorrow afternoon is fine, thank you."

She still had two more days before her leave was over. She had a bad feeling and suspected her period would not show up after all. She wasn't sure whether to be excited or petrified. On the one hand, she hoped she was pregnant; that meant it wasn't cancer. And Arik wasn't sterile, thank goodness. After all, it was never medically confirmed. On the other hand, what if she *was* pregnant? *What then?*

Chapter Forty-One

IT was just before three o'clock, during her lunch break that the new phone rang, while Ariella was resting at home. The sound jolted her; she still wasn't used to it, as if the phone's sharp ring could only bring bad news.

"Hello," she said, holding the black receiver slightly away from her ear.

"Is this Ariella Paz?"

"Yes."

"This is the clinic. Yes, the rabbit test proved it. It's positive; you're pregnant, *mazal tov*."

Ariella couldn't breathe; an unfamiliar tightness settled in her chest.

She was relieved but anxious all at once.

"You may want to make an appointment with your doctor to follow up."

Follow up? She wasn't sure what she wanted to do. One thing was obvious; she didn't want her family doctor to know, or Abba. She didn't want anybody to know. Except Arik. She had to speak to him. Had to.

Suddenly, her world collapsed. Pregnant. *She was pregnant.* How could it be? Arik had promised her it wouldn't happen. But it had.

I'm almost twenty-two, she thought, pregnant and not married. Well, this would speed things up a bit. Arik will get a divorce, we'll get married, and I'll have the baby—I'm having a baby! She had no idea how long it took to get a divorce. She didn't know anybody but Aunt Pearl who had gotten divorced. And it had taken her aunt about a year. All Ariella knew was that it was a big shame, at least in Israel. Would she have to wait a year now? And the baby…? She wasn't sure if she was scared or excited. A *baby*…a human being!

Doubts crept in; what if Arik's wife refused to give him a *get*, a Jewish divorce? Could this happen? What was the law? Ariella leaped from the chair and started pacing her bedroom. What would she do with a child by herself? Her eyes welling with tears, she felt weak at the knees and had to sit on the edge of the bed. What would she do if Arik didn't want a child at his age? His son, Boaz, was twenty-three already! What was she going to do? Oy, Ima, what am I going to do?

It was already three thirty, and Ariella had to return to

work, but she didn't feel well. She was weak and nauseated. When she was away in Athens, her colleagues had covered for her, and she knew that Yossie Lupo would be very angry if she took the afternoon off, but first she had to contact Arik.

In two years, Ariella had had no reason to call Arik, except maybe to clarify the London Paris confusion, but even that turned out fine. For the past two years, she had seen him every Tuesday—if he was in the country—and on some weekends. He always had told her ahead of time when their next meeting would be. He would call at the army base or her office.

She had no telephone number for him and no way to contact him. She wasn't going to go to Jerusalem to see Benny for that, nor would she call him; with his sensitivity, he'd feel that something was wrong. And she couldn't wait until next Tuesday; it was only Thursday.

There was only one person she could call: Ruth, the travel agent. But when would she call? She was on the bus back to the office now; it was almost four o'clock.

Both Goldberg and Lupo were in the office, and Ariella couldn't make the call. Neither could she call Ruth the following morning, Friday, as she had to leave the house for work at seven thirty, and the travel agency only opened at eight. She had no option but to ask to leave the office at twelve thirty instead of one. She said that she had a one o'clock appointment at the doctor's. Goldberg was out, and when she asked Lupo, he narrowed his eyes in suspicion, his eyebrows becoming one long bushy line. "One o'clock on a Friday? Don't clinics close at one?"

"My doctor said he'd wait for me. He knows that I'm working but had said to be there by one at the latest. I still need to take the bus." She hated it when Yossi Lupo interfered in her business and Goldberg wasn't there to stop him.

"Can you stay on Sunday half an hour longer to make up for it?" Lupo pressed on.

"*Beseder,*" all right, Ariella replied nonchalantly, even though she boiled inside. I won't give him the pleasure of seeing me mad. At twelve thirty she said *Shabbat shalom* to everybody and walked out, pretending to go to the bus stop. Shosh and Etty followed her out with their eyes.

Instead, she stopped by the post office two blocks down, where two public telephones were attached to the wall under a sound hood.

"*Shalom,* Ruth, it's Ariella Paz," she said into the receiver, after she found some tokens in her purse.

"*Shalom,* Ariella, you caught me just as I was going to lock up. How can I help you?" Ruth said kindly.

"I need to get hold of Arik. Can you believe it? I don't have his telephone number. I've never had to get hold of him before. Is there a way you can call him and give him the number here? I'm by the post office. I'll give you the number." She knew that she sounded desperate but had no other choice.

"Let me check his file. I think he flew to London again." Ruth made some noise with papers, and Ariella had to add a token into the phone to keep from being disconnected. London? He never told me he was going to London this week—

"Yes, I was right. He flew yesterday and will be back on Monday." Ruth was murmuring something else that Ariella couldn't hear; the phone made some hissing noises.

"We have a bad connection, Ruth. You said that he'll be back on Monday?" Ariella knew she had to hurry; Goldberg and the others would be coming out of the office soon and might come this way and see her.

"Yes, Monday," Ruth said.

"All right, never mind. Thank you, Ruth, *Shabbat shalom.*" Ariella replaced the receiver. She zipped around the corner and raced to the next bus stop.

By the time the bus arrived, it was after one o'clock and it was full; she had no place to sit. People holding shopping bags placed them on the bus floor between their feet and held on to the overhead handles for dear life. Every time the bus took a corner, people would bend down to grab their bags, making sure nothing fell out.

There was constant movement, and Ariella thought she'd faint. It was July and at least thirty-seven degrees Celsius. People were sweating; the driver yelled for them to move in and make room for others, and the warm bodies pressing against her own nauseated her. She had no energy to think. Her mind was blank. All she wanted was to get home, shower, and lie down.

"Ariella, your cheeks are red. Why are you so flushed?" Yael was back from summer camp, sitting in Ima's armchair and reading a book.

"Look who's talking," Ariella said when she saw her sister, who also had red cheeks and a small wet rag on her forehead. "You look like a red tomato. I only walked from the bus stop. It's like an oven out there. Do we have cold water in the icebox?"

"Yes, and cold milk, too. Shall I cut you a piece of the babka Abba brought home? It's still warm, no wonder; there is no chance of anything cooling down today." Yael got up before Ariella even replied and strolled into the kitchen. "Abba is sleeping," she spoke softly. "Getting up at two thirty in the morning on a Friday to have the challahs ready by five can't be easy. Poor Abba."

Ariella was pleased to see Yael in a cheerful mood. Since Eitan and Rachel's wedding, it seemed like Yael and her had grown closer. Or was her little sister just growing up?

Ariella went to take a shower. Under the water, washing her short hair and letting cool water wash over her, she thought, Tuesday, I can only talk to Arik next Tuesday. There's nothing, nothing I can do before then.

Chapter Forty-Two

WAITING for *Shabbat*, Sunday, and Monday to pass was agonizing for Ariella; she fought her nausea silently, placed wet rags on her forehead when she was home, blaming the heat, and at work, she kept drinking iced water to keep cool and calm.

On Tuesday she arrived at Benny's studio apartment in Old Jaffa at seven thirty. She let herself in and sat and waited, her mind churning at two hundred miles an hour. Arik wasn't sterile. There, she had proof. They'd have to hurry now and get married.

And then she heard the key in the door.

"Hi, *motek*, you're here already. Did you miss me?" Arik opened his arms, maybe expecting Ariella to run into them as she always did, but she didn't. She didn't even get up.

She had avoided Eitan and Rachel for the past week, didn't make eye contact with Abba the whole weekend, and kept out of Yael's way as much as she could. Now was the moment of truth.

"I'm pregnant," she said, not able to keep it in any longer.

She saw the blood drain from Arik's face. He stood by the closed door, his arms falling back to his sides, and just stared at her. She thought he'd stopped breathing, he was so pale.

"Isn't it wonderful news? So, you're not sterile, Arik, and don't even think for one tiny moment that this baby isn't yours." She tried to smile. "You know you're the only man I've ever been with. So now, come and sit down and let's discuss our future." She patted the seat next to hers. "We don't have a moment to lose."

But Arik sat down on the other side of the coffee table, his forehead dripping with sweat and his hair falling into his eyes. Suddenly, he looked old and gray.

"Ariella, there can't be a...there can't be a baby...a child...we can't...I can't...I can't raise a child with you. I'm not ready, Ariella, not yet, I'm married, I'm not ready..." He put his head in his hands, leaning his elbows on his knees, avoiding her eyes.

"Arik, I've been waiting for well over two years. I can't wait any longer. I don't know what to believe anymore. If your wife is sick, you must commit her. Arik!" She panted. "Talk to me, Arik, please, look at me, tell me you'll do it."

"Ella, how come it hasn't happened before? Are you sure?

Why now? Oh my God! Why now? Have you seen a doctor? What are we going to do?" He looked devastated, and she feared the worst was yet to come. He wasn't happy, and now neither was she. Her hands began sweat and her eyes stung. She felt short of breath; her head was spinning.

She watched him intently, knowing he would determine her future.

"Sweetie, this isn't the right time, no, no, no! Not now." He waved his hands in the air as if swatting flies. "It's just not the right time."

"It's never been the right time, Arik." She didn't know where her strength came from, but she kept going. "I thought *I'd* be your wife, *I'd* be Mrs. Emmanuel. I thought about it again and again over the past two years, but no, it didn't happen. I'm tired of hearing the same story."

For the first time since Ariella had met Arik, she felt contempt for him. Where was the tower of strength she leaned on when her mother had died? Where was her beautiful Arik? All she saw at that moment was a defeated man; a gray-faced, confused old man. As had happened many times over those two years, doubts swamped her. Would he really leave his wife? Would he ever commit to her? How many times did she need to beg and how many times had he promised? It was never the right time. But *now* was the time for the truth. Ariella felt it in her bones.

No. Never. He would never leave his wife; he would never be hers. Her heart kept warning her; her blood constantly hissed the message through her veins, every cell in her body cried out the truth; she knew, she knew; but she never listened. Never paid attention. Why was she ignoring them all?

She wanted to scream. She had loved him, utterly adored him, and he had betrayed her. Now she could see his *real* face, and it was ugly. She wanted to have nothing to do with him. She felt empty.

Ariella stood up, her fists clenched, her nails digging into her flesh. No. She wouldn't faint. She'd have to do what was best for her: she'd have another baby, another time, with another man.

She wasn't surprised to hear him say, "Wait." Arik jumped to his feet, approaching her. "We'll find a doctor who will take good care of your situation. I'll give you all the money you need."

"*My situation*?" She spat the words, her eyes stinging. "I don't want your money!"

Ariella marched to the door, threw the apartment key on the floor, and stormed out.

Chapter Forty-Three

RACHEL! She had to speak to Rachel; she needed her doctor. Rachel was the only one who could know what was happening.

Eitan and Rachel had rented a one-bedroom apartment but had no telephone. It was just after nine at night. What was she going to do? If she took the bus to Eitan and Rachel in that late hour, and told them her news, Eitan would know.

So Ariella took the bus home but got off two stops before and walked. She couldn't bring herself to go inside; Abba and Yael would be home. She crossed the road and took the bus back to Jaffa. On the way Ariella wondered what she was doing. Where was she going? She got off and walked toward the sea. The night's warm air enveloped her, and she could hear the swish of the waves gently crashing on the sand. People walked on the *Tayelet* with ice cream cones in their hands and teenagers rode their bicycles, weaving around pedestrians.

Hoping not to meet anybody she knew, Ariella sat on a bench. The same bench where she had promised herself to confront Arik. She looked far into the Mediterranean Sea, and let the tears roll down her cheeks.

Ariella had no idea how long she sat there, her blood sloshing in her ears. The sky was dark, so were the sea and the sand. People passed by like black silhouettes, her vision foggy. Her whole body was aching. Her throbbing temples made her feel like she was running a fever.

By the time she crept back in to her home, the apartment lights were off. Her face was wet, her neck sticky, her sandals dusted with sand. She got into the shower and stood there, the cold water washing over her like a comforting entity, whispering to herself that it would be okay, it would be okay— just like Ima would have said— "*Yhiye beseder, yhiye beseder.*"

* * *

"Ariella, aren't you going to work today?" Yael stood by her side, all washed and dressed.

Ariella awoke startled. Where was she? Was it a dream? Oh, no, it wasn't.

"*Od regah.*" Just one more minute. She said in a raspy voice as she pulled the cover sheet over her head.

"I must leave for school," Yael said. "Are you sick?"

Ariella pushed the sheet away and looked at her sister. "No, I'm not. You can go. I'll be up in a minute."

Life was unfair. Arik was unfair. Ariella called the office and told Etty she'd overslept and would be in soon. She'd work late today. Ariella felt numb, but she didn't care and went through the motions of washing and getting dressed and walked into the office an hour late. Goldberg wasn't in and Lupo raised an eyebrow. Or both. Ariella ignored him.

"Rachel, can we meet for lunch?" Ariella called her sister-in-law at the shoe shop.

"*Betach*, Ella." Sure. "Want to go to Shuk Bezalel for falafel?" Rachel asked.

Just the thought of fried falafel balls and the smell of hot oil made Ariella nauseated. "Could we go for ice cream instead?" She tried not to sound too odd. The heat bothered her tremendously. "It's so hot. I don't really want a warm, heavy meal."

"Ice cream for lunch? Every child's dream!" Rachel laughed. "All right, see you at Whitman's on Allenby at one thirty?"

"Yes. Good," Ariella said, and thanked the universe for putting Rachel in her path.

With deep pain she admitted in her heart of hearts that Rachel had been right all along.

The morning dragged. Ariella couldn't wait for lunchtime. As she approached Whitman's ice cream parlor, she found Rachel sitting outside under the red-and-white-striped awning, sipping her favorite mixed-flavored *gazoz.* It felt like the hottest and most humid Wednesday Ariella ever remembered; she was breathless and dripping with sweat. She longed for the *Hamsin,* the dry heat wave; the humidity was too much for her.

"*Shalom,* Ariella." Rachel lifted her head up.

"*Shalom.*" Ariella bent down to kiss her best friend's cheek and then plopped onto the small round metal chair by the metal table.

"What should I get you?" Rachel asked as she got up. Only one of them could leave the table to order; the other had to reserve their place.

Spoons in hand, they sat quietly and ate. Rachel scooped her cool vanilla treat slowly, and Ariella twisted her pink plastic spoon impatiently, staring at her melting strawberry ice cream. When Rachel finished, she took out an egg salad sandwich from her purse and offered half to Ariella. "I brought it from home. Here, take this." She looked at Ariella's ice cream. "What's wrong? You're not eating. Look, your ice cream is melting on the table."

Ariella took the sandwich but put it down on a napkin. "It's, it's too sweet." She wasn't sure how to begin. "I need to talk to you, Rachel." She tried.

"Are you all right? You look like you're shivering—are you sick? Is Abba all right? Yael? Pearl?"

"No, it's me." Ariella lowered her voice to a whisper, her

eyes full of tears. "I'm pregnant. I need to have an abortion. I need you please to help me find that...that...that doctor...you..."

"Oh, my goodness, not you, too! But I thought he couldn't—"

"Apparently he *could*. It's a fact." Her anger rose, and it felt so much better to be angry than depressed. "A nasty surprise, which under other circumstances could have been a wonderful blessing. But no, I'm done begging. He's not interested in my well-being, and I've left him." Ariella said this in one long breath, as curious people stared openly at the two young women sitting and whispering with their heads together. "*Yentas*." Busybodies. Ariella whispered under her breath in irritation.

"You what?" Rachel straightened up and placed one hand on her chest, as if to keep her heart in place, and the other on Ariella's hand. "Oh, Ariella, I don't know what to say. You knew I didn't approve of the relationship, but this is really awful. Of course I'll help you. But it's expensive...does your father know?"

Ariella shook her head. "No, and I don't want Eitan to know either, nor Yael. Only you." She wiped her eyes and sat up straight. "I need to have it done as quickly as possible. Please, Rachel, I have no time to waste."

"Okay, okay. Dr. Levy, yes, that's her name. I'll give you her number, and you can make an appointment to see her. But will Arik give you the money for it?"

"He offered, but I don't want his money. I don't want to

see him again, ever." She almost choked on her words. "I've been saving for a ticket for America." She looked down. "I guess I'll need to use it for this instead." Saying it out loud turned Ariella's stomach. It felt like her dream had shattered inside her. America. So far away; so hard to reach. She swallowed hard and looked Rachel in the eye now; she had to be realistic. "Do you have her number on you? I want to call from a payphone before I return to the office." It was hard to believe that one part of her brain was so devastated, while another stayed calm and practical.

Rachel took a small, black telephone book from her purse and looked up Levy. Ariella saw she had many Levys in her book. Rachel's eyes followed her index finger going down the list.

"Doctor, yes, there it is. Come, I'll walk you to the main post office. You can call from there."

Ariella made an appointment for a consultation on Friday at two o'clock, only two days away. The nurse explained that the doctor was working until one o'clock at the *Kupat Holim*—a health service organization—but starting at two, she was seeing patients in her private clinic. Ariella was satisfied; private clinics operated at their own hours, and she wouldn't have to ask for any more time off.

She could make it there by two on Friday, she'd told the nurse. Ariella asked Rachel if she'd accompany her, and Rachel agreed. Ariella didn't bother to take down the address of the clinic; Rachel would know where to go.

On Friday at one twenty in the afternoon, the girls met halfway between their work places, where the bus took them to a private clinic in Ramat Chen. *Ramat Chen?* Ariella was surprised. Where Arik lived! And Yom-Tov. It seemed like many IDF officers earned enough to be able to live in that small yet elite neighborhood. Luckily, Ariella figured there was no chance she'd run into Arik, not on a Friday afternoon at a women's clinic.

She turned her head from the bus window to look at Rachel seated next to her. "You never told me the clinic was in Ramat Chen," she said and immediately knew it sounded accusatory, but she was very nervous, and her hands shook. "I'd follow you blindfolded anywhere, you know that," she tried to soften the tone of her voice.

"I didn't want to go to some backstreet clinic," Rachel said. "Remember Mania from work? She recommended Dr. Levy, and I trusted her and the doctor. Don't worry." Rachel put her hand over Ariella's arm, making her jump. "You'll be in good hands."

It was almost two o'clock, and they had one more bus stop to go.

Chapter Forty-Four

THE girls sat in the waiting room, Ariella filling out the forms the nurse had handed her. A short woman in a white coat, with short black hair and black-rimmed eyeglasses, walked into the reception area. Ariella jumped nervously off her chair, and the papers she was filling out fell on the floor.

"Shalom." The smiling woman in the white coat extended her hand to Ariella. "I'm Dr. Levy. You must be Ariella Paz, yes? Nice to meet you. No need to be nervous. Come, let's talk."

Ariella tried to smile back and shook the doctor's hand, then she bent down and picked up the papers and handed them to the nurse behind the window.

Dr. Levy nodded to Rachel and walked out of the

reception area. Ariella looked at Rachel, shrugged, and followed the doctor. Strange, she didn't recognize Rachel, Ariella thought.

Dr. Levy entered an examination room and Ariella followed. There the doctor pointed at an examination table, and said, "Please sit here," and sat herself on a swivel chair.

The internal examination was surprisingly gentle, and Ariella felt trusting in this capable woman's hands; she seemed to know what she was doing, and Ariella liked her.

Dr. Levy took her gloves off. "Yes, you're definitely pregnant. Are you married?"

"No," Ariella whispered. She couldn't look the doctor in the eye. She remembered that the doctor had asked Rachel the same question.

"Does your boyfriend know that you're pregnant?" the doctor continued.

"Yes," she said quietly, "but he is...married..." Ariella's throat was dry. She sat up.

"Oh," the doctor paused. "Does he know that you're seeking an abortion?" Dr. Levy looked at her sympathetically and gained Ariella's trust immediately.

"Yes," Ariella answered willingly, glad to unburden herself. "You see, he had promised to divorce his wife and marry me." Ariella suddenly felt close to this kind, soft-spoken woman, and wanted to tell her everything. "But it seems that he's been lying all along." Ariella's eyes filled with tears; she longed for Ima. "When I told him that I was pregnant, it was his suggestion that I get an abortion, and he offered to pay for it." She had to take a deep breath now. "But I declined. I have enough savings of my own. I can pay you, no problem."

"That's brave and honorable of you, but if he has the means to help..." The doctor straightened in her chair. "Sorry, I didn't mean to pry."

"It's okay. He's a businessman," Ariella blurted out quickly. "Yes, he has a lot of money and travels to Europe often." Suddenly she couldn't stop herself. "He used to take me with him occasionally." Now she looked down at her own hands, teardrops falling down her cheeks. She was afraid she had divulged too much.

She looked up.

Dr. Levy frowned; her face contorted slightly. She turned away a bit, and when she returned her gaze, she seemed composed again. Or did Ariella just imagine it all, because the good doctor put her hand on Ariella's, and said, "Ariella, when do you want to have it done? You shouldn't wait too long."

"As soon as possible." She stopped crying. "Please."

"Tonight?" the doctor asked and raised an eyebrow. "At eight o'clock?"

Ariella didn't know that surgeries could be done at night; she was caught by surprise. That soon? Good. She nodded.

"Did you have a big lunch?" Dr. Levy asked as she got up from her swivel chair, indicating the consultation was over.

Ariella shook her head.

"Just make sure you don't eat for the rest of the day and have someone come with you." Dr. Levy was all business now.

"You'll bleed for a few days, just like when you have your period. You'll also have cramps, like menstrual cramps. Take painkillers if needed and rest for two to three days. Uh, and I'll need you to pay as soon as you come in, before the procedure, please." She told her the amount and Ariella flinched. Her anger at Arik rose again; he had stolen her dream of America. Doubts entered her mind, maybe she should have accepted his offer; even the doctor thought so.

The banks closed at one on Fridays. It was almost three o'clock! How would she get the money?

The doctor escorted her to the reception area and opened the door for her, saying, "See you tonight at eight." She closed the door behind Ariella without giving her another look.

As Ariella and Rachel exited the building, Ariella began panting. "I have to return at eight tonight, and I need to get the money now." She felt frantic.

"Tonight?! Let me think, let me think." Rachel rubbed her hands together the way she did when she became anxious.

"This is happening so quickly." Ariella was focused on her immediate problem. "I never expected it to be done today. She didn't even ask me if I wanted to think it over for a week, like she did with you and Eitan." But then she thought that the doctor hadn't asked her because she had said that her boyfriend was married. She came alone. Was she wrong in telling her that Arik was married? Ariella felt sick.

The girls walked to the bus stop and waited for a *Sherut* taxi as there were no more buses running after three on Fridays. An empty cab arrived, but they needed five more people to fill it. That's how it worked with a *Sherut* taxi; the driver wouldn't move until he had seven passengers.

Where should I go? Where can I get the money now?

Ariella and Rachel crawled to the back seat and sat quietly next to each other. They had less than five hours to get the money and return. Her stomach was in a knot.

It took about ten minutes before two young couples came to the bus stop, asking the shared-taxi driver, "To Tel Aviv?" The driver turned the engine on as a response. The two girls got into the middle bench and sat down, but the guys started arguing over who was going to sit by the driver. "Come on, fellows, do you want to get to Tel Aviv or not?" the driver said, annoyed. The taller guy pushed his friend in to sit by the girls, sat himself by the driver, and said, "*Sah.*" Go. Ariella felt her nails digging into her fisted hands.

"We need one more passenger...here he comes," said the driver, as a running man got in and sat beside Rachel.

It was quiet in the cab when Ariella blurted, "Aunt Pearl!" and quickly put her hand on her mouth. The youngsters in the cab were talking and making enough noise not to hear her, but Rachel did.

"What about her?" Rachel asked.

"Hey, listen," Ariella said louder to the driver. "Can you please drop us at the next corner?"

"*Betach.*" Sure. "Both of you?"

"Please stay with me today," Ariella said.

Rachel squeezed Ariella's hand in reply. "*Betach,*" she said. "I promise." The taxi stopped and they both got out.

"It's a five-minute walk to Aunt Pearl's from here," Ariella said. "She's the only person I can turn to now. Banks are closed, you and Eitan don't have that kind of cash on you, I don't want Abba or your parents to know, not even Eitan. So there's only Aunt Pearl. She must have cash."

"Ella." Rachel stopped walking suddenly. "I promised I'll stay with you today, but I have to tell Eitan where I am. Where will you go tonight after your procedure? You can't stay with your aunt—your father visits her often. You can come and stay with us, and Eitan will need to know. He'll never tell Abba if you ask him. You know your brother. Wild horses won't get secrets out of him. But don't you need to call Abba? Tell him you're staying with us for Shabbat?" Rachel was a quick thinker. "On Sunday you can call and say that you're sick," she continued rapidly. "But you'll need to tell him something."

Thankfully Abba's van wasn't in sight. Ariella rang her aunt's doorbell. No reply. She looked at Rachel wild-eyed. She tried again. Nobody was home. Ariella felt nauseated. She hadn't eaten the whole day; she was light-headed, and her heart wouldn't slow down. It was all too much. Thank goodness Rachel was beside her.

"She's not home. What am I going to do?" Ariella almost cried. The two of them sat down on the cool stairs before the apartment door and waited.

"Maybe you can offer the doctor a check? Do you have your checkbook with you?"

"Yes, I do. But she said that I need to pay her before the surgery."

"Did she specify that it had to be cash?"

"I'm not sure...I don't remember. I presume that's what she wants."

"But she knows that banks are closed, and nobody keeps cash at home, at least not young people like us. My parents keep small amounts at home," Rachel said, embarrassed, "under the mattress, in the linen closet, in old shoes. You know, like other Holocaust survivors do, in case they have to grab and run."

Ariella was familiar with the scenario, but she wouldn't dare go to Rachel's parents for this. "Yes, I'll give her a check! She can cash it on Sunday. I have no other way, I'll explain."

It was after six and they were done waiting. They walked outside the building and decided to take a *Sherut* taxi back to Ramat Chen. What a waste of money, taking a taxi back and forth...but how could she have known her aunt wouldn't be home—

"We have to make some calls first." Again, Rachel kept a straight head.

They looked for a post office with a pay phone.

"*Shalom,* Abba." Ariella so wanted to have her father by her side, to tell him everything, let him hold her, tell her that she'd be all right. But she only managed to tell him that she was going to spend the night at Eitan and Rachel's. He wasn't worried; she'd been absent many a night for the past two and a half years.

As Rachel took the receiver in her hand to call Eitan, Ariella had to lean on the wall so as not to collapse.

"*Shalom*, Eitan," Rachel said quietly; Eitan must have picked up the phone after one ring. "Listen, I'm with Ariella. We're on our way to see Dr. Levy. You know, the one I went to last year." Rachel paused. She must have been listening to Eitan. "Yes, she is having it done tonight, and I'll bring her home afterwards by taxi. It will be late, maybe eleven or twelve by the time we get home." Rachel stopped again and listened. "No, we don't need you to come. Can you just make the bed for her in the living room, on the couch? And listen, Eitan, not a word to anybody, please, especially Abba." She waited. Then she said, "Yes, I know, I'll tell her, see you later." She listened. "All right."

Rachel put her arm through Ariella's, and together they walked arm-in-arm to the bus stop to take the *Sherut* taxi. On their way she said, "Eitan says not to worry. She is top notch. You're in good hands." She smiled encouragingly. "I told you."

Ariella tried to smile back.

Chapter Forty-Five

ARIELLA and Rachel arrived at the clinic ten minutes early.

"Let's go upstairs and wait for the doctor there." Ariella was anxious to get it all over with.

"I can't see a thing. There isn't any light on. Let's wait here. She hasn't arrived yet." Rachel sat on the wide steps in front of the building.

"Ooph. The air is so sticky." Ariella felt most uncomfortable.

It was almost eight thirty by the time Ariella saw a white car pull up. Three figures came out and the driver seemed to hesitate before taking off.

"*Shalom*, Ariella. Oh, hello there, I see you've brought

your friend. That's good." Dr. Levy wore a summer dress and looked very pretty. "Sorry we're late."

"I'm Rachel Paz. I was Rachel Bernstein when I saw you last year for the...the..." Rachel stammered in embarrassment.

"Oh, yes, now I remember. Are you friends?"

"We're sisters-in-law now," Rachel said proudly. "I'm married to her brother. You've met him. He came with me—"

"Yes, *mazal tov*," Dr. Levy said. "I'm very happy for you." She turned to Ariella. "I'd like you to meet the anesthetist, Doctor Regev." The young man who stood beside her shook the girls' hands. "And this is my nurse, Rivka. Come, let's all go upstairs."

They all walked into the dark building, Dr. Regev leading. Somebody pressed a red wall switch that glowed in the dark. It immediately lit the staircase.

Ariella was led into a tiny dressing room where she changed into a white dressing gown. There she left her clothes, her purse, and her jewelry: the ruby ring, the gold bangle from Arik, and her mother's gold watch.

Once ready, the nurse led her to a small operating room. Ariella lay on the bed, and Dr. Regev placed a pill in the palm of her hand. "Just to relax you," he said.

The nurse brought her water and said, "Take just a little sip. It's a short procedure and will be over in no time."

Dr. Regev put a needle in the back of Ariella's hand, and just before she felt her head floating up to the ceiling, she thought she heard, "Thanks for coming on such short notice, Regev. It's a huge favor I owe —" She didn't hear the end.

Ariella woke up confused. She felt hungry and sick at the same time. The bright light above the surgical bed was off now, but there was a small wall light that illuminated a figure leaning on the wall, watching her. Ariella moaned and tried to turn on her side.

"Regev!" she heard Dr. Levy call out as she moved from the wall and opened the door. "She's up. Rivka, come let's get her dressed and out of here." Now she approached Ariella. "You did really well, Ariella. Everything is fine. You came to me just in time."

Ariella felt some pain in her abdomen.

"Come, come, you have a sanitary napkin between your legs now. Don't worry, you won't bleed on the floor. Come, let's get you dressed, and your friend can take you home to rest. It's just past ten o'clock." The doctor helped her get up, and Ariella winced. She walked slowly between Dr. Levy and the nurse, Dr. Regev watching her.

"Well, she's wide awake and walking. I'm off. Remember, Sara, you owe me one." And he was gone.

Ariella was back in the dressing room by herself. She slowly got dressed and wanted to put her jewelry back on. She put on her ring and watch, but didn't she bring her gold bangle, too? Did she give it to Rachel for safekeeping? She bent down to look in her purse, and a sharp pain sent her to the floor. She sat there for a moment, and once she caught her breath, she opened her purse. The gold bangle wasn't there, but her checkbook was. Oh, she forgot to pay!

They all seemed to be in such a hurry. She'd give her the check now. Ariella got off the floor and opened the door. Where was her bangle? The corridor was dark, but there was some light coming out from under a door. She walked slowly and carefully toward that light, touching the wall for support, and opened the door.

Dr. Levy sat at her office desk. She had something in her hand, which she turned around and around. Ariella recognized her bangle.

"Oh, you found it, thank you. I must have dropped it." Ariella tried to smile at the doctor and put her hand out to take it but quickly withdrew it, remembering. "I never paid you, here." She took the checkbook out of her purse, hoping to get her bangle back as soon as she paid.

Dr. Levy put her palm up to stop her. She looked at the inside of the bangle and read out loud the inscription, "To my beloved AP, with all my heart, ADE." She looked at Ariella with narrow eyes. "AP is Ariella Paz, right?"

Ariella nodded as fear gripped her. What was going on?

"And ADE?" the doctor asked as she stood up. Her face was as white as the wall behind her, her eyes narrowing, and her voice hoarse. "I have the same bangle. I don't want your money, Ariella," she said quietly. "You can pay me by getting out, please." She threw the bangle at Ariella. "Out of my clinic and out of Arik's life." She said his name with clenched teeth.

Ariella caught the bangle with shaking hands and almost fell over, losing her balance. She held on to the doctor's desk and looked up at the wall behind it. On it, above the doctor's head, she saw a framed picture. It was of women soldiers and underneath was a bold inscription in black:

To dear Dr. Sara Levy-Emmanuel, with appreciation for your service, all the—

The words became blurry and the room started spinning. Ariella almost fainted. "You...you...you're his...oh my God! You're well, you...you're a doctor..." She stumbled out to find Rachel, and fell into her arms, her knees buckling under her.

Chapter Forty-Six

ARIELLA opened her eyes the next morning and found herself on Eitan and Rachel's couch in the living room. She heard somebody moaning. Then it stopped.

"It's okay. It's okay, Ella, you're fine. It'll pass." Rachel sat beside her on the couch, holding a wet rag on her forehead. "Here, take these." Rachel handed her two Palgin and helped her sit up. Supporting Ariella's back with one hand, she handed her a glass of water with the other.

"Who was moaning?" Ariella asked, listening intently.

"It was you." Rachel smiled. "You woke yourself. I've never seen you like that. But you'll be fine. It's not even twenty-four hours yet. The first two days are awful. I know you'll be okay by tomorrow."

"Twenty-four hours? What time is it? What day is it? Oh, Goldberg—"

"Don't worry. It's only Saturday night. Tomorrow morning I'll call your office and tell Goldberg that you ate something bad on Shabbat and you're constantly running to the restroom. He'll understand you must stay home a day. By Monday you'll be fine and go to work." She got up and went to the kitchen, returning with a tray of three glasses of grapefruit juice and a bread basket. "Eitan, she's up," Rachel called out. "You can bring the goulash and the rice."

She turned back to Ariella. "I called Abba and told him that you have a cold, and Eitan and I are spoiling you, so he shouldn't worry. He asked if Eitan and I were okay, and I said yes. He said we should be careful not to catch your cold." She smiled.

Eitan came from the kitchen with two full plates and returned to bring the third one.

Rachel continued talking while setting the silverware and napkins on the living room coffee table. "I'm worried about you, Ella. The doctor said you almost fainted because you'd lost a lot of blood and because you hadn't eaten all day. She said that your blood sugar or something was too low. I don't know what it means, but she also said you need to rest and eat red meat because of the blood loss, so I made goulash."

"How are you feeling?" Eitan kissed Ariella on the forehead.

She smiled back. "Better, thanks. You two are angels."

They all sat in the living room and ate in silence. Ariella felt ravenous after two days of fasting. When they finished, and Ariella's cramps returned, Rachel told her to lie back down and took the dishes off the table for Eitan to wash up.

That's when it all came back. Ariella started shivering. She couldn't control it, and her moaning and sobbing started anew. Rachel returned to the living room and got into bed with her and hugged her. It felt so good. Nobody had hugged her in such a long time.

Arik's face appeared behind Ariella's closed eyelids as she thought, Arik, what did you do to me? Why did you lie to me like that? Your wife is well. Why did you make up such a horrible story? While Ariella'd visualized his poor, sick wife wearing a house gown and sitting staring at the walls, Dr. Levy-Emmanuel was a healthy woman, an active and successful physician. Ariella felt sick.

She'd fallen like a ripe fruit into his hand, and he'd squeezed hard. He had swept her up and away from the devastating drama she was living at home, back when Ima was dying, and Abba so withdrawn. It was her most vulnerable time.

Yes, at times she loved the danger and secrecy, but now she was full of remorse, and humiliation, and pain. She wanted to die; she felt alone and stupid. That was the worst of all. Feeling stupid. The confusion of what she'd discovered, the shame of what she'd lived through and what she'd done, and the urge to tell Rachel what she knew now, sent her back into waves of sleep. *Escape, escape.*

Ariella felt better when she awoke early on Sunday morning and found Eitan sitting by her on the couch, holding two cups of coffee.

"*Boker tov.*" Good morning. "Feeling better?" Eitan offered her a cup, its warm delicious scent rising in swirls of steam. She nodded, sat up, and took the coffee from him. While she drank, he told her about work. She loved her non-judgmental brother and wished she could find a guy just like him. Lucky Rachel. When she needed to get up for the bathroom, he stood up too, hugged her, said goodbye, and left.

Rachel got ready to go to work, too. "Make yourself comfortable," she said as she picked up her purse. "I'll be back at lunchtime and will bring you ice cream. Oh, no, it will melt by the time I get home. It's so hot and humid already. Never mind, I'll still see you on my lunch break." She waved, blew Ariella a kiss, and left.

Ariella couldn't believe it. The toilet was full of blood. She used two new pads and returned to the couch. She made sure to follow orders and put her feet up on the back of the sofa, making sure they were higher than her buttocks.

When Rachel came home for lunch, Ariella told her about the bleeding.

Rachel frowned and said, "I'm worried, Ariella. I didn't bleed nearly as much. Maybe you need a blood transfusion?

Maybe we should go back and see the doctor?"

Ariella panicked. "No, no, I'm not going back to her!"

"Why? She's a reputable surgeon," Rachel asked in surprise while she heated some goulash from the day before and took out a chopped Israeli salad from the refrigerator.

Ariella's hands began to sweat; she wasn't sure how to start.

"You need to eat. You hadn't eaten the whole—" Rachel stopped. She stared at Ariella. "What?"

"I can't go back to her, Rachel." Ariella hesitated. "I know who she is." She couldn't say it. She just couldn't. She placed her face in her hands.

"What do you mean, you know who she is? We both know. Ariella, you're scaring me."

"Her full name is Sara Levy-Emmanuel. She goes by her maiden name, Dr. Levy, maybe because she became a doctor before she married." Ariella took a deep breath. "I didn't know until after the surgery, when I entered her office, but she's Sara Emmanuel... she's... she's Arik's wife."

Rachel's hands stopped serving in midair. "What?!" She looked up at Ariella, her eyes red and narrow. "The bastard!" She almost broke the plate as she placed it back on the table with a bang. "Cheat! Liar! Thief! Scum!" She seemed to be looking for more words to use, but apparently this was the extent of her bad words, which she had never used before, as far as Ariella knew. Then she blurted, "*Cholera Psha Krev!*" They were the worst Polish swear words Ariella had ever heard. "How could he?!" Rachel continued pacing. "What a con man;

almost everybody was caught in his net. Good Heavens, I feel so stupid for not pulling you out by force!"

"I have to go home, Rachel. I must see Abba and Yael. It's been three days already." She also knew it was time to take charge of her life. She had to make a drastic change.

"You're very brave, Ariella." Rachel's eyes softened. "I have to go back to work soon, but I won't be able to stop thinking of you. What an animal he is! I wish he was here, so I could spit in his face! He never intended on leaving her, did he? And he said he was going to institutionalize her?! Bastard! I'm sorry Ella; I had no idea. How could I have known? And Mania also didn't—" She stopped abruptly, looking at Ariella's face. "She *did* mention the name Emmanuel once, now I remember, but who could have connected...? It's also a first name...oh my God!"

It was three thirty, and Rachel said, "I really have to go back to work. Please don't go yet. Wait for me. Eitan and I will take you home tonight—" She yelled her last words as she ran out the door and toward the stairs to catch the bus back to work.

Ariella sat down in the living room. Then she got up and went to the bathroom, happy to see that the bleeding had subsided. She slowly folded her sheets and put it all in the wash basket on the small balcony outside the bathroom. Then she found the broom and took her time sweeping. She felt better; stronger, useful. When she was done, she went into the kitchen and washed the lunch dishes and made a fresh salad for dinner.

She crept downstairs to the small *Makolet*, the neighborhood grocery store, which was located on the ground floor of the building. Getting out of the apartment felt so good, although the hot air hit her as soon as she stepped out. Ariella enjoyed moving her limbs after being cooped up in bed. The grocer held a kerchief to his face, wiping his sweaty forehead as he approached her. She bought some Bulgarian cheese, green olives, six large eggs, fresh pita, and *labne*, fermented buttermilk. She'd surprise her brother and sister-in-law with a small thank-you dinner.

Tomorrow she'd go back to work, but she knew she'd have to be late. She didn't care about Lupo.

There was something she had to do first.

Chapter Forty-Seven

EITAN and Rachel dropped Ariella at home after ten o'clock that night. They decided that Abba would probably be sleeping already, so they left, but Ariella saw light under his door, and knocked.

"*Ken?*" Yes. Abba said.

Ariella opened the door and walked in. "*Shalom,* Abba. Can we talk?"

"*Shvi.*" Sit down. Abba moved and made room for Ariella to sit by him.

"I have to tell you something, Abba. You may hate me or be disgusted with me, but I've decided that I need to talk with you. It's time."

"Yes, what is it?" Abba lifted his eyes in interest but didn't seem alarmed. "Are you feeling better?"

"It's not that, Abba." She took a deep breath. "I had an affair with a married man, Abba. For two and a half years." Ariella swallowed hard. "But now I've ended it."

Abba's eyes were red. Was he tired?

"I knew something was very wrong." He shook his head. He didn't look shocked.

"You *knew what*?"

Abba sighed. "I suspected him when he didn't take you to Tivon because he had a family emergency." He looked her in the eye now. "And I noticed your jewelry and new clothes, which meant he was well-to-do, and much older."

Ariella didn't know what to say.

"I knew something wasn't kosher, Ella. I'm not stupid, but you never talked to me. You mentioned him by name just once, and you never brought him home although I've asked about him several times." He rubbed his eyes with the palms of his hands, as if trying to wipe off a memory. "I suspected he was married because he always took you out of town, as if he didn't want to be seen with you in Tel Aviv." He shook his head in sadness. "Also, I suspected he was about Yom-Tov's age, being his friend, although you only said that he had known him. But to be honest, I hoped that he was divorced, or a widower. I wasn't sure he was married, until —"

"—until Aunt Pearl told you," Ariella said.

"Aunt Pearl?" Abba looked surprised. "Told me what? What does she have to do with it?" *Now* he sounded alarmed.

"That Arik was...is...married."

"Pearl? How does *she* know?" Abba looked confused.

"I told her, and we had a fight. She didn't tell you?" Ariella was astounded.

"You two had a fight?" Abba scratched his head. "She never said a word about a fight or about knowing that Arik was married." Abba looked at Ariella with concern. "Why did you two fight? What was the fight about?" Abba's faced dropped.

"I told her about Arik a few months ago, when Yom-Tov died, and she said that I wasn't behaving properly." Ariella didn't divulge more.

"Yom-Tov died? When? She never said a word to me. And neither did you." Abba was the one who needed to take a deep breath now. "I got suspicious when you didn't invite Arik to Eitan's wedding..." Abba looked thoughtful.

It was odd to hear him say Arik's name.

"...I wasn't sure if he was travelling or what, but I thought that it was a good opportunity for him to come out from behind his shadow, and when this didn't happen, I suspected he was hiding something." Abba's concern touched Ariella. "There were many clues. Tell me, what happened now that you've ended it?"

"He lied to me, Abba. He kept telling me his wife was mentally ill. Incapacitated and in need of institutionalization. He was going to commit her, get a divorce, and marry me."

"Did you know that, according to Jewish law, you can't obtain a *get*, a Jewish divorce, from a mentally ill person? It's because that person is not in their right mind to give it. It's very complicated." Abba looked very tired. "And was it all true?"

"No." Ariella couldn't continue; she couldn't tell Abba who Arik's wife really was, not yet. She suddenly felt exhausted.

"I'm very tired, Abba," she said, standing up. "Can we talk another time?"

As she turned to walk out, he asked, "Did you just have a cold, Ella?"

She stood by the door and stared back at her father. Her first confession had been much too hard for her; she had no energy for another. She put her head down and walked out of his room. He didn't stop her.

* * *

In the morning Ariella rose early and left the house at six thirty. She went straight to 71 Ha'yarkon Street, to the US Embassy in Tel Aviv, and stood in line for two hours until her turn came to speak to the person behind the little window.

"Good morning," Ariella smiled at the short-haired blonde woman. "My name is Ariella Paz. Here is my identity document and here are my military discharge papers."

"How can I help you?"

"Oh, yes." Ariella felt her cheeks becoming hot. "I would like to apply for a student visa so I can study in the United States."

"Do you have family in the States?"

"Yes, yes! My cousin lives in Los Angeles."

"And would she sponsor you?"

"Yes. And she offered me a place to stay. With her and her family."

The woman handed Ariella a form and told her to bring it back with two photographs, her passport, and a fee. Visa issuing hours were from Monday to Friday, eight to eleven.

"Thank you, I'll be back," Ariella said in English, and the clerk smiled.

Ariella shivered with excitement; she still had her savings, as Dr. Levy didn't want her money, and it played perfectly with her plans.

Ariella was almost two hours late to work.

"Here you are! Welcome back, how are you?" Shosh greeted her with glee.

"We weren't sure you'd come today." Etty came forward to hug her.

"Welcome, welcome. Feeling better?" Goldberg sat behind his desk, a pen in hand and glasses perched at the tip of his nose. He smiled broadly. "Come sit; I have work for you."

"*Shalom*, everybody." Ariella smiled at them. "Yes, thank you, I'm much better and so glad to be back."

She immediately entered Goldberg's office and sat at his desk to listen to what she'd missed. From the corner of her eye, Ariella saw Yossi Lupo at his desk in his office. He stared at her and looked back at his watch. He didn't greet her nor asked how she was. Well, they had had no chemistry from the get-go. She refocused on Goldberg and when he was finished updating her, she threw herself into work, trying to keep up with the others.

Just before they took their midday break, Etty approached Ariella. "Want to go for a sandwich, or are you going home for lunch?"

Ariella still didn't feel like herself and wanted to go home to rest for an hour but knowing that Shosh and Etty had taken over her work for the past two days, made her say, "Sure, I'd love to go for a sandwich with you."

"Somebody has been calling you these past two days but wouldn't leave a message." Etty followed Ariella as she went into her office to take her purse.

Ariella whirled around in alarm. Etty knew Sara. What if her affair with Arik was exposed? And her abortion by his wife? It was all too much.

"I'm sorry, Etty," Ariella said, "I dated this guy, but we broke up. He must be the one calling. If he calls again, please don't give him any information about me. If I'm here or away, please just say I'm busy and you'll give me his message if he leaves one."

"Sure, I can do that."

"Thank you, I appreciate your help, Etty, I really do. I know it's not part of your job, but it's a personal favor." She couldn't look her in the eye. "It's really been hard."

"No problem," Etty said.

Shosh walked into Ariella's office. "Coming for lunch? We've missed you," she said. "I promise we'll eat something healthy, so you won't get food poisoning again." Shosh laughed.

Ariella tried to smile; it was good to feel wanted, but she

was worried. She took her purse and followed.

* * *

Ariella's chest x-ray looked good, and the American consulate doctor gave her a clean bill of health. With the forms filled out, two passport photographs, her Israeli passport, and her military discharge certificate, she made her way back to the American embassy.

She'd also obtained a letter from the University of Judaism in Los Angeles stating they would accept her as an international student. Cousin Sonia and her husband Max wrote in another letter that Ariella Paz was family and they would take care of her financial and health needs while she studied at an American college. Cousin Sonia must have gone ahead with the sponsorship, although Ariella hadn't requested it. So much was happening. Cousin Sonia was a smart woman.

Three weeks later, Ariella received a student visa in the mail for one year beginning September. It was August already. She jumped with glee. Arik was no longer in control of her life. She was.

She had to tell Abba, Eitan and Rachel, and young Yael. She had to buy a plane ticket—so much to do! Ariella also planned to give notice in two weeks as she wanted to work as long as possible.

But that evening, as she walked out of the office building with Etty and Shosh, leaning on his white car, smoking, stood

Arik.

She almost didn't recognize him; he'd lost weight since she'd seen him last. She stopped, as did her colleagues who were walking with her to the bus stop. They all stood staring at each other. Arik stomped his cigarette out on the sidewalk and approached her. Ariella's body went stiff, paralyzed with anxiety, but Etty and Shosh must have sensed something because they both took one step forward as if to protect her.

"Arik?" Etty exclaimed.

Arik stared at her, looking confused. Ariella had never seen this expression on his face. As if he had seen a ghost.

"Aren't you Arik Emmanuel? Sara's husband? Sara Levy? I mean, Sara Emmanuel?" Etty turned to Ariella and Shosh, "Do you know Arik, girls?"

Arik ignored her and turned to Ariella. "Ariella, I need to talk with you, now." Some passersby stared. Ariella's throat felt dry. She grieved for the man she had loved and couldn't believe he was the one in front of her; this man looked older, shriveled, his face drawn in, and his hair grayer than she'd remembered. As she began to walk away, and Arik tried to follow, a passerby approached them. "Is this man bothering you, ladies?"

"We're okay, I think, thank you," Shosh was quick to reply. The man looked at Arik doubtfully, and left.

Arik tried to grab Ariella by her wrist, saying, "Come with me. I need you, Ella. I can't go on without you." He was pleading. He looked strange and somewhat scary.

Ariella pulled her arm back, yelling, "No!"

Several passersby stopped walking and stared.

"Arik, what are you doing? Aren't you ashamed?" Etty interfered with her hoarse voice. She turned to Ariella. "I wish you had told me who that 'boyfriend' of yours was." She turned back to Arik. "Go home, Arik. Go home to your wife. You don't deserve her, I swear!"

Shosh looked mesmerized; she stared wild eyed from Etty to Ariella, and back. She eventually took Ariella by her arm and Etty by her hand, pulled them both, and started walking.

Ariella noticed that people turned around to stare, and she stared back. She didn't look at Arik. Her legs just kept walking like independent entities.

The three staggered away silently, and by the time they arrived at the bus stop, Ariella had somewhat calmed down and regained her composure. She faced Etty and Shosh and said, "You're both the best friends a girl could have; thank you. You can go ahead now. I'm fine. I'm going in the opposite direction. My brother and sister-in-law are expecting me for dinner."

Shosh looked at her doubtfully but let go.

Ariella crossed the road and looked back to make sure Arik wasn't following her. Neither he nor his car were anywhere to be seen. She found a seat on the bus and noticed her hands were shaking. So was her bottom lip. She put her fingers on her mouth to stop the shaking, leaned her head on the glass window, and looked at the cars below crawling by.

She realized that she needed help, but whom should she turn to? Maybe Abba? Or Uncle Rafael? She had to keep Arik out of her life for just another month.

Chapter Forty-Eight

SITTING in the living room, holding an open book on her lap after dinner, Ariella looked on at her supportive family with gratitude: Abba, Eitan, Yael, and Rachel, and even her Aunt Pearl. They were all reading quietly as the doorbell rang. It startled them, and they all looked up.

"I'll get it," Yael said as she jumped up to open the door.

"*Shalom, Kulahm.*" Hello, everybody. Uncle Rafael's voice boomed over Yael's head. He bent down to kiss her as Dalia ruffled her hair and went to hug everybody. Ariella noticed her uncle exchange looks and a smile with Abba.

Eitan brought two chairs from the kitchen. Ariella went to make tea, and Rachel followed to help. She looked at Ariella questioningly, and Ariella shrugged.

For a while they all sat drinking tea and eating the chocolate cake Abba had brought when he unexpectedly shot up from his chair. He strode into the kitchen and brought a bottle of brandy and eight small glasses on a tray.

"I want to thank you all for being here," Abba said, pouring a little brandy into the glasses. Everybody stopped talking and looked at each other with surprised expressions.

"Oh, a celebration?" Yael asked, and quickly went into the kitchen and brought the bottle of banana liqueur Abba kept there. "May I have some?" she asked.

"A drop, my little fourteen-year-old," Abba said, smiling.

Once each little glass was half-filled, Abba stood up, raised his glass, cleared his throat, and said ceremonially, "My dear family, again, thank you for coming." His voice filled with emotion as he turned to face Aunt Pearl. "I'd like to announce that Pearl and I are planning to get married."

What?! Ariella's heart skipped a beat.

His voice quivering, Abba smiled at Aunt Pearl like Ariella had never seen him smile at Ima. Or did he used to smile at her like that when they were young? Her chest tightened; she felt a mixture of jealousy and sadness, but also relief.

Abba looked from one family member to another, his eyes shining and a proud smile on his face. "We're engaged."

"*Mazal tov*!" Uncle Rafael stood up and cheered. "So from being my brother-in-law, now you'll be my...brother-in-law!"

Everybody laughed. Almost everybody. It sounded like a nervous laugh, Ariella thought. An odd situation indeed.

"When?" Ariella asked. She suddenly felt weightless, like she was tied to a hot air balloon rising and flying away. Everybody looked at her, then at Abba again.

Ariella's question stood for a moment in the air with no reply. She was free. Abba would have a wife, and Yael would have somebody to look after her. I can go to America without guilt, she thought. She stayed standing after everybody settled down again and said, "There is another reason to raise a glass."

The room went quiet and everybody looked at her.

"The reason I asked 'when' was that...was that...I may not be here for the wedding." She looked at their faces, anticipating a harsh reaction.

Abba frowned, not understanding. Aunt Pearl raised an eyebrow in surprise, and Rachel and Yael asked at the same time, "What?!"

Ariella swallowed. "I'm leaving for America...soon...very soon...at the end of the month, actually." she decided to be brave and say it out loud, at long last.

Rachel jumped up. "Ella! You're really doing it! You're really going to America!"

"You knew?" Eitan and Yael said simultaneously.

"You told me about this dream so long ago," Rachel said, ignoring Eitan and Yael. "And you're doing it! I didn't know that you'd secretly prepared for it, you little rascal! Oh, my goodness, you're really leaving. But at the end of the month? Why so soon?"

She scanned their faces. Everybody stared at her.

"Yes, why so soon?" Everybody was asking at once.

Everyone but Abba.

Ariella turned to face her father. "Abba," she started, then stopped.

He looked at her with tears in his eyes, trying to smile.

"I have a student visa. I applied and was accepted to the University of Judaism in Los Angeles," she talked fast, not wanting to lose the momentum. "Cousin Sonia is sponsoring me and has offered me a room in her house, at least for the beginning." She swallowed hard. "I feel so fortunate. She was wonderful in helping me arrange everything."

Ariella felt her eyes tearing up, too, but continued, "My dream is coming true, Abba. You have taught me to love the whole world, to spread my wings and be adventurous. You've lived on three continents and did the best you could in each of them. I want to do it, too."

Abba got up and hugged her. "I suspected it would happen one day but didn't know it would be so soon. Cousin Sonia hinted at something in a letter," he said with a smile. "She told me that she'd offered to have you come but didn't add details. I guess she wanted to prepare me in a way and still be loyal to your secret."

"She did?" Ariella was genuinely surprised, but not upset; this way it wasn't a shock for Abba. "Maybe it's better that she did. I'm sorry I kept it a secret. I've kept too many secrets lately. It's exhausting. But I was afraid to jinx it, and I was waiting to have the visa in my hand first." She felt relieved but nervous. "School begins in October. I need to register, buy books, get used to the place. There's a lot to be done." She felt the nervousness leave her, and the excitement take over.

"Wait, everybody." Eitan raised his voice to be heard above everybody's noise. "I hope you all have a spare drop in your glasses." He stood up and went to Rachel, who stood now with the glass in her hand, her liquor untouched. "Rachel and I have a reason to celebrate, too, and as you can see, she is not drinking," he said and kissed the tip of her nose.

Rachel flushed and placed her head on Eitan's shoulder.

"Rachel!" Ariella yelled. "When did that happen?" Her face burned with embarrassment at her silly question, she wasn't sure if everybody was laughing at her.

"Maybe last night!" came Uncle Rafael's joke as a reply, and everybody burst out laughing again. The room was filled with love and joy.

"*Be'sha'ah Tova.*" All in good time. Abba hugged Eitan and then Rachel, blessing them with the customary Jewish blessing when hearing of a baby on the way.

Ariella's eyes stung as Rachel came over and hugged her, as if she knew the storm this news had stirred in her. Ariella controlled her tears. She wasn't going to cry anymore for the baby she could have had and for the life she thought she'd wanted to lead, because she knew well enough that it was only a fantasy. It wasn't to be.

She hugged Rachel tightly, and whispered in her ear, "I'm so happy for you, my sweet Rachel. You deserve it."

Rachel said softly, "Go, Ella, find Prince Charming, just like I did. Get married and have a baby. You deserve it, too."

As everyone sat and talked, Ariella looked around the room and knew she'd miss them all.

Chapter Forty-Nine

ARIELLA was two weeks away from leaving for America, when she was visiting two of her favorite people. Eitan and Rachel were both in the kitchen of their little rented apartment when the phone rang. Ariella picked it up.

"Hello?"

"Ariella…Ariella…Abba, uh, Aunt Pearl…the police are here because of the accident…come home, Ariella, please…" Yael sounded hysterical through her sobs.

"Yael?" Ariella's body went numb. "An accident? Abba and Aunt Pearl?"

"Yes, can you…can you please come home?" Yael was pleading. "The policeman said…he said that we need to go to the hospital. They...they are injured, the ambulance took them. Please come, Ariella..."

Ariella's chest felt tight; it was an effort to breathe, but she knew she first had to calm her sister.

"All right, sweetie...we're on our way home," she tried to say as calmly as she could.

Eitan, who stood beside her, narrowed his eyes in confusion and concern. He jangled the car keys in his hand, seeming to understand a phone call at ten at night meant something was very wrong. Rachel followed behind him and rested her hand on Ariella's shoulder.

Ariella felt better with them by her side and continued speaking to her younger sister. "Just stay where you are. Don't go anywhere with anybody. Make yourself some tea and try to calm down; if the ambulance took them to the hospital, they're being taken care of." She tried to be logical for her own sake too. "We'll be with you very soon, *motek.* We'll pick you up and go to the hospital together." Her hand shook as she replaced the receiver.

About ten days earlier, Ariella had spoken to her Uncle Rafi who worked at the bank. She'd filled him on her history with Arik, but never told him about the abortion. Uncle Rafi told her he'd known of one Arik David Emmanuel, who had an account in a Swiss bank. It was a criminal offense. Benny Sarkowski, a blind painter, had suspected Arik was cheating him out of commission and complained to the bank, that involved the police. An investigation was being processed.

Ariella didn't mention that she had met Benny.

A few days later, Abba's two front tires were slashed while his car was parked overnight in front of their apartment building. When he replaced them, they were slashed again. Ariella suspected Arik but had no proof. Abba wanted to contact the police.

Could this accident somehow be related to him as well?

"You'll tell us in the car exactly what has happened." Eitan said before he rushed out the door, jumping down the stairs two at a time, Ariella ran down the four flights of stairs while Rachel descending carefully, holding on to her belly with one hand and the railing with the other.

"Tell us what she told you," Eitan said as he drove. The streets were almost empty; the roads were wet and slippery.

Ariella repeated what Yael had told her when Rachel suddenly screamed, "Eitan, slow down." She held on tight to the strap above the car door. "It won't help anybody if we also have a car accident. And the baby—"

Eitan slowed his little Fiat 600. He hadn't changed his tires since he bought the car five years ago, and Ariella felt the skidding every time he took a corner. By the time they arrived at her home, Yael was sitting by herself in the kitchen hugging a full cup of hot tea.

As she saw them, Yael let go of the cup and rushed to hug her sister. Ariella held her shivering sister tightly, kissed her wet cheek and said, "Do you want to sit in the living room and tell us what happened?"

"No," Yael said. "We have to go to the hospital."

Back in the car Ariella held her fourteen-year-old sister's hand. "Tell us everything."

"About an hour ago," Yael started and sniffed, "a policeman came to the door." She took a deep breath and continued, her voice shaking. "He asked me if Daniel Paz lived here. I said yes. He asked me if I was alone, and I said yes, again. 'Where is your mother?' he asked. I told him she was dead." Yael wiped her dripping nose with the back of her hand. "'Do you have any siblings?' he asked. I said I have a sister who is visiting my married brother. 'Do you have a telephone?' he asked. I said yes again. I was so scared. I'd never spoken to a policeman before." She stopped again to take a deep breath but seemed calmer now.

Ariella patted her head and said, "Neither have I. It must have been very scary."

Yael continued, "So he told me to call you and tell you to come home and pick me up and that we should all go to Hadassah Hospital because Abba was in a car accident and there was a woman with him who had been hurt." She stopped before she thoughtfully continued. "I remembered that Abba said that he was going to pick up Aunt Pearl, and they were going to the movies at seven, and he'd be late." Yael put her head on Ariella's shoulder and cried.

"I hope he's not dead." She whispered onto Ariella's shoulder.

Chapter Fifty

"ABBA!" Ariella was the first one to see him. Five other people stood in the small emergency waiting room, probably waiting to hear about loved ones. There were several cubicles surrounded by closed curtains. She heard murmurs coming from behind them.

Abba sat bent with his elbows on his thighs and his head in his hands. He looked unhurt aside from some dry blood on his shirt, on the left shoulder, and collar. It was very late, and Ariella realized he must have been up since five a.m. She stood before him.

"Ariella, oy, Ariella." Abba lifted his head and extended his hand to her. She sat next to him, holding his hand in both of hers. Eitan sat on Abba's other side, and Rachel and Yael stood in front of him, hugging each other's shoulders, looking at him questioningly.

"*Mah karah*, Abba?" What happened? Eitan placed his hand on Abba's shoulder. "You're hurt. Why don't they attend to you?"

Ariella noticed an adhesive bandage taped on the left side of his forehead and a few little dry cuts next to it. She saw dried blood on his ear, too.

"You have cuts, Abba," Yael said. "Where is Aunt Pearl?" She looked around.

"She's in surgery. I'm fine. I don't know how hurt she really is. They won't tell me. All I saw was blood. She's much worse than me...I know that for sure. I'm fine. I only cut my forehead and have some stitches, but she was injured badly." Abba choked on his tears.

Yael cried softly in Rachel's arms, so Rachel led her to a seat next to Ariella, who now took Yael's hand in hers and held it tightly. "Abba is okay, you see?" Ariella whispered to Yael and smiled.

"What happened, Abba?" Eitan repeated. "Please tell us."

"Aunt Pearl and I went to the movies at seven, and when we came out there was pouring rain. In August! The streets were oily and slippery after a long hot summer. First rains are so dangerous, you know." Abba sounded distracted. He rubbed his eyes with his fists and continued.

"I wanted to drive home, and we were almost there, but Pearl wanted to go to Café Kassite or Roval for coffee," he said.

"As I passed the house I noticed a car on my tail. Every time I looked in the rearview mirror, I saw its bright lights. It was blinding me."

Ariella froze with horror.

"I don't know why he drove so close to me." Abba continued. "I felt a bit scared. When I arrived at the stop sign—Boom!" he slapped his hands together. "He bumped into me. Of course, he didn't have enough space between us to stop; the idiot was too close. Next thing I knew, he pulled back and was gone, but not before he shoved me into the middle of the intersection. When he pushed my little van, I lost my footing on the clutch. The gearbox got stuck. I couldn't press the clutch in. We were stuck—in the middle of an intersection!" Abba took a deep breath before he continued. "Suddenly I saw bright lights coming from the right. The bastard wouldn't stop! Then again—Bam! I felt a tremendous crash. The car smashed right into me! Into us! On purpose! I swear! Into Pearl. She started screaming. I banged the left side of my head on the side window and broke it. But Pearl was screaming so much I didn't even notice that I cut myself. I tried to help her out, but her right leg was stuck between the dashboard and her door." Abba stopped and rubbed his head wildly with both hands, as if to erase the memory. He breathed heavily. "Do you have a cigarette?" he asked no one in particular. Eitan shook his head, but Ariella, her hands shaking, took a box out of her purse, offered Abba a cigarette, and lit it for him.

"So, Aunt Pearl broke her leg?" Eitan asked.

"I'm not sure. I think that her left arm looked crooked,

too. Oy, was she screaming from pain until the Magen David Adom arrived! And there was so much blood! It was horrible."

"Who called the police? And the ambulance?" asked Rachel, ever the practical one.

"I'm not sure," Abba continued. "There were a few cars on the road by then, and somebody must have knocked on a resident's door asking them to call for help. It was late, but some people came out of their homes to see what'd happened. We were brought here, and the police followed us for questioning. They let the doctor clean me and stitch me up, and then I had to give them the report." Abba started coughing and crushed the cigarette under his shoe. He was perspiring.

He must be exhausted, Ariella thought. "Do you want some water?" she asked and got up. Abba nodded.

On her way to ask a nurse for a cup of water for her father, Ariella passed a cubicle with a half-open curtain. She saw a man on a bed, most of his head covered with a large bandage, only one eye showing. Ariella thought she saw a woman with short black hair sitting next to him.

She stopped. Was she seeing things?

She wanted to go back. Maybe even draw back the curtain to make sure, but she couldn't move. So she stood on the outside of the thin curtain and listened.

"No, Sara, I wasn't drinking, you know I don't drink," the bandaged man said to the woman. She knew that voice. "I told you...it was the bloody rain."

"You could have killed someone, Arik."

Ariella's legs started shaking.

"Yes...yes...but I didn't, did I?" he said and moaned with pain.

Ariella ran to the restroom. She heaved and vomited repeatedly like she'd never done before in her life. After she washed her face, she leaned on the sink for support and looked into the mirror. She saw the horror in her eyes. She wanted to sit down on the cold floor but didn't; she had to go back.

This time she pulled the curtain back with one swift move.

Arik lay in the bed, his head bandaged, and a cast extended from his right shoulder all the way down to his hand. Sara wasn't there anymore. He opened his one eye. The shock on his face was obvious.

"You...you...you're...okay?" Arik stammered in surprise.

Ariella wanted to hit him or spit on him. She clenched her fists to contain herself.

"Me?" And then she got it, her anger exploding in her throat. "*Me?*" she asked again. "Of course I'm fine—why are you asking *me*? Did you think it was *me in the car*? You almost killed my father and my aunt!" she yelled uncontrollably.

A nurse came running. "Hey, you! What are you doing? You're not allowed in here."

Ariella turned to face her. "I wanted to see the face of the person who tried to kill me, or my father," she hissed. "But I can only see an eye. An evil eye." She turned back to Arik and said, "You just wait, you criminal, you evil person. Wait until the police hear *my* side of the story."

The nurse looked at her oddly, shaking her head and pulling Ariella out.

Ariella walked slowly back to her father. She felt like her temples were being held in a vice grip. Her legs shook; she had to hold onto the wall to steady herself.

Then she noticed a doctor in a white coat standing and talking with Abba. Ariella saw Eitan and Rachel look at her for a moment, and then back at the doctor. She wondered if anybody had heard the commotion.

Ariella approached them. Aunt Pearl would be fine, the doctor was saying; she'd broken her right leg and her left wrist. She was very lucky, he continued; they'd put both her limbs in casts. She also had bruises and cuts. They wanted her to stay overnight for observation, to make sure she had no internal bleeding.

Abba was also lucky, the doctor added. They stitched the cut on his forehead and said it would heal in no time. The rest of them could go home and come back tomorrow to pick up Aunt Pearl if all went well.

Eitan drove them all home; Abba sat quietly next to him, and Yael sat squashed at the back of the little Fiat, between Rachel and Ariella. Ariella hugged her sister with one arm, and worked hard to contain her shaking, thinking of Arik. He must have been confronted by Uncle Rafi, or Benny, or the tax collector. He might be financially ruined now; no wonder he crashed Abba's car, trying to hurt him. Or was he trying to hurt her?

She shook her head; the deep guilt and sadness for the pain she'd brought on her family by letting Arik into her life crushed her. She balled her hands into tight fists, hoping he was hurting just as much, if not more so, than she was.

Yael must have felt the tension in Ariella's arms. She lifted her head and looked at her sister. "Why are you so tense, Ella? Abba is alright."

"*Ken, motek.*" Yes, sweetie. "I'm so relieved he's alright and coming home with us." Ariella tried to sound calm. How could she tell her sister what she'd just discovered? She kissed Yael on her forehead. "Everything will be okay, Yulinka," Ariella whispered and tried to smile despite doubting her own words. It was all her fault.

Ariella's plane ticket was for ten days from now. What would she have done if Arik had hurt her? How could he do something so terrible? The guilt was so painful she wished she could forget it all. Her poor Aunt Pearl! Ariella decided that there was nothing she could do. She'd leave it to Abba and Aunt Pearl to press charges, but first she had to tell Abba.

"I know who crashed into you, Abba," Ariella said in a low voice as she sat at the kitchen table with her family drinking tea and smoking. The clock read two a.m., and Abba had already tucked Yael into bed.

"You do? Who?"

Eitan and Rachel stared at her as well.

"Oh, no!" Abba's eyes suddenly lit up in horror.

"Yes. When I went to get you some water, I passed a cubicle and saw Arik in bed with a cast from his right shoulder to his hand, and a bandage over his head. He looked shocked, although only one of his eyes was uncovered. I think he was surprised to see me standing upright." She stopped. Was Abba following what she was saying?

"What a coincidence!" Eitan said. "But why was he surprised to see you—oh my God! Was it intentional?! Was *he* the guy who crashed into Abba?" Eitan stood up, as if he couldn't contain the news sitting down.

"He could have killed him! Or Aunt Pearl!" Rachel's eyes filled with tears and horror. "He wanted to hurt *you*...?"

Ariella nodded, unable to speak. The thought that Aunt Pearl could have been killed because of her haunted her.

"Yes," Abba said in a shaky voice. "You and Aunt Pearl really look alike. You always have since you were a baby. And Arik must have found out about me and Uncle Rafael investigating him—"

"We have to go to the police," Eitan said as he paced the small kitchen.

"Yes, in the morning," Ariella said and looked at her watch. There wasn't much time left for sleep.

"Ariella and I will go," Abba said. "We'll press charges and make sure he gets what he deserves. Eitan and Rachel, go home to sleep now; Rachel needs her rest," he said and patted her hand. "Ariella and I will try to sleep a few hours, and in the morning, we'll take a cab to the police station on Dizengoff Street. Don't worry, justice will be served."

"What about America?" Rachel asked at the door. She must have known Ariella was worried.

"No problem, she'll go as planned," Abba said as he saw them to the door. "I won't let him ruin her life."

Ariella looked at him with love and gratitude.

"You just give your testimony to the police and tell them you've had an affair with this man, and I'm sure they'll let you go. I'll hire a lawyer and take it from there. Between me and Uncle Rafael, it will be enough to prosecute him. Don't make any changes to your plans, Ariella. Your life should go on as you planned it."

Eitan and Rachel nodded and left, but Ariella felt her emotions surging and started crying; she had *never* heard Abba so assertively protect her, support her, and love her. She knew she was forgiven.

But now she had to tell strangers about her affair with a married man.

Chapter Fifty-One

AFTER receiving an excellent letter of recommendation full of praise and compliments, Ariella said a teary goodbye to Goldberg. He told her that he liked Etty a lot and offered her Ariella's job, against Lupo's advice, and hired a new typist. Lupo shook Ariella's hand and wished her "bon voyage." Etty and Shosh bought her a new suitcase, a parting gift, and she promised she'd write.

She couldn't wait to start her new life in Los Angeles.

* * *

The night before Ariella left, she said her goodbyes to

Eitan and Rachel. The hugs and tears and promises to write were genuine.

"Go, Ella, go in peace and make peace with your life," Rachel said as she held Ariella's hands in hers, squeezing her fingers.

The lump in Ariella's throat didn't allow her to say a word. She hugged Rachel and held her close for a long time, saying nothing.

"Write," Rachel managed to whisper, choking on her word.

"*Be'hatzlacha.*" Best of luck. Eitan put a brave smile on his face. "I'm sure you'll enjoy your studies. Make lots of friends. Come visit." That was her Eitan, short and to the point.

Just before she awoke in the morning, Ariella had a dream. She and her mother sat at a small, round, marble-like table. Three slices of different cakes rested in front of them, each one cut in half, along with two glasses of hot tea nestled in silver holders. The table was the only one in the middle of a large hospital room surrounded by about twenty beds. There was no hospital scent, Ariella noticed. On the contrary, the fragrance of lilies filled the air. Ima wore a pretty green dress, the color of her eyes, just like the one she wore for her sister Pearl's wedding to Irwin. She looked much younger than Ariella had remembered, her hair short and shiny.

"I'm leaving again, Ima."

"I know, Ella. I'm coming with you."

"You are? I miss you so much, Ima."

"I'll always live in your heart, Ella. We call it love."

"It's wonderful to see you, again, Ima. It's been so hard since you've left, but I had some good moments, too."

"Yes, sometimes one has to pay a heavy price for good moments."

"You know about that?

"I do."

"And you couldn't stop me?"

"It wasn't my place. You had to live through it."

The hospital beds disappeared.

"I'm a little scared to leave again, Ima. Do you think it's the right thing to do?" She reached out to touch Ima's hand—but there was nothing there.

"Anything you do, everything that happens, is supposed to happen; otherwise, it wouldn't happen."

Ariella opened her eyes. She could hear the quickened beating of her racing heart. She felt as if her mother were still beside her; it felt so real. She closed her eyes again, wishing Ima were really hovering over her and coming with her to America. She felt like a little girl again, full of fear and doubt.

Later that morning, Aunt Pearl moved into Abba's apartment, so that he and Yael could take care of her. It all made sense; they were adults, getting married in four months. She was going to share the room with Yael and sleep in Ariella's bed until she healed.

After lunch, when Ariella hugged and kissed her goodbye,

Ariella cried soft tears on her aunt's shoulder.

Aunt Pearl pulled back, patted Ariella's cheek with her good hand, and said, "Go with a smile, Ella, not with tears. I have a surprise for you." She smiled and extended an envelope. Ariella stopped crying. "We'll see you back in December." She laughed as Ariella opened her big eyes in surprise. "I bought you a ticket for December, so you can be here at the wedding. This is my good luck gift to you." With a sad expression she added, "Then you can go back to your studies in America."

Ariella resumed her crying; she was heartbroken that her aunt had suffered because of her huge mistake, but she was thankful that she was alive. She hugged her aunt gently so as not to hurt her and kissed her cheeks again and again, as she whispered, "thank you, thank you."

Abba and Yael sat in the secondhand van Abba had bought last week, after the accident. They were ready to take Ariella to the airport. She was flying to New York via London, and on to Los Angeles.

At the airport, Abba held her tightly for a long moment.

"Have fun, my child," he said, tears in his eyes. "I wish your mother could see what a beautiful and courageous daughter she raised. I'm proud of you, Ella. Go and succeed."

"I'll miss you so much, Abba. I hope your courage will settle in my bones." She looked him in the eye. "And I wish you lots of happiness with Aunt Pearl. I know she loves you deeply."

Ariella turned to her sister, who was the same height as her now, and hugged her tightly.

"I'll miss you, Ella. Write me lots of letters in English. I need to practice for school."

"I'll see you soon, Yulinka." She held her for as long as Yael let her.

Ariella took her seat by the window on the El-Al flight to London. She had her book ready on her lap and her seat belt fastened. The plane was filling up rapidly. Men in suits and ties and women dressed in the latest fashions came on board. She noticed a tall, handsome young man approaching her row. He took the aisle seat and left the seat between them empty. Something in his face caught her attention, and she glanced at him through the corner of her eye. The first thing she noticed was his straight nose. She turned to look.

He looked back and smiled at her, most probably feeling her gaze. A broad and friendly smile displaying white, healthy teeth. She noticed deep-set, light brown eyes; well-cut, brown hair above his ears; and a chiseled jawline. So familiar.

Ariella had to swallow hard; her mouth going dry.

She noticed his tanned left hand had a faint white band of skin on one finger.

He couldn't have avoided her stare, because he smiled broadly, cocked his head to one side and extended his right hand.

"Hello. My name is Boaz..."

Ariella shook his hand reluctantly, said a faint "*shalom,*" and fumbled to open her book, indicating she wasn't interested in a conversation.

I know who you are, but you'll never know who I am. She

closed her eyes and placed the open book on her chest, as if to protect her heart. The plane pulled back, turned, and started to taxi.

She heard a soft whisper in her head, Ima's familiar voice: Anything you do, anything that happens, is supposed to happen. Otherwise, it wouldn't happen.

ACKNOWLEDGMENTS

I love teachers. They're amongst my favorite people. I remember my freshman year in high school, *Ironit Aleph*, in Tel Aviv, Israel, when the beautiful and pregnant HAMUTAL BAR-YOSEF walked into our classroom. She was our Hebrew literature teacher. She made me fall in love with the subject, and with the idea of becoming a teacher. That was the beginning.

Having good teachers is a lifelong gift. It took many, many years before I encountered the wonderful teacher, poet, and author MAI-LON GITTELSOHN in Del Mar, California. One day, in her writing class, she gave us a prompt: 'What Does She Want?' It was a 20-minute, quick-writing exercise. I scribbled a story I'd heard about many years ago. Towards the end of the semester, Mrs. Gittelsohn asked us to choose one of our quick-writes and expand it to 8 pages. I chose that one story and named it THE AFFAIR. As I wrote, added, and expanded, I felt a fire being lit under me.

By the time I joined a Read-and-Critique class at SDSU, run by the talented teacher/author/TV presenter KATHI DIAMANT, I knew what I was going to work on. Kathi's gentle critique style, her precise rules and guidance were so encouraging, that my 8-page story evolved into 20,000 words!

But this wordcount did not a novel make, yet, said the successful author of 12 novels, TAMMY GREENWOOD, when I came to her class at SD WRITERS' INK. This was home. This was where I found my people. My supportive, loving-but-harsh 'critiquers,' honest-to-the-bone brothers and sisters, who helped me, under the guidance of our leader, to write my novel. Tammy was my first content editor. Thank you, T. Greenwood, Bridget Myhro, Dave Oei, Shawna Yaley, Christopher Penney, Jan Steele, Erin McGlone, and especially Chih Wang, who copy edited my book. Thank you, guys. You'll forever be engraved on my heart.

A special thank you to my beloved and talented son, Gil Sery, who read, proofread, and edited my manuscript several times, and never stopped rooting for me. He's a writer in his own right.

I'm grateful to my loyal and talented writing group members, Sally Polack and Kerry Ojeda, who have been diligently coming to my house weekly for years to share in writing feelings, memories, and secrets. It's a sacred space we hold for each other. Thank you, Sally, for reading and commenting on my last draft.

Thank you to the people who read parts of my first drafts, including my sister Ora Etner, my uncle Shimon Bar-Zlil, Anna Taksar, and Susan Buxbaum. And to my generous Beta Readers: the diligent Carole Finn, my friends Edna Yedid, Orit Carmi, Mark and Isabella Wilf, and author R. D. Kardon.

Many thanks to Annette Driesen, my dear friend in Israel, who read my manuscript, made sure I got the facts right, and encouraged me with love and care.

Thank you to my publishers, best-selling authors Jessica Therrien and Holly Kammier, founders and co-owners of Acorn Publishing LLC. Thank you, Holly, for the tough-love editing style you employed when editing my manuscript, which was both honest and smart.

I thank Regina Wamba of Maeidesign, for designing my stunning book cover, as well as Christa Yelich-Koth and Zan Strumfeld, for formatting and corrections.

To my beloved daughter, Natalie Sery Cruz, who kept tapping my shoulder lovingly, saying, "get the book out, Mom." To my son-in-law, Oscar Cruz, and to my grandsons who kept asking me "How do you do it?" and to my supportive and encouraging husband of 50 years, Joe Sery—thank you, from the bottom of my heart.